A BRICK TO REMEMBER

VS Gardner

Enjoy this memory mystery!

VS Gardner

i

Copyright @ 2022 VS Gardner

All rights reserved.

This book is a work of fiction.
Names, characters, places, and incidents either are products
of the author's imagination or are used fictitiously.

Scripture quotations are from The Holy Bible,
New International Version® Copyright© 1973, 1978, 1984
by International Bible Society. Used by permission of Zondervan.
All rights reserved.

Cover Painting by Steve Gardner
Cover Design created by Germancreative

ISBN 9798763454956

Printed in the United States of America

This book is DEDICATED to my father
~ *George L. Lilly* ~

Many things go into publishing a first novel. One of the most important factors, for me, was my dad's opinion.

After writing six chapters of what I hoped would become my first novel I read them to my parents. Since my dad has always been an avid reader I was very interested in his response. After listening to what I'd written dad said simply, "I would buy this book." And, as they say, the rest is history.

When dad asked what my sisters thought of my book he was surprised to learn I hadn't told them. I shared that I simply didn't know if it was any good. I didn't know if I would even finish it. He looked me in the eyes and said "*Yes! It's good* and *you are* going to finish it. Now tell your sisters."

While dad's encouragement played a huge part in the publication of my first novel, A Killing on Hardee Street in 2020, its dedication was already set in my mind. Similarly, from word one, the dedication of this, my second novel, A Brick to Remember has always been to my father.

Dad,
I treasure the memories of growing up as your baby girl.
I thank God every day for blessing me with you.
The love, laughter and family life we share are precious to me.
Thank you for your lifelong dedication to mom and your three daughters.
Thank you for being the best husband, dad, grandpa,
great-grandpa and now great-great grandpa (wow!) out there.
Thank you for holding fast to your faith, family and friends.
Your unwavering belief in, dedication to, service and
love for God are your legacy,
along with your sense of humor and fun-loving spirit.
I am so proud that such a godly, good, caring and loving man is my dad.
Words cannot express how much your
support and encouragement mean to me.

Thank you for believing in me as an Author.

I love you, dad.

~ ACKNOWLEDGEMENTS ~

~ My **Readers** – To those who read my first novel <u>A Killing on Hardee Street</u> - Thank you for taking a chance on this first time author! My deepest thanks to each one who has given feedback, referred the book to others, posted a review on Amazon, followed my Facebook Author page (VS Gardner) and posted /or allowed the posting of your selfie with my book. Such fun! To those who've waited patiently for my second novel - *thank you for being my fan base!* Your support means the world to me! You, dear reader, are such an exciting part of this journey. It's so fun to hear from and/or meet so many of you! Thank you for enjoying my stories.

~ Each **Merchant** who has made shelf space for my first book <u>A Killing on Hardee Street</u> - as we add <u>A Brick to Remember</u> I just have to say again *Thank you!* Your support means so much to me!

~ My supportive and loving **Family,** Steven, Jeremy, Janet, Nathan, Megan, Sam, Amber, Dan, Jovie, Jaxson, Ellie, Matthew, Aiden, George, Debbie, Mike, Monica, my nephews, nieces, cousins and all extended family *–Thank you!* I am so thankful we're family and I love each of you so very much!

~ My **Mom,** Dorma Lee (Williams) Lilly, whose earthly journey ended August 15, 2021. ~ I loved your excitement and support in each step of my writing journey. You would have been my first phone call when this book was published. I miss you mom.

For the investment of your time, input and guidance – *THANK YOU!*
BETA Readers: Mary McCoy, T Moise
Proofreaders: Mitch & Morgan Webber
Encourager: Megan GF Choe
Something Else: Deb Troiano

~ Above all I'm thankful to God, my loving Father, for the fulfillment of my lifelong dream to be an Author, the many blessings He continuously pours into my life and for giving me the gift of faith and a way with words.
~ My appreciation knows no bounds ~

ALSO BY VS GARDNER

A Killing on Hardee Street

You may notice I write butterflies into my stories
I've always loved my name ~ Vanessa
it's of Ancient Greek origin meaning ~ butterfly
Already beautiful the butterfly's meaningful symbolism
makes it even more precious.

~ butterfly ~

The butterfly is a great symbol of Christ
it begins its life walking the ground amongst us.
It then 'dies' and is wrapped in a shroud
until it rises again, glorified!

The butterfly is also a reminder
of people who have left us,
been made whole and are now
free of the worries of this world.

-copied/author unknown-

A Brick to Remember

VS Gardner

CHAPTER 1

Denvel's heart was full as he watched his little girl pretending in the makeshift play area. His childhood hadn't been happy. He'd grown up extremely poor, the son of an abusive father and disengaged mother. He could never have imagined his life would turn out to be this good. It left him feeling especially blessed.

He loved his wife, Megan, beyond expression. Eager to escape the trials of their youth, they had set out on their own earlier than most. They wanted nothing more than to leave that life behind them.

Knowing the odds were against them made them even more determined to make it. At first it was a real struggle just to keep the bills paid, but with a lot of hard work they were finally able to start saving. Eventually, they had managed to purchase their small house only fifteen miles from his job down on the docks. Never having aspired to be wealthy they were excited to reach a level of living comfortably. What mattered most was that they were happy.

Denvel was proud of his ability to provide for their small family and his wife loved staying at home with the children. She prepared delicious and nutritious meals on a tight budget and kept the house clean. She loved giving their children a happy life. The life neither of them had enjoyed as children.

Megan was at the grocery store now. She had taken their older child, their son, with her. It was raining and a bit cold. The basement he was sitting in was large enough to keep the children's riding toys. It had ample space for them to really move about.

Denvel was home with the baby, their little girl, who had just turned four. She loved playing outside more than anything. But that wasn't happening today.

"Watch me, daddy!" she suddenly exclaimed as she climbed onto her tricycle. She began to ride in a circle around the support posts and furnace that were standing in the center of the large room. He clapped his hands together, smiling and cheering her on as she giggled. Her eyes brightened and her face beamed proudly with each turn she took.

When the spin cycle on the washing machine stopped, he got out of the easy chair and went to move the clothes into the dryer. He had no qualms with doing 'women's work' as most of the men in his generation did. There was nothing he wouldn't do for the good of his family. He knew of no reason a man shouldn't help his wife. This was especially true, when that wife would work as hard as any man to better their life together. He started the dryer cycle and put another load in to wash all while keeping an eye on his little girl. He then returned to the easy chair.

Watching as she rode her tricycle in a large circle, he marveled at what a beautiful creature she was. Her fair skin and curly light brown hair replicated her mother's. The deep brown eyes, thin nose and full lips were his. She was the perfect combination of the two of them. She would be a lovely woman one day. Outward beauty wasn't what mattered to Denvel though. What he wanted for his daughter was for her to have a beautiful spirit, just like her mother's.

There was no one on God's green earth with a more beautiful spirit than his Megan. And you want to talk about strength? No woman alive was stronger than she. It was her strength that had helped him through the darkest days of his young life.

The two of them were neighbors who grew up as friends. He wasn't sure he would've survived his upbringing if not for that. Her strength was what had drawn him to fall in love with her as they became young adults. It was her strength, not his own, that had carried him through the hard times. He liked to think he could've overcome on his own but, in truth, he knew he never would have.

He needed some of her strength now but his fear of putting her in danger was keeping him from confiding in her. For her, and the children's sake, he needed to untangle this mess on his own. With that thought he reached into his pocket and ran his thumb over the flash drive he had put there earlier.

What should he do with it? He had to put it somewhere; somewhere safe, where no one would find it. No one must know what he knew, *what*

2

he wished he didn't know, until he could figure out what to do about it. Until then he must protect himself and his family.

Denvel was afraid.

There was no denying it. This was the kind of thing that could cost a person everything, even his own life.

His life had been going so well. He didn't need this kind of complication. Why did this have to happen? He wanted nothing to do with any of it. But it was the hand he'd been dealt.

All he could do was hope and pray no one was the wiser until he decided what to do. He wished he could just forget about it, but he couldn't. Even if he could, that wouldn't be right and he could never live with himself if he didn't do what was right.

Despite his unseemly upbringing and small place in the world he was a man of great integrity. To his way of thinking a man had nothing if he didn't have that. It was his wife's strength that had drawn him to her. Likewise, though he didn't realize it, it was his integrity that had drawn her to him.

Denvel had been keenly keeping an eye on his daughter during all this deliberation. He continued watching her as she moved over to the small area beneath the stairway.

In years past, a chimney had run upward at that spot. There had been a fireplace on the main level above him, and another in the master bedroom on the floor above that. With the modernization of the house a furnace had been installed, nullifying the need for the fireplaces. When he and his wife purchased the house they painted the cement floor and added a clear sealant so the children could play in a clean place. This was when they noticed the sealed fireplace located under the stairs, on the one brick wall in the basement, where she was now playing.

"Daddy," she called out to him, "come help me." He got up and went to see what she needed.

"Help me move it," she pleaded as she pulled on the toy baby bed set up under the stairwell for her baby dolls. "I want her to sleep over there," she said, pointing to the main part of the room.

"Oh, we can't do that," he answered. "It would be in the way when mommy's carrying laundry up and down the stairs. We have to keep it under the stairwell. I'm sorry, baby girl. How about if we just move it over to this side though?" he asked as he picked up the baby bed. He bent at the knees to

3

get under the stairs and placed the toy bed on the opposite side of the play area.

Her face lit up and she hurried over to get the baby blankets and her other baby dolls. Content with the new location she went about putting them all to bed chattering happily as she played.

As he backed out of the tight space he remembered the last time he had played here with his daughter and a thought began to take shape. Returning to the easy chair he watched her play and continued thinking it through.

A few moments later he said, "Hey, little Dove, come here a minute."

She hurried over to her daddy excited to see what he wanted.

"Do you remember the hideaway we found for your little toys last time daddy played under the stairs with you?" Her head cocked to the side and her soft curls spilled across her shoulders as she puzzled the question over.

He waited patiently.

"Oh, yes!" she suddenly said and turned away from him to hurry back to the play area. She stood facing the wall and ran her hands along the brick just as he had shown her the last time. Watching her movements he felt a sense of pride at how smart his little girl was.

He was impressed!

She missed it the first time so she stood back again, studying the bricks and thinking.

Again, he waited patiently.

Ready to try again she placed her little hands on the surface of the brick. Slowly and gently she moved them sideways across the bricks. Suddenly she stopped and turned her head to look at him. Smiling broadly, she said, "I feel it, daddy!"

He chuckled and answered, "Good job, little Dove! What do you do now?"

Grinning happily she turned back to face the brick wall. She placed her little fingers at the edge of the brick she had felt jutting out ever so slightly. Poking around gently, she wedged her finger into the loose mortar at the lower left corner of the brick. The pressure caused the right side of the brick to protrude outward at an angle. Gently she pulled on that end of the brick until it began to slide out.

Her father laughed as he got up from the easy chair and walked over to join her. Kneeling beside her he told her how proud she had made him.

A Brick to Remember

Together they pulled the brick out and put it on the floor beside her feet, clad in small pink tennis shoes.

She squealed with delight as she saw the row of small toys she had placed inside when they first discovered this hiding place.

Her father smiled. He had forgotten how spacious the shelf behind the sealed fireplace actually was. He supposed the chimney mortar had simply broken away with age. He could only assume that after noticing the loose bricks and realizing they had excess cement after pouring the floor, the renovators had simply removed the bricks and poured the extra cement into the area behind the original fireplace. The cement filled the open space. As it settled it created a flat shelf behind the bricks. The loose brick he and his daughter found just hadn't sealed well. When they pulled it out they discovered the perfect hideaway for a child's tiny toys.

His little girl's eyes shone with excitement as she removed the toys she had hidden before.

"Now, why don't you choose what to put in the hideaway this time?"

Her father's question sent her hurrying over to the toy box to make her choices. A few minutes later she returned with her hands full. Some of the toys she'd chosen were too big to fit into the space so Denvel helped her narrow it down to the four smallest.

Both of them were smiling as he coached her in maneuvering the small items into place. Each time she successfully left one standing on the shelf she clapped and jumped up and down. He loved this little girl so much! She found such joy in each accomplishment!

After standing the last toy in place she bent down to pick up the brick.

"Wait," her father said softly prompting her to turn and look at him curiously.

"Daddy has a toy he wants to put with yours. Is that okay?"

Her eyes grew wide and she clapped her hands together in innocent glee.

"Oh, yes, daddy! What fun!" she all but shouted, throwing her arms around his neck in a tight hug.

Smiling, she stood back and waited to see her daddy's toy.

Reaching into his pocket he wondered if this was wise. He wasn't at all sure it was. Withdrawing his hand he looked down at the grey flash drive nestled inside the plastic protective covering he had taped around it. After running his thumb over it one last time he handed it to his little girl.

5

CHAPTER 2
(Twenty years later)

Leanza Williams rushed through the Stokesbury, South Carolina airport terminal alternatively glancing from left to right quickly. After retrieving her luggage she hurried toward the rental car counter. Fifteen minutes later, keys in hand, the slender young woman headed to the parking garage. Settling into the black Chevy Impala she started the vehicle and expertly guided it away from the airport and headed towards downtown.

All she wanted was a good meal and hot shower, but both would have to wait. She was expected at a meeting with representatives from the FBI National Missing Persons DNA Database and ViCAP - the Violent Criminal Apprehension Program - in less than twenty minutes. Her earlier fears of missing the deadline had subsided. She was going to make it! In fact the timing was right on point.

She drank a protein shake as she drove since there was no time to eat and she desperately needed fuel to keep going.

She'd had a long week, a long month. Actually, it had been *a long year*, but all of her hard work was about to pay off.

Leanza's deep brown eyes, thin nose and full mouth were framed perfectly by soft waves of light brown hair. The curls of her childhood had calmed during adolescence, about the same time the boys had started taking notice of her. She showed them no interest. Leanza was intelligent and intuitive and she had big plans for her future. She wasn't about to get sidetracked by some handsome young fellow.

As soon as she was old enough to watch such television programs Leanza had literally absorbed missing persons, forensic files and cold case studies. By the time she was fifteen Leanza knew this was her chosen career.

A Brick to Remember

Her mother, Megan, stood firm in her conviction that Vocational Schools didn't get the credit they deserved. From an early age, she began explaining to both of her children the benefits of Vocational Education. The programs give students an excellent skill set with which to build a successful career without the financial burden of four year colleges. Following in her older brother, Wade's footsteps, Leanza had entered the Criminal Justice curriculum at the Accredited Vocational Center in their home town of Norfolk, Virginia.

Wade had used that school as a stepping stone, going on to obtain his Law Degree after graduating high school. Wade was ambitious, resourceful and hardworking, not to mention determined. All of which contributed to him becoming the successful Attorney he was today.

Leanza's vocational education in Criminal Justice led her to a job in the police department. As quickly as possible after her first several advancements she became an advocate for missing persons. In her new role Leanza gladly took on unsolved cases that had gone cold. At only twenty four years of age she was known for having solved the highest number of missing person cases in her county, to date. Today's meeting was the top of the upward climb in her career. It was the first time she'd been assigned a case of this magnitude. She would be working hand-in-hand with the two FBI departments she was meeting with today as the leader of the A413TF, an acronym for the Advocates for Thirteen Task Force. The goal of the Task Force was to solve the cases of thirteen missing people.

Her briefcase contained copies of every pertinent piece of evidence. Leanza had been over each document herself multiple times and with colleagues repeatedly. She had also gone over it in conference calls and zoom meetings with the agents she was now about to meet face-to-face.

Today they were all meeting in Stokesbury, the place where all the evidence converged. The town of Stokesbury is located between Myrtle Beach and Logan, South Carolina. The once small, rural community of Stokesbury has grown quickly. More and more people seeking the benefits of living near the ocean without the congestion of Myrtle Beach and its traffic were choosing to settle in Stokesbury.

It was still a bit unclear which of the two cities, Stokesbury or Myrtle Beach, these cases centered around. Either way, this was the end of the line. It may take some time to put the pieces in place but this looked to be the last leg of the journey. At least, Leanza prayed it was, for the sake of the families and loved ones of the victims.

Arriving at her destination she entered the parking garage. Exiting the car a few moments later she took the time to smooth her pencil skirt, re-tuck her blouse, put on her suit jacket, run a comb through her hair and touch-up her lipstick. Gathering her purse and briefcase she then walked confidently to the elevator which would take her into the massive building.

Exiting the elevator onto the eighteenth floor, she could see the conference room at the end of the extensive hallway stretching out before her. Mentally preparing for the meeting she straightened her shoulders, focused her mind completely on the task at hand and walked the entire length of the hallway. Entering the room a few moments later Leanza was the picture of professionalism.

Her vocation was more than just a job to her. It was about people's lives, those who were missing and those they'd left behind. There was nothing more serious in the world to her at that moment. It was this resolve that had led to her success.

The Leanza Williams of years before had not been mistaken in believing this to be her calling. It truly was.

CHAPTER 3

Vonda Graham was missing her dear neighbor and friend. Doreen had temporarily moved back to Massachusetts to be near her aging mother who needed her. It was strange seeing Doreen's condo sitting empty at the end of Anderson Street and Vonda didn't like it.

She and Doreen had met one morning while walking in the neighborhood. The two ladies chatted enjoyably on the way back toward their homes where they realized they only lived four houses apart. They quickly became walking partners after that. Vonda could hardly believe a year had already passed since their first meeting.

You need to stop being grumpy about this. She told herself as she set out alone on her morning walk. Everyone must do what they must do. And, as you've already seen, life's about change and nothing ever stays the same! Well, nothing except for God's love. Thank heavens that never changes! Vonda thought gratefully. Knowing she was free to talk with God about the way she was feeling Vonda did exactly that. By the time she had walked past the baseball field, around the public swimming pool and circled back toward home she'd had quite the talk with her heavenly Father.

As always, Vonda was feeling better after their time together.

Reaching the intersection where she and Doreen usually parted ways Vonda noticed a dark Chevy Impala parked at the front of the condo. It caught her attention right away. She was still wondering about it when she arrived home.

Lilly, her large, long-haired, white cat greeted her with a welcoming meow as she opened the front door and deactivated the alarm system. Lilly matched her every step down the hallway toward the open concept living room, dining and kitchen area.

It had now been just over four years since Vonda's dear husband, Stanley, had passed away. She and Lilly had gotten through that together. Vonda still missed him. But God had helped her through those grief-filled early days and been with her every day since.

They hadn't lived in Logan very long when Stanley passed away and Vonda became very lonely once he was gone. But God, and time, brought new friendships into her life. Quite by accident she had become good friends with Marshall, the owner of Davidson Construction Inc. the company that was building new homes in her neighborhood. Through that friendship Vonda met Marshall's family, many of his employees and his baseball teammates. Her life was now filled with acquaintances and friendships and for the most part she felt happy. She was very blessed and she knew it, but recently she'd been feeling a little lonely again.

As she continued processing her feelings Vonda realized, for the first time, that part of her loneliness may be from missing Marshall. She hadn't even considered that possibility. But now that she was, it made sense.

Marshall had become very important in her life. If she were honest, she'd have to admit he was the person she turned to first these days; her sounding board when she needed to work something through, the one she shared her concerns with and the first person she wanted to tell her good news to. There was no doubt Marshall had become her best friend and favorite companion over the past few years.

She hadn't given it much thought until right now but a new construction project had been keeping Marshall pretty tied up recently. Years ago he had founded Davidson Construction as a residential building company. As the years went by, and the company grew, it expanded in commercial building as well. Both branches of the company had since become quite successful.

The Hardee Street Project, a residential housing project in Vonda's own neighborhood, was still being completed by the residential branch of the company. As the vacant lots were purchased new homes were put up. Eight homes had been added since Vonda's move there and twice as many lots were still available.

Just a couple of months ago Marshall and his partners, Manny and Saul, had entered a bid for the contract to build an addition to the main branch of the Myrtle Beach General Hospital for the healthcare system. The company was abuzz with excitement when they were awarded the contract. Marshall had pizza, drinks and desserts delivered to every work site for an all-staff celebration the day the announcement was made. He and the partners had then treated the corporate staff, along with their guests, to a formal evening of dining and dancing at a very elegant restaurant. Vonda was Marshall's invited guest for the evening. While she wasn't accustomed to formal gatherings she had to admit to having had a wonderful time.

Since this was the largest commercial project Davidson Construction had taken on to date, Marshall was overseeing every aspect of it. Needless to say, that was adding quite a bit to his already full schedule. Vonda hadn't really thought about that until just now.

Along with the void created by Marshall's busier schedule Vonda was feeling the absence of her friend, Doreen. She would adjust in time. She knew that. She was just having a rough time of it right now. Having now made the connection to Marshall she could better understand her own discontent. Knowledge really is power Vonda thought, and relaxed a little bit with the realization.

Settling into her recliner to read this month's book club selection she pulled the soft throw cover over herself and patted her leg, inviting Lilly to join her.

Not needing to be asked twice Lilly obliged quickly. Padding her way softly across the chair and onto Vonda's lap she began to knead the throw cover as Vonda petted her. The entire length of Lilly's body dipped and rose with each stroke of Vonda's hand across her soft fur. Vonda smiled when at last Lilly stopped kneading. Her purring reaching an even higher volume than usual she curled up in a circle on Vonda's lap. The cat was soon asleep and it wasn't long before Vonda was caught up in the adventure on the pages as she read.

VS Gardner

CHAPTER 4

With her head tilted backward Leanza let the warm water of the shower spray directly onto her face. Eyes closed she cupped her hands to her face and gently pushed the water back. Following the shape of her head her hands tightened and squeezed down the length of her hair. Standing perfectly still she continued letting the water pour over her. It wasn't just rinsing away the shampoo and conditioner it was rinsing away her thoughts. This was the first time she'd been completely relaxed since her arrival five hours ago.

Within moments of entering the conference room Leanza had taken complete charge. After introducing herself she spearheaded the introductions of each of the five other members of the newly formed team. She then reiterated the purpose and goals of the Task Force and they set to work.

One by one, a picture of each one of the thirteen missing persons included in this investigation was passed around the room. The details of each disappearance were shared and discussed. As she taped the last picture onto the board Leanza was struck again with the enormity of their task.

She could have used a computer projection to display the missing but there was something to be said for the old way of doing things. Leanza wanted this assignment to touch a personal cord within each agent. The impact of holding each victim's picture in their own hands and looking closely into each face made the victims real. It was her hope that would ensure they weren't easily forgotten.

After months of digging through the lives of missing people, the previous investigators had determined that these thirteen were tied together through their vacations in the Myrtle Beach area. That is when their names were submitted to Leanza and the request for a special team had been made.

Once the pertinent evidence was laid out for the new team, Leanza began to ask the vital questions; were they all missing for the same reason? If so, what was it? Exactly what was behind all of these disappearances? Was this the work of a serial killer, some type of slave/trade operation, something else entirely, or was it all just a massive set of coincidences?

The one similarity tying all of them together was that each had vacationed in this area within three months of their disappearance. It was now up to the best of the best - Leanza Williams and these five carefully chosen agents - to solve this set of cases.

Over the next several hours they hashed out an agenda detailing the direction each agent would take in this operation. After settling on a schedule and choosing the day and time of their next meeting the group was dismissed.

Leanza had initially been slated to stay at a hotel in Stokesbury for the assignment's duration. She, however, had a different plan. If she was expected to eat, sleep and breathe this case for the next six months she was willing to do it on one condition; that she live in a nearby rural community.

Leanza knew herself well enough to know living and working downtown would be counterproductive. She needed open spaces, nature and a quiet environment if she was to be buried in casework. It was the only way she could keep her sanity. She simply had to be able to step away into at least a somewhat normal life. The short commute to a new setting would help her make that happen.

Leanza had repeatedly proven herself in the past, so her superiors knew what they were getting. That was the reason she'd put it out there. It was also the reason strings were pulled until she got exactly what she had asked for. A condominium being offered as a short-term rental in a nearby small town had been located and secured as her residence throughout the duration of this case.

After the meeting ended Leanza stopped at a Chinese take-out place and made several selections. She then entered the rental address into the Impala's GPS system and headed for Logan, South Carolina. Twenty minutes later she parked the vehicle, walked to the front of the floor level condominium, opened the door and entered her new temporary home.

Refreshed by her shower and comfortable in her night shirt Leanza retrieved the takeout containers from the refrigerator. She had purposely chosen a variety of dishes, planning for leftover meals until she could make a grocery run. It was later than she usually ate but that had been unavoidable.

Seated at the dining room table Leanza enjoyed her meal and let her eyes lazily take in her new surroundings. The place had a homey feel that appealed to her. It wasn't elegant or overdone but there was definitely a certain style to it. Yes, this condo would do quite nicely. She looked forward to seeing her outside surroundings in the morning.

After putting the extra food away and clearing the dishes Leanza settled comfortably into the recliner with her laptop. Typing in her daily personal journal was a nightly habit that had begun in her youth. Well, it had actually been a handwritten journal back then. The practice had remained a constant through the years. Spiral notebooks were replaced with hardback journals which were later changed to typewritten pages and finally computer files. Today had been full, which meant her head now dipped and bobbed with sleepiness even as she typed.

Awaking with a start Leanza found her fingers relaxed on the keyboard. She was totally unaware of how much time had passed since she'd nodded off. This wasn't the first time she'd fallen asleep while typing and it wouldn't be the last.

Experience had proven there was no point in trying again so she set the computer aside, turned off the living room lamp and made her way to the bedroom. She would backtrack and catch up on her journaling tomorrow.

Leanza barely took time to thank God for her life, her health and her purpose while pulling the covers back and climbing into bed. In less than a full moment she was sound asleep.

CHAPTER 5

Vonda opened her bag chair and set it up on the lawn not far from the stage where the bluegrass band was tuning up.

She saw Marshall pulling into the parking area and waved. When he reached her a few minutes later they shared a brief hug. Marshall set his chair next to hers and the two of them chatted pleasantly with other community members for the next five minutes. Marshall's brother, Mason, and his wife Stacy, along with their two boys soon joined them. All of them were surprised and excited, when Mitch, the brothers' only other sibling, arrived just before the show would start. After accepting a new job in North Carolina six months ago, Mitch had moved four hours away. It made it harder for him to join them in pleasant activities like this one. His announcement that he was staying for the weekend was met with cheers from the boys and overall excitement.

It wasn't long before Jack Murphy took the stage and welcomed everyone to the <u>Down at the Barbershop</u> live radio show. Jack owned the local WLSC Tiger Radio station which featured this program every Friday morning. The show took place behind the Logan Barbershop on the outdoor Big Bang Boom Stage with spectators sitting under the old Elm tree. For two hours Jack humbly shared his own musical talents and other local talent. He voiced advertisements for local Logan businesses sponsoring the show and shared music history and a weekly Mayberry Trivia quiz over the airwaves.

Once the Pickadilloes band was introduced the toe tapping began: guitarist Gary Long, Doug Bell on the mandolin and bass player Gary Cole kept the audience entertained with their bluegrass selections. Today's show also featured Joe Register whose smooth voice gently crooned country tunes to everyone's enjoyment. As was true each week, musician, Normand Beaudette, played a medley of songs on his accordion halfway through the broadcast. Jack Murphy's humorous comments throughout the show never failed to bring smiles and laughter. With a good bit of ribbing, he introduced Jack Johnson as the last entertainer of today's segment. Jack soon had everyone clapping, if not singing, along.

While enjoying the program Vonda noticed a pretty, slender woman with long light brown hair walking by on the nearby sidewalk. She stopped to listen for a moment. Obviously enjoying the music, she leaned against the light post and tapped her foot in time.

When the show ended Vonda said her goodbyes while bagging up her chair and slung it over her shoulder. Out of the corner of her eye she saw the woman she'd noticed earlier turning to leave. The two women arrived at the same spot on the sidewalk at the exact same moment. They smiled casually to one another and fell into step heading in the same direction.

"The music was quite good today, didn't you think?" Vonda asked.

"I did," the young woman answered without looking in Vonda's direction. "I'd just started taking a look around the area earlier today when I noticed they were setting up. Once I finished, I made it a point to come back to see what was going on."

"Oh, it was your first time attending then?" Vonda asked her.

"Yes, it was. I heard the DJ say it's a weekly broadcast. That's really nice."

"Yes, it is. I try to come every week." Vonda answered, noticing that they were still walking in the same direction.

"You said you were just taking a look around, are you new to Logan?"

This time the young woman turned to look directly at Vonda as she answered "I am. I actually just arrived yesterday."

"Oh, well, welcome to Logan then!" Vonda said with a smile. "Let me introduce myself. I'm Vonda Graham."

"Leanza Williams," Leanza answered with a smile of her own. "Have you lived here long?"

"I've been here just short of five years now," Vonda replied. "But Logan has completely become my home. It's a lovely place to live."

Vonda was surprised the young woman hadn't turned away yet as they were now approaching Anderson Avenue. The condominiums across the street from Vonda's home were the last dwellings in this direction beyond which there was just woodland. Leanza turned onto Anderson with Vonda, which caused her to look at the young woman in surprise.

"I'm sorry if I'm being too forward here, but where exactly are you heading?" Vonda asked.

"I was actually wondering the same thing about you," Leanza answered before adding, "I'm staying there for now." She was pointing to Doreen's condominium.

So this is the tenant renting Doreen's place, Vonda thought, but said instead, "Well, how about that? Welcome to the neighborhood."

Vonda immediately turned and pointed four houses down on the opposite side of the street while saying, "My house is the last one. See the country blue place with the windmill palm trees in the front yard?" She had a definite sense of Déjà vu. The morning she'd met Doreen the two of them had stood in this same location. Not knowing that the year to come would see them become walking partners and close friends Vonda had spoken the exact same words. Perhaps she was looking into the face of another such friend right now.

CHAPTER 6

Driving through the Hospital parking lot Marshall Davidson took the farthest turn onto the dirt road leading to the construction site for the new addition. He couldn't help it, he felt positively exhilarated that Davidson Construction had landed the contract for the largest hospital expansion project to be completed in Myrtle Beach, to date. It was an exciting time for Marshall and his partners, most specifically for Saul: the Director of Commercial Building.

They had just broken ground on the project and gotten the big equipment brought in. Supplies were on order and as soon as the foundation was laid construction of the new wing would begin. This new addition would add two hundred and fifty beds to the existing three hundred bed structure, resulting in a five hundred and fifty bed acute care facility. It would be the largest in Horry County. Marshall was proud his company was building the new addition. He felt honored since this facility would provide vital health care to the people living in the area he loved so much.

The number of meetings Marshall had attended to get to this point was staggering. He'd expected to work closely with the Chief Executive Officer of the Hospital and, of course, the architect. He had not expected so many other people to be involved in the process. The Hospital board members were to be kept up-to-date on all aspects of the addition. The medical staff had not only been included, but their objections and approvals had resulted in changes to the architectural plans. Marshall was astonished that hospital leadership treated the opinions of staff with such respect. In his opinion that spoke very highly of the CEO, COO and board members.

Marshall's professional network was definitely expanding through this venture. When submitting the bid he had vastly underestimated the expansive network involved in this project. Due to the extensive interaction and time involved, Marshall was getting very comfortable with the staff of

A Brick to Remember

Myrtle Beach General Hospital on every level, from the janitorial and cafeteria staff all the way up to the CEO. He couldn't be more pleased with how it was all working out. He found himself spending a little time with at least one person on the medical staff daily while at the job site. Since initially having been introduced to some of the department leaders they were now quick to join him over a cup of coffee or lunch whenever he was spotted in the cafeteria. Many had joined him, either individually or as a group, on more than one occasion. Each person was a pleasure to be with and he was continuously impressed by their professionalism.

Marshall would never divulge this but he found himself enjoying the occasional impromptu chats with one particular staff member more than any of the others. A not-far-from-retirement member of the maintenance crew named George El. George had come on staff right out of high school in the janitorial department. He moved into maintenance a few years later and had since spent his entire career taking care of the building.

There was no denying the actual affection in his words and voice whenever George spoke of the 'old girl' - his affectionate nickname for the hospital building itself.

George openly shared how grateful he was to have spent his life working for the South Carolina healthcare system. Its provision of good income and medical benefits had allowed George to provide comfortably for his family. His children were born there and he and his and dear wife had been cared for by the medical staff on many occasions through the years.

George was filled with memories of events and conversations that had taken place within the walls of Myrtle Beach General Hospital. He shared experiences from that vast storehouse whenever the occasion presented itself. Close to retirement, and getting closer all the time, George couldn't be more pleased to be on hand to see the hospital expand.

The project was to be completed within a period of eight months. George was happy it was bringing opportunities for people, just like him, to become employees of what was, to his mind, the greatest healthcare system in existence.

George spoke favorably of most everyone whose name came up. Marshall did notice that when George had nothing good to say he simply stayed silent. He was obviously a man of integrity and kindness. While humble, he was definitely proud to be among the staff of Myrtle Beach

General. Anyone who knew Marshall Davidson would see similarities between the two men. It was completely understandable that Marshall would be drawn to George. They seemed to be cut from the same cloth.

Marshall's purpose today was to quickly survey the new construction area. He would be spending the bulk of his time at this location over the next six to eight months and wanted to be comfortable there.

Heading back to his truck, after a quick walk through, Marshall glanced over at the existing hospital. He and his little brothers had been born within her walls. Years later, on the exact same day and at almost the same time, his parents had died there.

The facility was soundly constructed when it was built and had been updated frequently throughout the years. The new addition would add significant value. Through this expansion the healthcare system was adding more quality medical care to the people of the Myrtle Beach community, including the many tourists who came annually.

It was an exciting time for the medical staff, the Davidson Construction company and the Myrtle Beach community as a whole.

CHAPTER 7

Leanza stood up, stretched and walked away from the table. Having spent the last four hours studying the contents of the case file spread over it in a semi-organized fashion she needed a break.

To anyone else the table would look like a garbled mess but to Leanza it made perfect sense. She had a system and it worked for her. She'd done this for so long and had such a natural talent for it that when she looked at the evidence her mind categorically organized it.

It was as though her brain could look at what was laid out, pick it up, move it around and consider it until something clicked into place. She didn't know how it worked. She just knew it did.

Leanza had purchased a white board soon after her arrival. Between the table contents and the white board notes she fully expected to find the elusive answer. But after four hours without a breakthrough she needed to step away.

Another investment she had made was a coffee maker. Individual K-cup coffee brewers were sufficient for daily life but for casework she needed an entire pot of coffee! She now went to the kitchen and put a new pot on to brew. It promised to be a long day.

Once the coffee was ready Leanza poured a cup and took it to the living room. She drew her legs up beneath her while settling into the easy chair. She then sat staring into space silently sipping the hot liquid. Her mind was churning through the activities of Jessica Gunther and the interview statements taken from her acquaintances after she went missing.

Jessica had vacationed in Myrtle Beach for just short of two weeks the summer before her final year of College. She met up with a group of friends and the majority of her time was spent on the beach. She did, however, take in a few tourist attractions: a dolphin cruise, parasailing and a couple of popular shows in between dining out quite often and visiting a few clubs.

21

The only unusual thing that happened was when she stepped on broken glass while barefoot. The cut warranted a visit to the hospital emergency room. She was stitched up and sent on her way hobbling a bit but still able to enjoy the remaining two days of her trip.

The answer to her disappearance was here. But where and what was it exactly? This was the most grueling part of the process. Knowing the answer was staring you right in the face but still eluding you.

Leanza had been here before. The only thing to do was to keep going over it until the answer made itself clear. She would spend the rest of today on Jessica's file. Tomorrow she'd move on to her next missing person.

She had four cases to study as did three of the other agents. The fifth agent, Jeremy Alan, would chase down anything the other agents found that was questionable. Somewhere in the activities of these thirteen missing person case files lay the commonality that would explain their disappearance.

By early evening Leanza needed to get out of the house. Having been cooped up too long she needed fresh air and sunshine. A walk would do the trick. She put on her walking shoes, locked the door behind her and set off in the direction of Main Street. Getting closer to downtown she could smell burgers frying. Where was that heavenly scent coming from? Turning at the town center just before reaching the railroad track she spotted Betty's Grill. It looked to have a walk-up window beside the entrance. She opted for going inside instead and found herself a booth.

The young waitress was friendly and Leanza loved her thick southern accent. She was obviously a hometown girl. Leanza chose a burger, fries and diet soda. She enjoyed people-watching as she waited for her meal. Patrons were talking and laughing loudly at each table, obviously enjoying the company and food. Still others arrived at the pick-up window, retrieved their order, paid and went on their way. This seemed to be a very popular spot in Logan. Once her meal arrived and she started eating Leanza understood how Betty's could be a town favorite. Her burger was top notch and the fries were delicious. Fully satisfied with the experience Leanza left a generous tip, wished her waitress a good evening and headed home.

After a good night's sleep she was back at it early the next morning. This time the case before her was that of Donald Collins. Donald was part of a group of single young construction workers. Four of the men who worked on the same crew had opted to take a Myrtle Beach vacation together between jobs. Leanza flipped the white board, set up the card table she'd located in the spare bedroom and began laying out the evidence. Four hours later she was again in need of a break and more fresh coffee to get her through another long day of case study.

She was well into her second hour of reading through interview statements when something caught her attention. One of Donald's friends was giving a run-down of events the group had participated in together. In the middle his statement read: "Oh wait, Donald didn't make it to that one. He was a no-show that day. He didn't stay at the same hotel as the rest of us. So when he didn't show up we just figured he had changed his mind." He then continued to list the rest of the activities.

Leanza's mind went into overdrive. What did Donald do during the time the others were on that chartered fishing boat? Was this segment of Donald's time in Myrtle Beach accounted for anywhere else in his file? Leanza went into search mode trying to locate the missing information. An hour later, satisfied that the segment of Donald's time was indeed unaccounted for, she made several notes for the A413TF meeting which was taking place on Friday. She would share the information with the entire group and it would fall to Jeremy to find out where Donald had actually been during that time.

CHAPTER 8

While advancing through the ranks from New York City Police Officer to Detective, to Sergeant, and prior to making the crossover into the FBI, Jeremy Alan had come up against a number of intense criminals. The trend had continued during the three years he worked as an FBI agent prior to taking his current position within the Violent Criminal Apprehension Program. Working in ViCAP for the past five years he'd witnessed the worst of what humanity has to offer. With that job change Jeremy had relocated from New York to South Carolina and his personal life became more peaceful. Simultaneously, his professional life became more intense. Jeremy could tell you in no uncertain terms that working in ViCAP was no joke.

His days of saying he'd seen it all were now long passed. Having been proven wrong time and again made it feel as if he were tempting fate each time he said it. He had just about had his fill of violence, depravity and evil prior to joining ViCap. After that his investigations covered even more despicable acts making it necessary to reevaluate his use of the phrase. When his job continued to prove he indeed *had not* seen it all Jeremy decided it was time to stop saying he had.

After five years his time in ViCAP was beginning to wear on him. He now wanted, perhaps even needed, to see good in humanity again. He was getting to a point of questioning if that was even possible when word came through that a temporary new team was being formed.

The purpose of the team was to investigate a number of missing person cases somehow tied to the Stokesbury/Myrtle Beach area. Jeremy was immediately interested and wanted to toss his hat in the ring.

As it turned out - it wasn't that simple. Interested parties had to apply for the position by submitting a detailed report in the form of an essay stating why they were interested and what they could bring to the table.

A Brick to Remember

The synopsis given was that each agent would study a limited number of the original case files. The team would then meet, discuss each agent's findings and decide the best mode of investigation to determine the cause of these disappearances. Since they were acting as advocates for thirteen missing persons the new team was to be called the A413TF team, essentially the "Advocates for 13" Task Force. Jeremy really liked that acronym. He wanted in. Actually, he wanted in badly. He needed to do something beyond tracking down American's most depraved criminals. He liked the idea of being an advocate. It felt hopeful and he hadn't felt hopeful in years. If, as these things had a way of doing, the investigation revealed depravity, evil and death, at least he could help bring closure to the families of the missing. It wasn't much but it was still a positive in the outcome.

Setting out to apply for the coveted position Jeremy felt strongly that he needed an angle. He needed something that would make him invaluable to Leanza Williams, who was not only heading up the A413TF but choosing its agents.

Jeremy could think of nothing else until he came up with an angle he believed could secure his place on the team. He wasn't sure it was perfect but felt confident enough to pin all his hopes on it.

After compiling the essay detailing his years of investigative work and listing specific accomplishments Jeremy ended with the following paragraph: "After looking back over all the teams I've worked on in the past I can see that one thing has been missing. That missing element is what I believe will guarantee the success of the A413 Task Force. What's needed is for the team to have one team member whose sole contribution to the project is to follow up on and resolve loose ends. In all my years of investigative work loose ends have been the most bothersome part of the job. They are always time consuming and often involve backtracking. Having one agent whose sole purpose is to follow up and resolve anything and everything team members come up against is vital to the timely resolution of this operation. Furthermore, I volunteer to be that agent. If you give me the chance you won't be disappointed. I will chase down every lead regardless of how small or encompassing. I'll do whatever it takes, as quickly as possible, to resolve the details of the investigation. By this clarification we may be able to ensure that the person or persons behind these disappearances is not only stopped, but brought to justice once and for all."

After completing the application and interview process Jeremy was thrilled to receive an email from Leanza Williams inviting him to join the investigating team. He was proud to be a member of the A413TF and considered it the most important accomplishment of his career, to date.

After repeated exposure to an overwhelming amount of violent photographic and video images, documentation, criminal interviews and trial presentations he was ready for comprehensive investigative work. It had been a long while since he'd been able to lose himself in the process and he was looking forward to the change.

Jeremy had felt excited about the investigative aspect of the job. Now that he had secured the position he was determined to prove that the team and the families of the missing could count on him. He was determined not to let anyone down.

CHAPTER 9

Vonda was relaxing in a lawn chair in her front yard. While enjoying the cool evening breeze she looked up to see Leanza approaching from across the street.

"Well, hello there neighbor," she called out.

"Hello! Are you up for a visitor?"

"Absolutely! I welcome the company," Vonda answered, gesturing toward the empty chair beside her.

Crossing the yard Leanza took the seat and asked, "It's a beautiful evening, isn't it?"

"It certainly is. I absolutely love end-of-summer weather in South Carolina. The hot days still allow for summer clothes while the evenings are pleasant without being so cold we need a sweater."

"I haven't been to South Carolina at this time of year before. I'm looking forward to it, but truthfully, I've been wondering what type of clothing I'll need."

"How long do you expect to be in the area?" Vonda asked, remembering that Doreen wasn't returning until next summer.

"My current work assignment is six months so I'll be here at least that long. I'm probably looking to leave in March or April of next year depending on how the case pans out."

The two women conversed about Leanza's needed wardrobe before moving on to chat about the houses on Anderson Avenue. Vonda filled Leanza in on how she and her late husband, Stanley, had come to be there. She then shared what little she knew about the people occupying the surrounding homes. She pointed out the newest houses which were all part of the Hardee Street Project of home constructions taking place on the many vacant lots.

27

Vonda asked a few questions about Leanza's life in an effort to get to know her better. She was excited to have another woman in the neighborhood. The companionship would be nice.

It was interesting to learn about Leanza's background. Her line of work sounded fascinating and it was obvious she had a passion for it. Vonda commented on that and Leanza looked away thoughtfully before replying.

"There's a reason for that," she said. "My father disappeared when I was four years old. He's never been seen or heard from again and his case has never been solved."

"Wow," Vonda responded with a slight whistle. "I imagine that had a huge impact on your life. Thank you for sharing that with me, Leanza."

"And you would be right," Leanza answered. "I don't remember much about what my mother went through at the time but I've watched her live with it since. Obviously this has given me first-hand experience as to what the families of missing persons go through. I wonder, since I was so young at the time, if I even have any real memories of my dad. I know certain things about him, of course, and I'd like to think I remember him but...." her voice trailed off sadly as she looked out across the horizon.

Vonda sat studying the young woman's face. She felt a strong compassion for Leanza and immediately began asking God to meet her new friend's emotional needs and give her peace.

A few seconds passed before the conversation picked up again. The two women talked enjoyably until dusk began to fall. They wished each other a good evening and Leanza headed across the street. Lilly greeted Vonda with some soft meowing as soon as she entered the house. Vonda picked Lilly up, walked to the front window and stood petting her while watching Leanza finish the short walk back to her condo.

Once inside Leanza found herself feeling a bit reflective as she settled into the recliner with her computer. She was intent on catching up on her daily personal journal. Reading over her last entry she had to chuckle at the incoherent sentences she had typed while falling asleep the night before. Leanza had come to fondly refer to such entries as sleep-typing. She couldn't say exactly when it had begun but at some point as her life had become more demanding she'd started nodding off while filling in her journal. The next time she went to make an entry she would find it. *It* - being whatever she had typed while falling asleep. *It* never made any sense.

More often than not *it* included words that tied to her past. Whether the very distant past or just earlier the same day. Many times *it* contained words that made no sense to her at all.

There were even a few words and phrases that seemed to show up repeatedly. Leanza had puzzled over them at times. They simply didn't make any sense. The phrase 'Little Dove' showed up regularly as did some mention of bricks and a hideaway. None of it made sense to her at all. Not long after she'd noticed this trend of falling asleep while typing, Leanza had made the decision not to delete her sleep-typed sentences. Instead, she chose to leave them as part of the journal. She did begin to highlight them in yellow & italicize the entries. She did this so she knew to skip over that section on the rare occasions when she read back over her journal. She wasn't even sure why she insisted on keeping the sleep-typing.

No, that wasn't true.

She kept them because many times her sleep-typing contained a reference to her dad. The references were in the form of the words, dad or daddy. It was as though, deep in the recesses of her mind, her inner child, if you will, remembered the man she had lost so early in her life. There was something comforting in that. Even though her conscious mind didn't recall her dad or, at least, nothing specific about him, Leanza liked the fact that somewhere inside her there was a little girl who still remembered her father.

CHAPTER 10

Leanza hurried down the long hallway toward the conference room on her way to the second A413TF meeting. She was eager to share her findings and see what the rest of the agents had come up with.

At the same time, she was looking forward to this meeting being over, as if that made any sense.

Outside of the effort it had taken to adapt to her new surroundings over the past two weeks, every ounce of her energy had been given to studying case files. She was ready to give the most significant part of that information to Jeremy. His follow up promised to take them one step closer to solving these cases. Work was all that had consumed her thinking for days and she needed a break; *a real break*. She wasn't sure how to achieve that yet, but as soon as today was over she intended to figure it out.

Once all the agents were gathered Leanza called the meeting to order, explained today's format and got started. Over the next three hours the white board became covered with important markings as each investigating agent took turns summarizing their four cases for the rest of the group. Each agent had come up against a variety of unknowns.

Jeremy was systematically given those loose ends to follow up on throughout the presentations. He wasted no time utilizing every technological resource available to begin immediately chasing down the missing information.

Having designated the entire day for this meeting they had collectively agreed that after every agent presented their findings a two hour lunch break would be taken. This would give them the chance to clear their minds with a little fresh air, sunshine and food from their choice of the many local eateries before getting back to it.

A Brick to Remember

During that two hour break getting lunch was the furthest thing from Jeremy's mind. He had leads to follow up on and information to gather. These agents were counting on him and he wasn't about to fail them.

When two-thirty rolled around and the meeting reconvened Jeremy was ready to present his findings. He'd managed to find answers to a good twenty percent of the questions the team had brought to the table during the morning session. Of course he had tackled the most relevant issues first. The remaining information would take days, if not weeks, to track down. He'd be presenting his findings at each meeting until all issues were resolved. If any discovery seemed of major importance before they gathered he could share with the team through email or texts. An unscheduled meeting could always be pulled together in the event of a major development coming to light.

Once everyone had taken their places Jeremy delved in. Things took an interesting turn when he began to address his findings on Donald Collins. This was the case file in which Leanza had realized there was an entire day unaccounted for during Donald's Myrtle Beach vacation with his three co-workers. Although the four had planned the trip as a team Donald had chosen to stay in a hotel he'd frequented in the past instead of with the others.

On the day in question the other three men met early, as previously planned, to spend the day on a chartered fishing boat for deep sea fishing. Donald never showed up. Jeremy telephoned the man who had made the original statements when interviewed. He gave Jeremy the missing information. Either it hadn't been mentioned in the original interview or the interviewing officer had neglected to put it in the report.

The other agents were amazed at how quickly Jeremy was able to ascertain what had actually happened. As was his daily habit, Donald rose early and headed out for a jog. He was running on the beach when his foot landed in a low spot in the sand causing his leg to twist. He immediately heard a loud pop and felt intense pain in his knee. After slowly and painfully retracing his steps he arrived back at his hotel. He inquired of the hotel clerk for the location of the nearest Urgent Care where the Dr. ordered x-rays. They revealed a slightly torn meniscus. Donald was given a cortisone shot, instructions for at-home care and told to follow up with his family doctor upon completion of his vacation. Obviously, his day on the chartered fishing boat wouldn't have happened anyway but the rest of the men were already gone by the time he returned to the hotel. At that point he was unable to let them know he wasn't coming. Donald then spent the day resting his leg in his hotel room.

Thinking through the other case presentations Leanza remembered mention of a few other accidents among the other missing persons. As the agents began their end-of-day discussions it became obvious that she wasn't the only one making this connection. Files began to be pulled open as the agents searched out which emergency rooms and urgent care facilities had been visited.

Could they be onto something here?

CHAPTER 11

I don't remember the first time I consciously chose wrong over right. I doubt if anyone ever remembers that. We're all prone to selfishness from birth. It's just our natural instinct to reach for whatever we want and take it even if someone else already has it.

No one has to teach us to choose what's easiest or most lucrative for us. Isn't this the very reason parents start trying to direct their little ones to share and be kind so very early in life?

It's the very definition of the terrible twos, isn't it? A little toddler rips a coveted toy out of another child's hand simply because he wants it. He's not turning it loose regardless of the other child's complaint, tears or even fighting back. Two toddlers can be quite vicious in their battle over one toy. Mothers all through the ages have had to step in and separate them. It stems from our instinct to take what we want regardless of how it affects others.

I've thought about this a lot, simply because of the choices I've made in my own life.

No, I really don't remember the first time I purposely chose wrong over right. I am, however, acutely aware of countless times I've done it since then.

Obviously, we choose selfishly as toddlers, it's purely instinctual then. But what about later, after we've realized there *is such a thing* as right and wrong: once we have that understanding, once we're aware of that consciousness that rises up to prick us when we go against what's right. How is it that some of us purposefully continue to choose what's wrong?

I've often found myself wondering about this.

At what point is instinct replaced with conscious choice? How much do the reactions of adults and treatment from adults impact a child's ultimate reluctance and/or willingness, to repeat the wrong choice?

I haven't been able to pinpoint the answer. Nor can I deny how different situations may play themselves out when we're very young.

Sometimes I try to figure out when and why I went wrong. How much of the blame can I place on the adults in my life? How much of the blame must I accept as my own?

My sixth grade school year was a pivotal year in my life. I distinctly remember it and I think about it a lot. I often wonder how much of my moral judgment was formed or went awry due to the events of that year.

That was the school year in which I was first required to do a presentation in front of my classmates. It was a scientific experiment for my Science class. My assignment involved liquid being put into beakers. There was copper wiring attached to two cylindrical pieces which were to be dropped into the beakers of liquid: two different beakers, two different liquids, two different cylindrical pieces, each with its own piece of wiring wrapped around it, each on which one end of wiring would stick up out of the liquid while the rest was submerged.

Not knowing exactly what day I would be called upon I read the assignment at home and followed the instructions. Just as the textbook said would happen one of the wires turned blue and the other did not. Okay, I thought to myself, it worked. Easy-peasy. I'll do exactly what the book describes. Everyone will see that one wire turned blue while the other one didn't. It's as simple as that. I closed my text book and put everything away.

Science class was the last period of my school day. Two days after my practice run at home my name was called and I walked to the front of the classroom. I was feeling good. While performing the experiment I spoke confidently as I clearly explained my every move to my fellow students. Putting the required liquid into each of the beakers I pronounced the name of each liquid perfectly. I then placed one of the cylindrical shapes with its connected wire into the first beaker. Ever so gently I placed the second cylindrical shape into the second beaker.

Feeling comfortable, and a bit more confident, I watched closely. Speaking loud and clear I pointed out that the liquid around both cylinders was reacting to the wire. Small air bubbles were forming on both wires. Within a few moments the one wire had only a few air bubbles still clinging to it. It had otherwise changed not at all. The air bubbles were basically the same on the second wire but its copper colored hue had begun to change into a very distinct shade of baby blue. A few seconds later, in a loud voice and with great authority, I announced that the entire wire had changed from copper to blue.

Voila! Successful experiment! A+ in Science! Take a bow. All done and moving on now! Or so I thought....

To my great surprise my science teacher spoke up from behind me. He was wondering why the wire had reacted differently to each liquid he said simply. Would I care to explain?

What? My mind asked as I tried to maintain my composure and continue to exhibit an air of confidence.

Well, of course, I explained, that had to do with the difference in the two liquids being used. I was careful to repeat the names of each liquid correctly again while explaining that they were two distinct liquids and so, of course, the wiring would react differently. In all my words there was however, not even one word that offered a good explanation since I simply did not know the answer.

My teacher, Mr. Strong, had by this point realized I'd done only what was necessary to complete the experiment, and none of what was necessary to *actually understand* the experiment.

Based on that realization he made a choice. He chose to humiliate me to the depth of my very soul in front of the other students. I suppose it was an attempt to keep me from ever slacking off again and ultimately that did work. Unfortunately, instead of teaching me to care about my school work and be more diligent in the future what he actually taught me was how to hate; from that day forward I despised him.

Looking back over the remainder of that year I'd now wager the feeling was mutual.

Mr. Strong proceeded not only to question me in great detail but to encourage my classmates to do the same. I, of course, gave answers which made no sense until ultimately I gave no answer at all. Proving without a doubt I had no idea what I was doing. In the end I was reduced to a timid shell of my former self. Standing red-faced I quietly uttered the words "I don't know."

Mr. Strong could have, at that juncture, shown mercy and allowed me to slink away to my seat. Instead, he chose to further humiliate me by making an example of me.

I was forced to continue standing in front of the class as he towered over me. He belabored the point that a good student would do more than just follow the steps in the textbook. A good student would work hard to understand the experiment, digging deep to answer all ensuing questions at home during preparation so as to be able to answer when posed with them later on.

"Exactly," he went on to say pointing his boney finger at me "as this student did *not* do."

Upon finally dismissing me to take my seat he added smugly, "If the rest of you are wise you will not follow this piss-poor example. "

All of the other children burst out in laughter. What he had said was funny to sixth grade children. Naturally, I took their laughter to be at me. In the years since I've come to wonder if they were laughing at me or simply laughing at his choice of words.

It matters not.

The die was cast and the events which followed can never be changed.

CHAPTER 12

Vonda had just passed the condo on her way to the Thursday night Old Timer's baseball game when she saw Leanza pull into the parking lot. On a whim she stopped and stood watching as Leanza parked the Impala.

Not noticing Vonda at all, Leanza got out and stood by the open front door. Placing her purse over her shoulder she then picked up her briefcase. Reaching back inside she gathered the wrapping from the Wendy's hamburger she'd eaten on her way home, the used napkin and her empty drink cup. After shoving the trash into the Wendy's bag she turned to find Vonda patiently waiting not far from her.

"Oh, hi Vonda," she said in a surprised voice. "I didn't see you there."

"No problem," Vonda answered with a smile. "It looks like you might've had a busy day today?"

"Oh, I sure have! I've been in a meeting, literally, all day long. I can't tell you how ready I am to think about something else, *anything* else, really!" she added with a laugh.

"How about baseball?" Vonda asked quickly. "Any chance you'd want to walk to a ball game with me? I'm heading that way now."

"Oh? You are?" Leanza looked at the items in her hand, made a quick mental assessment, glanced at the condo and made a decision.

"Sure! Actually, I'd love to. Let me just put these things inside. Uh, any chance you can give me just a few minutes to change into jeans and tennis shoes?"

"Absolutely!" Vonda answered, happy to know she was going to have a companion tonight. "I'm so glad you're going to join me. I'll be right here whenever you're ready."

Half an hour later, after having chatted comfortably the entire way there, the two women arrived at the ball field. As they found their seats Vonda introduced Leanza to a few of the other spectators. She then shared with

Leanza that she'd begun attending little league ball games in an attempt to feel more at home in Logan the year after Stanley passed away.

As the game got started Marshall walked to the pitcher's mound. Vonda told Leanza she'd met him at a little league game and continued to see him when she began attending these evening games. Through those encounters their friendship had grown. The ball field had quickly become a connection to others in her community. It was an important part of Vonda's life in Logan.

The women chatted easily in between cheering for the fellas on both teams as the evening passed. Once the game ended they stayed around long enough for Vonda to introduce Leanza to Marshall and several of the other players.

As they walked home Leanza admired the new homes on Hardee Street. This prompted Vonda to share that Marshall owned the company that was building them.

As the two women conversed and enjoyed one another's company Vonda asked Leanza what was on her agenda for the coming weekend.

"I don't actually have anything specific planned but I'd really like to. I've done nothing but work since my arrival. My job can be quite intense and sometimes I just really need a break from it.

Things were pretty hectic leading up to this move and the case I'm on demands my undivided attention most of the time. Now that I think about this I'm actually overdue for some serious disengagement. I love nature so I enjoy hiking in the woods or being on the water. Living away from home I'm kind of at a loss as far as sporting equipment goes. I haven't got my golf clubs, my bicycle or my kayak. At home there are endless possibilities of places to go and things to do but I'm new to this area. I have no idea where to even start."

While listening Vonda was reminded of the wonderful times she and Stanley had spent together doing the very things Leanza was mentioning. She found herself deeply missing the comradery, friendship and love she and Stanley had always shared. She seldom gave it much thought but she was saddened now to realize she hadn't been hiking at Myrtle Beach State Park or canoeing on Spivey Lake in over four years.

Before she knew it Vonda heard herself admitting to enjoying those same activities. She quickly added that she hadn't done them since she'd lost

Stanley. Never being one to invite the pity of others Vonda usually didn't mention things like this. She didn't know what had come over her to mention it now. The more she thought about it the more she realized how much she truly missed hiking and boating.

The next thing she knew Vonda was telling Leanza about their canoe. It was one thing Vonda hadn't been able to bring herself to part with after Stanley's death. It was still on the trailer Stanley had hauled behind his car. He'd always stored the canoe on the trailer near the shed in the backyard. And that was where it still remained. They'd had so many fun times on Spivey Lake, the Little Pee Dee and the Waccamaw Rivers in that canoe together. Vonda felt herself smiling with the memories. Stanley would fish and Vonda would take pictures and read. She actually hadn't thought about those times in a very long while.

"So what you're saying is - you've got *a perfectly good canoe* just wasting away in your backyard? Are you telling me it hasn't touched the water in over four years? There's nothing wrong with it, is there? It doesn't leak, right?"

"Yes. Yes! That is what I'm telling you and no, it doesn't leak. It's nothing like that. Canoeing was just something we did together. It weighs a hundred pounds so it's not like it was something I could do by myself even if I had been inclined to, which I wasn't. It's got a wheel on one end and a handle on the other. It can easily be pulled to the water's edge and back to the car. Stanley and I did it together all the time."

Leanza stopped walking and touched Vonda's arm causing Vonda to stop walking, too. Leanza then stood facing Vonda.

"Vonda," Leanza said looking intently into her new friend's face. "Are you telling me you and I could take the canoe out together? Is that something you'd be comfortable doing?"

Vonda hadn't known until just this moment what she had actually been saying. She stood there looking into the eyes of her lovely new, young friend. She felt an old but familiar excitement rising up inside her. She turned and started walking again and Leanza fell in step with her.

"Yes," she said a few seconds later after coming to a decision. "That is exactly what I'm telling you. If you're willing to try taking the canoe out with me I'm very willing to see if it's something the two of us can manage to do together. I think it would make Stanley happy if we managed to get that old canoe back out on the water again."

"Okay then!" Leanza said as an expression of excitement spread across her face and the two of them arrived at Vonda's driveway.

"I'm game if you are!" Leanza added. "Let's plan it for this Saturday! *I'm so excited!"* she said while heading across the front lawn toward her condo. At the edge of the yard she turned and waved goodbye.

Vonda felt light in spirit as she walked the few steps up her front walk, unlocked the front door, stepped inside and disarmed the security system.

Lilly came meowing up to her and rubbed her body against Vonda's calf. Leaning down to pet her Vonda said "Guess what, old girl. The Verna Mae's coming out of retirement!!"

Stanley had affectionately referred to Vonda as Verna Mae the many times they'd worked side-by-side on renovation projects they'd done together. He had no idea why. It was just a fun nickname he'd taken to using for her while raising their family. When they bought the canoe in their older years they laughed together as he christened it 'The Verna Mae.' With the return of such happy memories Vonda's heart felt light and playful. She could almost see Stanley's teasing smile as she walked through the hallway to her bedroom and went about her nightly routine.

Just before drifting off to sleep she remembered the complaining she had done when Doreen left to help her family. Of course she wanted her friend to be there for her mother. It was just hard to see past the void Doreen's absence was leaving in her own life. She realized now and could actually admit to herself, and to God, how selfish she had been.

With the possibility of a new friendship she was seeing things a bit differently. So many times we focus on what we're losing instead of what we may gain when things change. Vonda had faced that struggle before. No doubt, she would face it again in the future, probably many times. Continuing to talk things over with God she thanked Him for helping her see things in a different light.

It had been too long since she'd had occasion to look forward to getting out on the lake in The Verna Mae. When she lost Stanley she assumed that part of her life was over but now it seemed that wasn't necessarily true. As her body and mind began to relax she said sleepily, "Thank you God, for the blessing of a new friendship. Please help me be a good friend to Leanza."

A Brick to Remember

If there was one thing Vonda's life had taught her it was that people come and go in our lives. A select few are there for the duration while most are seasonal. The circumstances indicated that Leanza was only going to be in her life for a short season but it was lining up to be a good one. And Vonda intended to enjoy it!

CHAPTER 13

The hospital cafeteria was full when Marshall walked in. It didn't take him long to realize a staff event was taking place. One tell-tale sign was the tables lining the front of the room covered in white linens. Further verification was the food on elegant serving trays being laid out in a decorative manner. Adding that the dishes themselves were specialty items like pinwheels, vegetable sushi, various crackers surrounding cheese balls with tiny serving knives left no doubt of the matter. At the end of the table was a chocolate fountain with an array of dessert items for dipping. In the corner was an elaborate fountain with streams of lemonade circulating freely. People were randomly walking up to hold out their clear plastic cups for filling.

It was quite the set-up and Marshall was about to back out of the room when the hospital CEO Daniel Travis spotted him and rushed to his side.

"Stop right there Marshall," he barked in a playful voice.

"No need for you to leave, in fact, I'm quite pleased you've stumbled into our month-end staff luncheon today. The hospital administrative team and board members are dubbing this a 'celebration luncheon' in note of several important goals being met. It wasn't highlighted in the invitation email but the new hospital addition is well worth celebrating as well. I have every intention of touching on it in my comments shortly. Please stay and join the festivities. Many of our staff members have yet to meet you and I know they'd like to."

"Well, if you're sure. Of course I'll stay." Marshall answered, now noticing the sign near the entrance announcing the staff luncheon and directing hospital guests to a separate section of the cafeteria. He didn't know how he had missed that. Daniel was now guiding him by the elbow to the head table while saying, "Very good, and yes, absolutely, I'm honored to have you join us. Please help yourself to lemonade and get comfortable. I'll join you right after I make the welcoming comments," and with that he went to stand at the front near the food table.

"Welcome everyone! Welcome!!" he called out as he clapped his hands loudly. The room immediately began to quiet down.

"As you can see we've done things up a bit for this month's staff luncheon. I believe you'll find it to your liking. Please be sure to thank the board members before you leave today. It was their unanimous decision that our chef should prepare the favorites you see spread out on the table. We're considering this a celebratory luncheon and want you all to enjoy it. As you're all aware we've achieved several long-term goals this month which were outlined in the email invitation. Congratulations everyone on a job well done!! And let's not forget about the hospital expansion! Exciting things are happening for our Myrtle Beach General Hospital family! And while I'm on that subject let me introduce the head of the new expansion construction project. Marshall, would you mind joining me for a moment?"

Marshall walked to the front of the room and stood at Daniel's side.

"This is Marshall Davidson everyone, the newest, albeit temporary, member of our family here. You'll be seeing him frequently during the next six to eight months as the building goes up. Please take every opportunity to make him feel welcome. And now let's enjoy these delicious appetizers. The board members of Myrtle Beach General, the administrative staff, and I, myself, extend a heartfelt thank you to each and every one of you! You're doing a great job – keep it up everyone!"

As the staff applauded he turned to Marshall and the two men walked to the food table and began choosing their items. Daniel turned toward the room and motioned for others to join them and the food line was formed. Everyone chatted amongst themselves as they made their selections.

Once they were seated Marshall asked Daniel how long he'd been with the hospital. The CEO shared that he had come on board almost twenty-five years ago. He was young and joined the staff as part of the IT department. After several years he was promoted to IT Director. Continuing his education he was then promoted to Hospital Administrator, then Chief Operating Officer and finally to Chief Executive Officer. Daniel shared that for the most part the administrative team members had all been on staff long-term. It was his belief, and Marshall immediately agreed, this spoke highly of the operations of the hospital. When there's poor management, people are less likely to remain on staff.

During the course of the luncheon many staff members took a few moments to introduce themselves to Marshall. It was a bit overwhelming and by the end of the luncheon Marshall knew he would never remember all of their names and roles. In the space of several hours he had formally met the Chief Financial Officer: David Minter, Human Resource Director: Amanda Brookes, Director of Registration: Mary McCoy, and Director of Housekeeping: Janet Kay. Of course, staff members were coming and going throughout the luncheon and there were many others Marshall wasn't formally introduced to. When he thought about it later in the evening, he was impressed with the professionalism and friendliness of everyone he had interacted with.

CHAPTER 14

At last Thursday's A413TF meeting Jeremy had hit the road running as soon as the agents started giving him loose ends. Knowing they were reconvening after the two hour lunch break he'd hoofed it to get a few things completed so he could present the results during the second session. Jeremy had always worked well under pressure and it usually paid off.

As the meeting wore on and his submissions for information came rolling in Jeremy was able to make a few important declarations. At the end of the day it seemed as if the team had been pleased with his accomplishments. It felt good to be on top of things.

Now that it was Friday things were getting a bit more challenging. Although he was well seasoned in tracking information down he wasn't used to having so many unrelated issues to follow up on simultaneously. Focusing on one case at a time was clearly a bit different from working thirteen different missing person cases being handled by four different agents. This was going to take a bit of juggling.

Hey, he told himself, you volunteered for this. You just need to figure it out. Get in there and prove to yourself and everyone else that you know what you're doing.

He had kept the issues in the same order they were given as the agents made their presentations the day before. The challenge now was to find the most time saving way to chase down all of the missing information. In truth - it felt a bit overwhelming. In all actuality - it was a daunting task. At least it would be for anyone who didn't have Jeremy's extensive experience and background.

He'd been staring at his list for ten minutes when he felt the answer begin to take shape. What he needed to do was to rearrange the information. It was imperative his list be compiled according to the amount of time each item would require. There were two ways of doing this but the perfect scenario would actually require a combination of the two.

Any follow up requiring research by someone on the other end - who would then have to get back with Jeremy - had to be at the top of the list. Yes, that made sense. Jeremy would reach out on those first. That would allow him to then move on to the next set of items while waiting for feedback.

Secondary to that would come the items requiring the least amount of legwork on his end. Once that information was gathered and submitted he could check those items completely off the list. At that point he could devote his full focus to the remaining issues. Perfect, he said to himself, as he began assessing each issue to estimate the amount of time and leg work each was going to require. Of course there were many factors that could play into the timing. Admittedly, this wasn't an exact science, but it felt good having a place to start.

As soon as the list was correctly compiled Jeremy began reaching out to the people on the other end. Phone contact was his preferred method since it may result in instantaneous resolution. Sometimes it worked. Sometimes it didn't. Each failure to immediately access a person required him to leave a voicemail. Every time this happened Jeremy shot off an email containing the exact same information as the voicemail. He made certain to clearly request the specific answers needed. In an ever-changing technologically-advancing society it's virtually impossible to guess which communication method any given person prefers. For this reason he left nothing to chance.

Now that the first issues on his loose-ends list had been tossed to the four winds, so to speak, it was just a matter of waiting to see what the wind would blow back in.

Jeremy settled in comfortably.

Anyone observing his behavior at this point might mistakenly assume he had totally forgotten about the whole thing. In reality Jeremy was mentally returning to the meeting. While comfortably lounging on his sectional he was actually going over the meeting in his mind. He didn't have an eidetic memory but he did have a high proficiency for detail. Jeremy had found over the course of his career that things often came into better focus and clearer perspective for him upon later reflection. This realization had resulted in his making a habit of quietly rethinking the initial source of

information. During this phase of the process it usually appeared to friends and family that he was being incredibly lazy and detached from his work.
Nothing could be further from the truth.

CHAPTER 15

Saturday morning found both Vonda and Leanza waking up early in anticipation of their day on the lake.

Vonda was a little worried about the two women being able to handle the canoe.

Leanza, on the other hand, was simply filled with excitement for this fun-filled day.

Leanza, independent young woman that she was, was used to getting herself and her sporting equipment where she needed to be. She had no qualms about backing the car up to the trailer.

Vonda had always filled the helper role. Still, she was surprised by how easily she slipped back into the position. She was ready to help lift and guide the trailer onto the hitch. Once it locked into place they secured it and loaded the back seat with the life jackets, seat backs and oars, all of which Vonda had located in Stanley's shed exactly where they'd always been. After a quick wipe down they were ready for use.

She hadn't done a thing with his shed after his passing. Dealing with everything inside the house, as she felt ready, had seemed more than enough to do. She saw no harm in leaving it the way it had always been so she just never forced herself to go through the shed. Besides there were occasions when she needed tools so it was handy still having them. She had never expected to be using the canoe equipment again but was thankful to find it easily now that she was.

Vonda took a small backpack containing her camera and book. That along with a bottle of water was all she had ever needed for canoeing with Stanley so it was all she took today. Leanza loaded a small cooler, small tackle box and one fishing pole into the car. Once she knew this was going to happen she had made a few purchases. They included a North Carolina fishing license since Mount Tabor was just over the state line. If she was going to get out on a lake she wanted to be ready for a good fishing day. With the boat trailer hooked up and the car loaded the two set off on their way.

It was still early morning when they arrived so a light haze was visible hanging over the water. Vonda hopped out but found she wasn't needed for directing as Leanza expertly backed the trailer down the loading dock. The most challenging part came next. Lifting and turning the canoe over. It actually went much smoother than Vonda had expected.

Soon they had the seat backs in place and everything else neatly packed inside the canoe. The very moment Vonda took her usual place up front the past four years simply fell away. Her mind settled back into the mornings she and Stanley had pushed off from this very dock, slipped their oars into the water and headed toward the center of the open lake.

The air felt the same; the horizon looked the same, the sense of adventure stirring inside her seemed the same. The only thing different was that *Stanley wasn't there.*

Leanza sat quietly in the back of the canoe gently dipping her oar, pulling it back and lifting it out of the calm water. She guided the canoe perfectly along the edge of the lake heading to the spot where it opened into a large body of water.

While thinking this trip over on Friday evening Leanza had realized it might not be as easy for Vonda as both women were assuming. It was then she had decided she would remain quiet and follow Vonda's lead until she saw exactly how Vonda was handling it. She was watching Vonda very closely now, trying to read her reactions.

Just as Leanza had suspected Vonda was going through a myriad of emotions. In those moments Leanza was the furthest thing from her mind. Leanza's silence gave Vonda the opportunity to just feel what she was feeling.

Vonda was silent. Without even realizing it she was giving herself the time she needed to grieve all over again. Unconsciously, she stopped rowing. If she had looked behind her she would have seen Leanza do exactly what Stanley had always done when Vonda got lost in the moment. Leanza simply continued to quietly row from side-to-side in order to keep the canoe on a straight path.

Drifting along so peacefully Vonda remembered Stanley and their times together in The Verna Mae. She felt again, the joy of spending those relaxed moments with him. And again she felt the sorrow of losing him. Eventually, as she came full circle back to the present her mind was willing, once again, to leave the past behind. Only then did her eyes begin to take in the beauty surrounding her. She had forgotten how much she loved the way everything was reflected as a mirror image in the water on calm mornings like this one: the moment when the heron suddenly took flight, the way ducks were so in tune with each other that they flew close to the water as a unified group before gradually flying higher and higher, turtle heads randomly spaced on the water's surface only to instantly drop as the canoe grew closer.

At some point Vonda instinctually reached for the camera hanging around her neck. She'd been snapping pictures over the last few moments when she excitedly said, "It's a perfect morning for this, isn't it, Leanza?"

"The best!" her new friend answered, thankful Vonda had worked through her feelings and was now present and enjoying their trip.

Vonda recommended a few spots where Leanza might try her hand at fishing and they maneuvered the canoe to the closest one. The two women chatted comfortably while Leanza got her fishing gear set and began casting the line.

Vonda was surprised when she looked at her watch and saw that an hour had already passed. She got her book out and kicked back to read.

Even as she read Vonda took notice that Leanza got a nibble now and then and so far was having no luck in actually catching anything. It didn't seem to be bothering her. She looked about as relaxed as possible. Talk about relaxing? It didn't get much better than this!

CHAPTER 16

Stanley and Vonda were always home by noon when they took the Verna Mae out. It took Vonda by surprise then to have Leanza ask whether she wanted to just stop on the lake or actually dock the canoe while they enjoyed their lunch. They decided to pull into a grove of trees where the beautiful Spanish moss hung freely from each limb. It created an oasis, almost a swamp area wonderland along one of the curves at the edge of the lake. It was just a typical southern scene really, so beautiful and welcoming.

Once the canoe was settled Vonda watched in amazement as Leanza opened the small cooler and proceeded to produce plastic tableware and napkins followed by a variety of small sandwiches, pickles, chips and fruit. It wasn't long before the two were enjoying their lunch as they swapped entertaining stories and their lighthearted laughter echoed across the lake.

After putting the lunch fixings away Leanza collected her fishing gear. They had decided to row across the lake so Vonda could show her friend what she and Stanley had concluded was probably the first home built on Spivey Lake. Sadly, it now sat empty with the gazebo and dock in terrible disrepair. As they worked together the canoe glided perfectly through the water and the woman talked comfortably.

Vonda complimented Leanza on her athletic skills and being an excellent sports woman and so independent. She shared that she herself had never been athletic and was often out of her comfort zone when participating in sports. Having struggled with fear throughout her life becoming independent had been an ongoing challenge. In this way she and Stanley were almost polar opposites.

Stanley had been a natural born athlete who excelled in literally everything he tried. He was adventurous and courageous. In the beginning of their relationship Vonda had taken golf and tennis lessons in a futile attempt to change her natural bend and make herself into an athlete.

51

She wanted to provide the sports competition she thought Stanley needed from her. Thankfully, Stanley loved her for who she was. He accepted that she wasn't likely to excel in those areas. He embraced their differences, realizing her limitations and never making her feel inadequate. Throughout their life together Stanley continued to enjoy all the sports he was good at. They worked together to discover those specific activities that worked for them as a couple.

In later years when the sensitivities of youth had passed, he playfully teased her and she comically exaggerated her inabilities for the sake of entertainment. In those years Vonda often accompanied Stanley on the golf course where she enjoyed her photography and he talked through his strokes with her. This resulted in both of them enjoying the game even when Vonda lagged behind to capture a butterfly or beautifully colored leaf on film. It worked for them and now added to Vonda's good memories of their happy marriage.

As to her struggles with fear and dependence Stanley often encouraged her to step outside of her comfort zone. Actually, Leanza would probably be shocked to know Vonda had once struggled with an intense fear of being on the water. The fact that she was out on a lake in a canoe at the moment was, in large part, due to Stanley's patient support in helping her overcome that particular fear. The rest of the credit went to God. Vonda had leaned on His commands not to be afraid but to instead call upon and trust in Him in the face of fear. Trusting Him had since become one of Vonda's go-to responses.

Taking the lead in the conversation at that point Leanza shared that her independence had been, not only taught, but modeled, by her own mother. With great emphasis she added that she had yet to meet another woman as strong as Megan Williams. Once she was old enough to somewhat understand the impact of having your husband disappear from your life with no explanation, Leanza had marveled at her mother's strength. Megan not only managed to keep her own sanity, she went on to raise her children in such a way that they would become two very well-adjusted adults.

Megan had never believed, not even for one moment, that her husband Denvel had left them of his own accord. His love and devotion to his family was beyond question. After all the obstacles the two of them had overcome and all the sacrifices they'd made to be together, there was

52

simply nothing that could have caused Denvel to willingly walk away. Theirs was a deep, true and lasting love through which they had been blessed with two healthy and beautiful children. They were well on their way to having the life they had dreamed of at the time of his disappearance so none of it made any sense.

Leanza and her mother had talked about this often. One of Megan's biggest frustrations came in remembering that Denvel had been unusually quiet during the weeks prior to his disappearance. Their lives were busy at that time so it wasn't until focusing on it later that Megan really saw it. She had since come to believe something was going on that he hadn't talked with her about. Without a hint as to what it was, Megan had nowhere to even start in an attempt to follow that trail. This left her feeling powerless.

Never finding answers or having proof that Denvel was either dead or alive must be a terrible burden. From her daughter's viewpoint Megan bore it with grace and dignity. Her husband's disappearance still remained an unsolved mystery, a terrible unfinished story that Megan lived with every waking moment of her life. Having Wade and Leanza to think of she had done what she had to do to move forward. Leanza admired her mother greatly in that despite everything she had never given in to hopelessness or despair.

Megan had been a stay-at-home mother when Denvel went missing. After several months with no answers the police investigation went cold. They encouraged Megan to accept the fact that she and her children had been abandoned. She told them all, in no uncertain terms, that *was not* what happened and as long as she lived she would never accept that explanation. Denvel loved his family! He would never abandon them.

Megan wasn't giving up on her husband nor was she giving up on the life he had wanted for their children. If that meant she had to give them that life on her own, and apparently it did, that's exactly what she would do.

When Wade and Leanza were older they questioned their mother on all that happened. She talked openly and honestly about all of it. She told them there was nothing worth returning to where she'd come from so that was never an option. Denvel had been the main source of income. Megan had no education or training after high school. She realized she would have to capitalize on what little skills she'd already obtained. Seeing that in the early twenty-first-century the world seemed to be quickly advancing in computer technology she set out to build on that.

Using her measly savings she invested in a high quality computer and Internet access. She began to research and subsequently to build her skill set in data entry. In the meantime, she became an at-home sales representative for a high-end cosmetic company. She was able to keep her family afloat from that income. It was only ten months after Denvel's disappearance that the world began to panic about the approach of the new millennium. That panic became known as Y2K, the shorthand term for "the year 2000." Y2K referred to a widespread computer programming shortcut that was expected to cause extensive havoc as the year changed from 1999 to 2000 at the turn of the Millennium. To prevent major impact, many companies hired data entry agents to manually change the dating in their existing files from the year 1999 to the year 2000, prior to the dawning of the New Year. Megan became proficient in this and was hired by multiple companies. It provided the income she needed to keep her household going without having to leave her children in the hands of strangers, which was one of her biggest fears, especially after mysteriously having lost Denvel.

Leanza was too young, at the time, to realize the cost at which her mother's self-education had come. She could now only imagine that Megan's life consisted of practically no sleep, long hours of child care and continuous hard work while surviving on almost nothing for many of those years.

It was clear her mom had done everything she could for the sake of the dream she and Denvel had for their children. The dream of building the good life they each were deprived of and desperately wanted for their family. Ultimately, Megan's actions and the explanation of her actions gave both of her children a clear understanding of strength in adversity.

When Leanza looked back at her childhood it was filled with happy memories: a sense of security, of being loved, of laughter and fun. At the same time, Leanza had been given responsibilities and held accountable. She was no stranger to hard work. Her mother taught her children the importance of an excellent work ethic, keeping your word, being kind and helping those less fortunate than yourself. Leanza's had been a well-rounded and happy upbringing.

A Brick to Remember

If Megan had times of despair Leanza never witnessed them. That's not to say she never saw her mother cry. She was just always assured that tears weren't the end of the matter. Megan told her children there are definitely times when life is hard, and those are the times we must realize 'this too shall pass'. God never promises anyone a trouble-free life. He only promises to be with us through it all, and contrary to humanity, God always keeps his promises. God *will* give us the strength we need *when* we need it. For Leanza, her own mother's life was all the proof she needed of that truth.

Leanza shared with Vonda that whenever a rainbow appeared in the sky Megan had, without fail, reacted with extreme excitement. Leanza laughed lightly as she added, "actually, she still does to this very day."

She went on to say Megan would pull the car over and they'd jump out of the car. If they were at home she would grab her children by the hands and they would run outside to look at the rainbow. Megan taking pictures and all the while telling her children that the sighting of a rainbow is literally the only time we, as human beings, can know the thoughts of God *in that very moment*. She would share from scripture Genesis 9:14-16, "Whenever I bring clouds over the earth and the rainbow appears in the clouds, I will *remember my covenant between me and you* and all living creatures of every kind. Never again will the waters become a flood to destroy all life. Whenever the rainbow appears in the clouds, I will *see it and remember* the everlasting covenant between God and all living creatures of every kind on the earth." Megan explained to the children that an everlasting covenant meant an unbreakable promise. Lastly, her mother would say, "What an awesome thing it is to know *at this very moment* God is *remembering* His promise to us!"

Leanza turned to Vonda and said, "You should see the look of wonder on my mother's face while telling us that."

Listening to Leanza's description had greatly lifted Vonda's spirits. She had no idea if she would ever actually meet Leanza's mother but she knew already she deeply admired her. It was no wonder Leanza was the strong, independent, confident, kind and caring woman she was today after being raised by a woman of such strength and faith!

CHAPTER 17

It didn't take long for Jeremy to realize volunteering for this position had put him at an advantage. Outside of the actual Task Force meetings the other agents were only privy to the information in the cases assigned specifically to them.

Jeremy, on the other hand, was getting information from all of the cases tossed his way constantly. As he chased down leads there were times he could see the whole picture even though it was still disjointed. His mind equated it to putting a puzzle together.

Jeremy would typically take the time to separate the puzzle by pieces. He would start by separating out all the edge pieces. He would then sort the remaining pieces into piles according to color or design. Once that was done he'd set about to complete all the edging after which he would have a completed rectangle edge to work from. Looking at his work space all he could see at that point was the puzzle's edge and the various piles of puzzle pieces. Jeremy knew once he'd taken the time and focus to put those pieces in place the final picture would come together as it should.

While still working the puzzle it was virtually impossible to see the actual picture prior to its completion. Over time he would begin to see it coming together but he wouldn't get the full effect until that last piece was placed.

The A413TF investigation he was currently working felt the same. The outside edging was now completed and the evidence was in separate piles. Jeremy just had to keep at it. He had a ways to go before the full picture would come into focus and even further before that last piece would be fitted in place. But it *was* coming together and when it was completed there would be an immense sense of satisfaction!

He was beginning to strongly suspect there was an unseen connection between the missing persons that somehow involved their hospital visits.

The team had now established that all thirteen vacationers had sought medical care. This just seemed too much of a coincidence. Being of rational mind Jeremy couldn't deny there was nothing criminal in it. Nor was it possible for one villain to cause thirteen random people, over a span of twenty years, to need medical treatment. That being the case it all begged one question; if the villain didn't cause this similarity, what did? What could all those emergency room or urgent care visits possibly have to do with the disappearances?

Despite the unanswered questions something was pulling at him about this and it wouldn't let go. For this reason and unbeknownst to the other agents Jeremy was digging deeper. To his way of thinking this was just another effort to see what similarities linked the cases. Jeremy believed something tied the missing together in a way no one had yet thought of. He realized this was probably a long shot but then he knew of multiple cases that had been solved by a long shot.

Following his instincts, he made the decision to utilize the opportunities he was being afforded. Whenever he was given a loose end on one of the cases he made it part of his task to look into what had sent that particular missing person for medical attention.

In this way he was killing two birds with one stone.

He had now investigated six such situations. Of those six, four had gone to the same Hospital emergency room: Myrtle Beach General Hospital. The other two had gone to the same urgent care facility: Myrtle Beach Doctors Care. Jeremy took immediate note of that. It would be much easier to follow up in more detail on all thirteen cases if each had utilized only these two facilities. He could see that happening. He could also see that the facility chosen hinged on the time frame. It was only logical that those vacationing in earlier years would all have gone to the emergency room since it wasn't until nineteen eighty one that the first urgent care facility was opened in South Carolina.

Another interesting revelation was that each of the six missing persons had gone for medical help for something other than an illness. In other words, they were hurt. Since the essence of an emergency or urgent medical situation is basically to treat something urgent, that makes sense. There again, something about the circumstances kept nagging at Jeremy's mind.

Jessica Gunther stepped on a piece of broken glass on the beach. Donald Collins twisted his leg tearing the meniscus in his knee. One of the others suffered from a vicious dog bite, another was treated for extreme sunburn, another suffered a sprained ankle and the last one had a reaction to a spider bite.

So far none of them had either a temporary or long-term illness. That seemed significant, but Jeremy didn't know how, at least, not yet.

In order to present all this information at a glance Jeremy created an excel spreadsheet listing the specifics of the medical care facility visits. The documented information was as follows: facility name - type and location, visit date, reason, diagnosis and treatment. He was very interested in seeing how the rest of the cases played out.

As he sat looking at the partially completed spreadsheet he believed he was onto something. Still he wasn't ready to put it out there, just in case he was only chasing feathers in the wind. Once he'd done similar research on all thirteen cases, and had more firm information, he would share it with the other agents.

Perhaps having five sets of eyes studying the results would more quickly bring something to light. He sure hoped so.

CHAPTER 18

Vonda was feeling a bit tired, but very happy, as she studied the young woman in the driver's seat.

Leanza looked different to her now.

She remembered, as a young girl, thinking a certain young man was very handsome. He was all she thought about for weeks. When the opportunity came to actually spend time with him she saw his unkind spirit and cruel nature and everything changed. Nothing in the young man's appearance was different but she no longer found him attractive. She had gotten to know the person he was on the inside and that was all it took.

Similarly, today had changed her view of Leanza. No longer was she just the professional, young, career woman Vonda had recently met. She was now beautiful and amazing. The combination of the innocent child of a strong mother and a father-gone-missing, the athletic, independent sportswoman, entertaining storyteller and investigator whose deeply rooted passion for finding the missing now made perfect sense.

There was so much to this young woman and Vonda found herself admiring it all.

Glancing her way Leanza asked simply "Did you enjoy our day, Vonda?"

"Without a doubt," Vonda answered quickly. "I don't think it could have been more perfect! I'm excited to get a look at my pictures, too. It's been so long since I've had a day to just enjoy nature like this. I enjoyed our lunch and our conversation so much. Oh, and your hilarious stories! Oh, my. I haven't laughed that hard in a long time!"

"Good." Leanza answered. "I loved it, too. I'm a little surprised by this, but I'm really beginning to feel at home in Logan. And that's thanks to you! Although I was excited about this assignment I wasn't really sure about the living situation. As you can imagine, I've traveled quite a bit in my line of work, but this is the first time I've completely uprooted to temporarily live where the job is. My whole plan was to focus on work during the week and have isolated outings on the weekends.

I'm being completely honest here; new friendships were *not* a part of my plan. I have to admit though, I'm really glad it's turning out this way. I never give it much thought but it's not often I get to simply enjoy another woman's friendship."

"Well, I'm so glad we can change that! We've got to get you away from those case files and into the joy of living sometimes." Vonda said with a laugh.

"After today that sounds great to me!" Leanza answered enthusiastically. "I look forward to whatever comes next!"

Arriving back at Vonda's they went about getting the trailer backed in and unhitched. Vonda unlocked Stanley's shed and they put everything away. Both women were ready to relax in their own homes so they said their goodbyes and Leanza walked home.

Vonda had a lot to tell Marshall when he called that evening to check in with her. He couldn't help smiling as he sat listening. Her voice was full of excitement and he could see her smile in his mind's eye. He knew Vonda had been missing her walking partner and he was happy she was making a new friend.

After they said good night Marshall sat alone thinking back over their friendship. Vonda had gone through quite a rough time just before he met her, and shortly after. She'd been blessed to have a strong and loving marriage with her husband. As her new friendship with Marshall continued to grow Vonda often shared her memories of life with Stanley. Those two had undoubtedly been very happy together and she was still deeply grieving his loss when Marshall came into her life.

It was hard to believe it had been almost three years since he and Vonda had first met. They hadn't realized it at the time but there was a tie between them – they were tied together through the mystery of Marshall's construction company accountant's disappearance. Unbeknownst to her, Vonda had witnessed something that put her in danger. As a result, Marshall became quite protective of her. Trying to distract her and to be sure she felt safe he began calling her every evening.

Vonda often attended the baseball games he played in and they were both involved in a church renovation project at that time. It was through all of those events that their friendship had grown. Now, several years later Marshall no longer called her nightly but he did call regularly and they often spent time together.

Their friendship was very important to him and he enjoyed her companionship immensely. Truthfully, Vonda had come to mean a great deal to him. Actually he wasn't completely sure his feelings for her could still be described as friendship. He'd been puzzling over that a bit recently.

Marshall had never married. In fact, he hadn't dated all that much and had never been in a deeply serious relationship. He had felt drawn to a few women through the years but his busy lifestyle didn't allow much time or energy for such a relationship.

When he was only twenty-five and just getting his new business off the ground his parents unexpectedly died as the result of a car accident. Without hesitation Marshall stepped in to finish raising his two younger brothers who were seventeen and fourteen at the time. Running his own construction company and raising his brothers gave him quite a load of responsibilities, which didn't leave much time for dating. Once the boys were out on their own Marshall devoted his time to the growth of Davidson Construction Inc. His life had always been busy and very full.

Through the years he did, of course, occasionally go out socially. He even dated steadily a few times; it just never amounted to anything serious. As he sat thinking all of this through his mind went back to Vonda Graham.

He'd been fond of Vonda from the moment they met, when she spilled soda on him. He couldn't keep from chuckling at that memory. He had immediately felt drawn to her. As they got better acquainted he was happy to quickly learn they shared a similar faith. It seemed as if no time had passed at all before he grew to consider her a good friend. He didn't think of her as anything more at the time which he now supposed was out of respect for her grief. He hadn't really thought about that in quite some time. Now that he was, it occurred to him that her grief had lifted quite a bit which was only natural with the passage of time. She still talked fondly of her husband, Stanley. Marshall supposed she always would. After all they had enjoyed a long and happy marriage and raised three children together.

Marshall had met Vonda's children and grandchildren during the past year and they were definitely good people. Vonda was very proud of her family and rightfully so. She enjoyed nothing more than having them visit or going to see them.

Remembering how delighted she was when they talked earlier in the evening Marshall smiled again. The sound of her laughter always brought him joy. In fact, he'd taken to making little jokes and witty comments as often as he could just to see her smile and hear her laugh. Sometimes she'd playfully swat his arm once she realized he was joking and they'd laugh together. He loved it when that happened.

Vonda had the most delightful ways of expressing herself. When she was especially pleased her eyes would brighten. Her entire face would light up, actually. She'd begin speaking very quickly and her hands would become quite animated. Even though he was alone Marshall couldn't keep from smiling. Just thinking about Vonda made him happy.

Was this what it meant to be in love?

He didn't know the answer and had only recently allowed himself to even ask that question.

He wasn't at all sure what he was dealing with here. The only thing he was sure of was that he wanted Vonda to be safe and happy. When she was happy he was happy.

It was as simple as that.

CHAPTER 19

Leanza dragged her eyes open and glanced at the bedside table. The lighted numbers on the clock in the still darkened room told her it was early; too early, especially considering it was Sunday. Her mind told her to wake up but her body refused to hear it. She pulled the covers more tightly around her and continued drifting in and out of sleep for the next fifteen minutes.

She was waking up now, albeit ever so slowly. She just wasn't ready to actually get up. There's no reason you really have to, her mind said. Grasping that truth she let herself keep laying there, eyes closed, mind resisting even as her body started to give in and began to stir. It wasn't often she allowed herself lazy moments like these. It felt good.

As her eyelids lifted ever so slightly, she sighed contentedly and basked in the pleasure of feeling cozy and warm. Her thoughts lazily drifted back to the previous day. Oh, what fun! Without question it was the best day she'd had in quite some time. Too much time had passed since she'd been surrounded by the beauty of nature, even longer since she'd spent time in a gratifying friendship. Truthfully, she'd lost sight of how important that can be.

Yes, her career mattered, especially because of the nature of the work; helping people find their loved ones, or at the very least find closure in the loss of their loved ones, was so important. It was easy to let it take precedent over everything else. Still, sometimes Leanza needed a day like yesterday to pull things back into perspective. It certainly seemed to have done the trick this time.

She meant every word she had said to Vonda about not having planned to form new friendships during this assignment. Still, there was no denying she was finding great satisfaction in the time she was spending with Vonda and her friends.

How funny and unexpected life can be. She thought. That's another lesson you've taught me, mom, she inwardly voiced. She hadn't talked about her mother in a long time. She hadn't thought about her mom in that much detail for a while either. Sharing what she had with Vonda had reawakened how very blessed she knew she was.

Leanza loved her mother deeply.

I'll give her a call today, she thought, as she stretched her long legs straight out, lifted her arms above her head and felt her body come to life. In fact, I'll take today and catch up on personal tasks she decided and mentally began to compile a list. Leanza was nothing if not organized and proficient, even when it came to things like calling mom and catching up on her personal journal.

An hour later, after a hot shower and a simple breakfast, she curled her legs beneath her, settled into the overstuffed easy chair and picked up the phone.

Megan recognized the number and answered on the first ring.

"Hey! It's my baby girl!" Leanza could hear the smile in her mother's voice.

"Yes, it is, your one and only!" Leanza answered warmly. "I miss you, mom."

"Oh, I miss you!" Megan answered in a voice full of emotion. "So tell me what's been going on. I want to hear everything! I just sat down with a mug of hot coffee and I've got all the time in the world."

And the two were off, filling each other in on the events in their lives as if they were seated across from one another in Megan's cozy living room. Time and distance fell away as mother and daughter talked and laughed together.

A little less than two hours later Leanza said, "I love you, mom. I know I don't tell you this enough but I am so thankful you're my mom. I'm so proud of you, too. Not only for everything you've come through in your life but for all you've accomplished. You did such a great job with Wade and me, especially having to do it all alone. No one else could've been the mom you were to us. No one could've done it better! I have such wonderful memories of my childhood. I always knew you loved me. I always know you love me now! No matter where I am, I know you're just a phone call away and you'd drop everything if I needed you. Not everyone has a mom like that and I want you to know I realize that. I'm so blessed to be your daughter, seriously mom. Thank you!"

There was silence on the other end of the line for just a few seconds while Megan swallowed her emotions.

"Oh, my sweet girl, I'm the one who's blessed," she finally said. "I can't tell you what it means being your mom. Hearing you say those things just proves you're exactly the kind of woman I already know you are.

It's strange, as a mom, how much it can mean to hear your grown children say they're proud of you. You and Wade are both so good to tell me what I've done right and how much it means to you. I don't know if other parents get that but I sure am thankful I do. I'm so thankful not only to be your mom, but your friend. What a wonderful blessing it's been to have my sweet, baby girl, grow up to become one of my best friends."

Neither woman could see the other as they brushed tears from their cheeks.

They quickly covered a few other topics, exchanged promises to talk again soon, said their cheerful goodbyes and ended the call.

Leanza wandered through the house a bit before getting a fresh cup of coffee and moving on to the next item on her list. Settling down at the card table/temporary desk with her personal laptop she began filling in her journal.

It was fun to recollect the details of the past few days, especially yesterday. Just prior to finishing up Leanza looked back over the past several weeks of entries. This was her way of ensuring her journal entries were caught up since she'd taken to skipping a few days at a time and filing them in during longer typing sessions. She couldn't help noticing the many highlighted and italicized entries. It made her chuckle to realize how often she fell asleep while typing.

She usually skipped right over those entries but this time she found herself reading through some of them. They could be quite entertaining, actually. They were, after all, incoherent sentences which amazingly combined past and recent events into complete sentences that made absolutely no sense. Like the one that started out talking about her schedule for the day but ended up saying 'she wondered why she hadn't been able and laughed as her daddy pulled the brick.' What in the world did that even mean? Oh my! Leanza chuckled as she asked herself where those thoughts could have possibly come from. Shaking her head in confusion she did a final save on the document and closed her laptop.

It was getting close to lunch so she went to inspect the refrigerator for something to satisfy her growing hunger.

CHAPTER 20

Marshall felt pleased as he walked through the hospital expansion construction site. The footers were laid and the steel framing for the walls was off to a good start. It wouldn't be long before the outline of the steel structure could be seen in the skyline as the framing for the upper floors came together.

Saul, the Director of Commercial Projects for the company, had scheduled this morning's meeting with the leaders of the HVAC, Electrical, Plumbing and Medical Technologies Systems. Marshall was impressed with how well the meeting had gone. Everyone seemed to be on top of things and fully committed to getting the job completed within the projected time frame.

This project was moving along right on schedule. After lunch this afternoon Marshall would be making sure everything was in compliance with South Carolina building code regulations.

There was definitely no shortage of things that needed done. Marshall had never been one to be put off by challenges. Being one who didn't focus on his own attributes he was unaware of how much that particular trait had contributed to the success of Davidson Construction Inc. Without being prideful Marshall was purposeful in putting forth excellence. He had met every challenge head-on and did what needed doing each step of the way. Marshall wholeheartedly believed God would reward a job well done. He had seen it proven true time and again and couldn't be more thankful for the way God was blessing his business.

A glance at his watch told him there was a reason he was beginning to feel hungry. With just over an hour free Marshall headed for the main facility to get lunch. Turning into the hallway toward the cafeteria he saw George El coming toward him.

"Well, hello there, Mr. Davidson," George greeted him. "How's the new construction going?"

"Going good, George. Going very good!' Marshall answered with an affirming nod. "How are things in Maintenance?"

"I'm glad to say the same," George answered changing directions to fall in step with Marshall.

"The old girl's still standing strong as she takes care of the sick and injured," George added. There was no mistaking the pride in his voice.

"Good to hear," Marshall said. "I'm heading to the cafeteria for lunch. Any chance today's schedule would allow you to join me?"

"Well, now," George answered, cocking his head to one side as he considered the question. "Yes, I do believe that can be managed today."

"That's great," Marshall said. A few moments later the two men entered the cafeteria, each grabbing a tray, they headed in different directions, made their lunch choices and met back up at an unoccupied table.

"How about we thank the good Lord for this food before we get started?" George asked as they took their seats.

"Absolutely," Marshall answered, gesturing for George to go ahead.

"Good afternoon, Lord," George said quite naturally. "Thank you for the warm sunshine today. It sure feels good. Thank you for this good food, Lord. Please bless the ones who made it. Use it to give us strength as we do our best work for you today. Thank you, Lord. Amen."

"Amen," Marshall echoed as he picked up his napkin and fork.

"Say George, you've spent a good many years here. How is it you're not the Director of Maintenance?"

"Oh, I always wanted that job to go to Gordy." George said with a huge smile. "I know you were meeting all the department heads when you first got this expansion job but I don't know if you've met the Director of Maintenance yet. Names Gordon El, but to me he's always been Gordy. He's my younger brother."

"Oh? No, I haven't had the pleasure." Marshall answered.

"See, I came on board here right after high school, like I told you before." George continued. "I was hired as a janitor. After a few years I moved into the Maintenance Department. I always planned to stay here a long time. Hoped to make a living here, you know? I sure am thankful for how that's worked out.

Well, Gordy, he's three years younger than me. He's tall, dark and handsome. Smart, too. He was a strong basketball player all through high school. He played football the last two years, too. Lots of girls were hoping to snag Gordy, let me tell you, but he only had eyes for one. She's the one

68

that got him, too. They fell in love young and married right out of school. The Lord blessed 'em with a baby right away. Gordy was working at the plastics factory then, just a little place. It didn't pay much and he was working nights. That meant leaving his young bride home alone and her expecting an all. That was hard for Gordy. I could see he was really struggling.

As soon as I heard a position had opened up here in Maintenance. I told him about it. I knew if he applied he'd get it and I was right, he sure did! He took right to it, just like I had. Of course, I did all I could to help him learn the ropes. It was good getting to work side-by-side with my brother. In fact, that's been a blessing all these many years.

Time went by, you know. The way it always does. And they had another little one by the time the position for Director of Maintenance came open. Gordy told me to apply for it.

I said, 'No, I don't think so. I believe the Lord's got you in mind for that job, Gordy.'

He says, 'No sir, George, you've been here longer than I have. You're my older brother. You taught me everything I know and that job goes to you.'

I told him, 'Now Gordy, you've got a wife and children. You need to take care of them. I haven't found my Mrs. yet. You work hard and you're gonna do a great job for this place. I want you to apply for it and being the worker you are, I know you'll get it. They'll know you're the right one."

I knew if he'd try, he'd get it and I was right! Yes sir! I couldn't have been more proud! And sure enough I met my Mrs. a bit later. My little Dorma Lee and over the next bit of years God blessed us with our girls. Like I've already told you, I've made a good living working here. The old girl has provided well for my family. And I've had the added blessing of working on Gordy's crew, isn't that great?"

"It sure is." Marshall answered.

"I'll tell you one sure thing," George said, "life is good. Even more than that - God is good."

"All the time." the two men said in unison.

VS Gardner

CHAPTER 21

The A413TF agents continued diligently working their individual cases. In their determination to learn exactly what happened to those who were missing each agent was meeting with family members. The families were thankful their loved ones' case was still being investigated. Retracing the actions of the missing as closely as possible each agent spoke again with the people who'd had contact with them during their Myrtle Beach vacation. None of the agents would leave even one stone unturned.

The thing with cold and missing person cases is repetition. You literally have to go over everything repeatedly. It's a search in progress until that vital piece of information finally surfaces or suddenly shows up. Usually you've looked at it from every angle and considered it multiple times before you can see where that final piece of the puzzle fits. That's when everything suddenly makes sense. Many times there's simply no rhyme or reason. It's just not clear until it's clear. The frustration of repetitious work is known for ending careers. It does some agents in. But not the good ones and Leanza had assembled the best of the best for this assignment. Jeremy had every confidence this team would solve the case.

In the meantime, he continued investigating the details of each of the missing seeking medical help. While tracking down that information, Jeremy discovered there was an urgent care facility located in Stokesbury. Four of the missing had gone to that facility for treatment. One was treated for food poisoning, another for an allergic reaction and the other two for random injuries. Jeremy now knew that all thirteen missing persons had been treated in one of three local medical facilities: the emergency room of Myrtle Beach General Hospital, Myrtle Beach Doctors Care or Urgent Care in Stokesbury.

Urgent Care in Stokesbury was one of the first urgent care facilities in all of South Carolina. Being a tourist area, Myrtle Beach had continued to spread. It was approximately ten years later that the need for an urgent care facility in the opposite direction from the existing hospital became obvious. That was when the Myrtle Beach Doctors care facility was opened.

Jeremy had considered everything carefully. He found it interesting that none of the missing were debilitated. None suffered from diabetes, heart disease or any other chronic illness.

Obviously, people with lifelong physical challenges go on vacations just like everyone else. Not only that, more often than not, such a person would need to visit an ER or Urgent Care due to a complication of their pre-existing condition. While it was true that each of the missing had to seek medical treatment during their vacation it was also true each was apparently overall a healthy individual.

The fact that each of these thirteen particular individuals experienced a medical emergency outside of your usual illness or chronic health condition seemed so extraordinary to Jeremy that he had a hard time calling it coincidental. If it weren't for the randomness and the huge time spans between each case Jeremy would believe these persons had been sought out for the express purpose of whatever end they'd met with. His mind kept going to something like slave labor or sex trafficking but this situation was obviously more streamlined. Whatever was actually going on was still eluding him.

Having completed his extensive research Jeremy was now ready to tell the rest of the group his findings.

Leanza welcomed everyone to today's meeting. She then thanked them, not only for being in attendance, but for the excellence and diligence each of them kept bringing to the table. She commended them for a job well done so far and expressed the importance of staying the course for what remained to be accomplished.

Unbeknownst to the other agents, Jeremy had previously approached Leanza requesting to be the first to make a presentation. Leanza was anxious to hear what he had to share. After a brief reminder that each person was to submit loose ends to Jeremy at any stage of the investigation she turned the meeting over to him.

Jeremy was a professional through and through and did not disappoint. He dove straight into telling them the plan he'd designed and put into practice on his own. He then presented each agent with a copy of his

71

completed spreadsheet detailing all of the emergency care visits: the facility name and date, the reason for the visit, the diagnostic result and treatment given.

He made a quick and informative presentation on the history of the three facilities. Jeremy shared his nagging conviction that this information was the common denominator which would lead to the resolution of the case. He emphasized his belief that they were getting closer to discovering that missing puzzle piece and asked that the five of them put their heads together. The other agents were impressed with the data, appreciative of his initiative and eager to grant his request.

Of course, each agent was especially interested in the details of the medical emergency visits of the missing persons which they personally were covering. They were anxious to place the information from each file into the spreadsheet and see how it fit in with the information they'd already studied. Each was hopeful this would put a new spin on things and bring them one step closer to the resolution of this case.

Leanza was very pleased. She could see almost immediately that Jeremy's presentation had brought fresh energy to the team. The other agents took turns making their presentations after which they circled back to Jeremy's data. While they still hadn't specifically solved anything by the end of the meeting there seemed to be renewed hope and determination. The general feeling was that the team was on the threshold of an important discovery. There was an actual air of excitement which hadn't been there in the past couple of meetings. Leanza was happy to see how the work was progressing

CHAPTER 22

I like to say I blame Mr. Strong for making me weak. I never actually say it to anyone else, but I sure say it to myself.

I think it's a clever play on words. Sometimes when I repeat it to myself I actually laugh out loud. Mr. Strong made me weak.

It's funny. I mean, sure, it's not funny, but at the same time, *it is*.

People don't think of me as weak. But they might if they really knew me. If they realized the things I keep hidden, the choices I've made that they would call wrong.

I think about that sometimes.

Although I like that clever play on words I don't see myself as weak, far from it, in fact.

When you don't stand up for what's right or protect other's above yourself people think you're weak. But I am *not* weak.

A weak person couldn't make the choices I've made and not let anyone know about it. A weak person couldn't fool people the way I do. I've been fooling people most of my life and I'm good at it!

They think I'm kind. They think I care. They think I'm looking out for them. I'm not. I've just done this for a very long time and I've gotten quite good at it. I've just about perfected my 'fooled you' skills and I can keep it up as long as I need to. As long as it benefits me, as long as I get what I want. In the end that's really all that matters.

I might not have always been this way. I don't know. I probably changed in my sixth grade school year. But did I really?

Maybe Mr. Strong isn't to blame. Maybe I would've made the same choices regardless of which grade teacher I had that year. I'll never know and it doesn't matter now.

Still I think about it sometimes.

I do know that the way Mr. Strong treated me impacted the way I saw myself and the way I saw myself back then has made me who I am today.

I never recovered from my epic science experiment failure. Mr. Strong made sure of that. With his approval a certain few classmates made sure of it, too. He never forgot, so they never forgot.

Worse yet, they never *let me* forget.

Mr. Strong never gave me a second chance. He refused to see me as anything but the student who only did the bare minimum. Some of the students continued to call me 'piss-poor' and Mr. Strong always grinned when they said it.

When he first called my name that day he looked at me kindly. After it was all over he rarely ever looked at me at all. Even when he acknowledged me he didn't actually look at me - let alone kindly. Up until the day of the experiment things had been alright. Afterward they were never alright again.

He ignored my raised hand when I knew the answers. He deliberately called on me when I didn't. I always avoided looking at him then. It wasn't until I was older and wiser that I realized that was my 'tell' and he knew it.

He took pleasure in embarrassing me. It was only when he already knew I didn't know the answer that he made me the center of attention. It was his way of continuing to heap humiliation upon me. Thus the science experiment trauma never ended. It happened early in the school year but he kept it going all year. He used it to ruin my entire sixth grade year.

Well that, and the class Christmas play. Mr. Strong was famous for having his class perform a Christmas play each year. It always involved an elaborate set; speaking parts, singing parts, stage set crew and extensive teamwork. It was quite the production.

His students would spend weeks learning their parts, rehearsing and finally performing for the other classes. There was even a special afternoon performance which parents and grandparents were invited to attend.

Everyone was excited to be assigned their job for the Christmas play. Naturally, I was, too. At the end of the first day of assignments I was happy. I was a train-set-up crew member. I didn't know exactly what that meant. I only know I hadn't been completely ignored. For once I was getting to participate! This was going to be so cool!

The following day we learned that the Christmas play was a story centered on an electric train. This meant we'd be setting up an electric train set complete with an entire village: grass, trees, mountains, houses and little people figures. There would be houses, street lights and lighted Christmas trees throughout the village. Of course, the train track would encircle the village. All of that would require an elaborate electrical system. All of it would be set up by the train-set-up crew members.

Wow! I was part of an important group!

Those with speaking and singing parts were given their lines and the songs they needed to learn. They huddled in groups memorizing and practicing while those of us on the train-set-up crew began putting the village together. I was elated to be included. I enjoyed working as part of the team.

With Mr. Strong's guidance and the provision of large wooden planks the train-set-up crew managed to create a large platform the village would be set on. The elaborate electrical wiring would be run underneath the boards. It would operate from one set of switches at the farthest end away from where the speaking and singing performances would take place.

It was the most enjoyable few weeks of my entire sixth grade school year. I loved painting the boards green and gluing the grass in place around the train track, sidewalks and roads. I enjoyed working with the other students on my team. Placing the houses, streetlights, trees, vehicles and people helped me come out of my shell. It was fun to see the village coming to life.

Mr. Strong was actually looking in my direction. He even spoke to me sometimes. He kept telling me to work closely with Benny and several other boys who were running all the electric wiring. We were all working together and it was fun. Benny and I spent a good deal of time on our knees taping the wiring in place on the underside of the boards. We made a good team. Everyone said so. Mr. Strong even took to calling us the electrical team. He still wouldn't look me in the eyes but at least he wasn't totally ignoring me like before.

Finally, the village was ready! Benny was given a copy of the script of the play. Mr. Strong had highlighted the lines Benny was to listen for so he'd know when to flip the appropriate switch to activate the correct lighting or train track according to what was happening in the story.

I wondered what important job I would be given as Benny proceeded to study what he was to do. Still not having been assigned my important job I found myself idly standing by. Looking at the various groups practicing together I began to feel like an outsider again.

It was a feeling I knew all too well.

One morning Mr. Strong announced that the electrical team was ready to demonstrate how the village worked. I stood up to join Benny since we were the electrical team. Immediately, Mr. Strong lifted his hand in my direction silently telling me to stop. For the second and last time, in my sixth grade school year, my teacher looked me directly in the eyes.

"No," he said in a voice only I could hear. "You are not a part of this. *You* take your seat."

Confused, I looked around at all the other children. Everyone had a part, a job, a role to play. Everyone had a place to be and something to do, everyone but me. Again, I lifted my eyes only to be met by his cold stare.

"Take your seat..... *now,*" he said forcefully when I hesitated to move. And so, of course, I did.

The next day the class began going through the entire play. Not wanting to draw attention to the fact that I was the only student with nothing to do, I put a chair next to Benny's and sat beside him throughout the rehearsals.

When I arrived the following morning there was a large sheet of material on my chair and a box of thumbtacks. Benny told me I was supposed to tack the material around the wood planks to cover up the area underneath the village. I was to leave an opening at the back where the electrical switches were. Happy to have a job again I went straight to work. I felt proud when I got the job done by the end of the day.

Every day for two weeks I sat beside Benny during play rehearsal. I loved the play and enjoyed watching everyone speak their parts and hearing them sing. By the time the two weeks of rehearsals had ended I knew every part in the entire play. I could've stepped in and taken anyone's place had that been needed.

Oftentimes throughout the play the entire class would stand together and sing songs that fit in with the storyline. Not Benny though and not me. I sometimes wondered why we were the only two students who didn't sing. The two of us sat in two chairs located at the back of the train set table near the electrical switches. Benny operated those switches as needed all throughout the play. If anyone wondered why I had no part or wasn't allowed to even sing with them they never mentioned it.

A Brick to Remember

The week before Christmas arrived. It was the last week of school before our Christmas break. All the children were excited to finally get to perform for the other classes. Mr. Strong sent invitations to the other classes in the building and the teachers all sent acceptances back. There was a buzz of excitement over the entire school building. The play would be performed for visiting classes twice each day, once in the morning and once in the afternoon. This would happen for two days. On the third day our parents and grandparents would come to the school to see the play in the afternoon.

Mr. Strong gave everyone a special invitation to take home to their parents.

Not Benny though, and not me.

I think about that sometimes.

I have to wonder what Benny must've done that put him on Mr. Strong's bad side. There must've been something. But it obviously wasn't as bad as what I did since he got a job and I didn't.

The first day of performances arrived and it was time for the first visiting class to come to our classroom. Everyone was ready and happily taking their places. I was excited to see the play in one uninterrupted performance, everyone in full costume, for the first time.

As the other students were talking together at the front of the room where they'd be performing Mr. Strong came to me and Benny. In a matter of fact voice he explained to us it would be distracting for those watching the play if they were able to see us sitting behind the village platform. It was for this reason that the switchboard Benny had been using for the lighting now had to be mounted under the table.

Mr. Strong said he knew that Benny and I had been sitting in chairs facing the switchboard each rehearsal. But today, he explained that wasn't going to work. He then turned the switchboard Benny used so that it was lower and facing the opposite direction.

Benny looked confused and said, "I can't turn the switches if it's that way." Mr. Strong said, "Of course you can't. Not from where you're sitting. That's why I want the two of you to get on the floor under the platform and under this skirting where no one can see you. That will be the best way." Confused, I looked at Benny and Benny looked at me. Was he really telling us we had to sit on the floor hidden from sight for five performances of the entire play? When we looked back at Mr. Strong he was motioning for us to climb under the table. Being obedient children, of course, we did as we were told.

And so it was that even though I knew every word of every one of my classmates' parts and all the words to every song in my sixth grade school play; I never even got to see the play performed. Instead, I sat unseen on the floor underneath the skirting I had put in place not knowing this was what it was intended for.

Each day, right before the other classes were ushered into the room Benny and I ducked under the platform skirting and sat on the floor beside each other. Through all five performances I watched as he expertly turned each switch to provide the perfect lighting and train track switching at just the moment each was needed.

Benny did a great job and at the end of every performance I told him so. Somehow I knew Mr. Strong wasn't going to and everyone needs to know when they've done a good job.

That's why I've always been sure to tell people I work with what a good job they're doing. In fact, I've always tried to treat people exactly the opposite of the way Mr. Strong treated me.

CHAPTER 23

After such a busy week Leanza was ready for some down time. She was so glad she and Vonda had touched base on Wednesday and come up with their plan for today. Dressed in jeans, a warm sweatshirt and hiking boots she was ready to go. Grabbing a winter hat she stepped out of the condo and saw Vonda coming through the yard.

"Good morning, neighbor," she called out. "It's not too cold for this, is it?"

"Not on your life!" Vonda replied. "The cool air will be good for our lungs. I've been looking forward to today ever since we talked. It's been too long since I've been to the Little Pee Dee State Park, or hiking anywhere, for that matter. I'm ready to hit the trails!"

"Good!" Leanza answered while locking the condo door. "I'm excited! From what I've heard it's a beautiful area."

"It really is!" Vonda agreed. "And it's such a pleasant drive to get there."

"I brought each of us a bottle of water and a granola bar." Leanza said motioning toward the backpack she was putting into the back seat of the Impala.

"I figured you would have that covered. All I brought was my camera." Vonda grinned while patting her camera case.

Leanza set the location into her GPS system and they headed out. Filled with autumn colors the surrounding scenery was even more vibrant than usual. When one wasn't pointing something out the other one was and the forty minute drive went by quickly. Before they knew it they were on the trail heading into the woods.

Vonda talked a bit before asking Leanza how things had been going for her.

Leanza mentioned the ongoing investigation before pointing out more for her own benefit than for Vonda's that weekends are for getting away from all of that.

Vonda readily agreed and asked what she'd rather talk about.

"Let's talk about the coming Holidays!" Leanza answered immediately asking what Vonda's plans were for Thanksgiving and Christmas.

"Well, normally I'd be having Thanksgiving with my children but this year they're all doing different things and no one's available to come my direction. My daughter's family welcomes me if I choose to join them but I'm just not sure I want to. Their plans are kind of special and I'm not sure I want to crash the party. They wouldn't see it that way, of course, but it kind of feels like it to me.

I had Thanksgiving dinner here last year and all of my children and grandchildren came. I included Marshall and his brothers and family. I wanted my children to meet them since they're all such an important part of my life. We had a lovely time. I could invite Marshall's family again but they may have their own day planned. I haven't asked Marshall what he's doing yet. As you know he's been very tied up with the new hospital expansion.

I really haven't thought much about the holidays, but you're right, it's just around the corner. I need to be thinking about it. Tell me what you'll be doing. Are you getting together with your family?"

"I actually don't have anything pinned down just yet either. I'm kind of thinking about going home to see my mom though. Is there a chance you'd like to join me? I've been thinking recently that I'd really like for you and mom to meet. If you're willing to go I'll be happy to buy your plane ticket. I'm thinking of flying out early on Wednesday and returning late Friday or early Saturday. That would give us an afternoon, all day on Thanksgiving and the following morning with the family. What do you think?"

"Really?" Vonda asked. She was a little surprised at the twinge of excitement she was feeling. "You'd like me to go to Virginia with you? Leanza, that's such a sweet invitation. My goodness, wow, humm I don't know but I'll certainly think about it. Are you sure your mom won't mind if I come?"

"Oh, not at all, mom would love it! I've told her all about our friendship and it makes her happy. She's always saying I work too much and need more human interaction outside of my job." Leanza laughed.

"She'd be thrilled to meet you. You won't find anyone more welcoming than my mom. I'm sure Wade will be coming so you'll get to meet my brother. He's absolutely the best! You'll love his wife and kids, too. I'm excited to see everyone, but I really would love to have you come with me."

"Wow," Vonda said again. "Well, you know what? I just might do it. Let me think about it and be sure there's nothing I need to be here for. I'll let you know soon, ok?"

"Of course," Leanza answered feeling hopeful.

The two continued chatting as they hiked and enjoyed the beauty of God's creation over the next several hours. While sitting on a log eating granola bars they laughed at the antics of a few squirrels nearby. A bit later they rounded a bend and came upon four deer grazing in the distance. Vonda was excited to get some great pictures throughout the day. All-in-all it was an incredible day for both women.

They'd just about made the entire circle back to where they'd started when they saw that straight ahead a little ways a tree had fallen. The tree trunk was lying at a long angle across the trail. They would have to step over it in several places to get past it. A young man was on the far side of it but his chocolate lab was hanging back. It was a very young dog if not still a puppy. Since it was a lab the pup was a bit large. The man had crossed over the log but the pup hadn't yet done so. It was scared and hesitating. When the women were about eight feet back from the pup, at their end of the fallen tree, they stopped. The pup was studying the situation hesitantly. On the other side of the log the pup's owner stood patiently coaxing the little guy to jump the obstructions. When the owner glanced at Vonda and Leanza they both smiled, thus assuring him they were prepared to wait patiently while that pup got enough courage to move ahead. His owner spoke to him in a gentle coaxing voice encouraging him to take that first leap forward.

The pup whined, paced a few steps back and forth, stared at the obstruction in the pathway and lowered his head. He then looked to his owner, took a step forward, whined again and took a few steps back again. The man on the other side of the fallen tree waited patiently. Not wanting to physically retrieve the dog he tried one more time by issuing strong words of encouragement. "Come boy, come!"

The pup jumped over the tree at the first spot, took a few steps and immediately jumped over it at the second spot where the path curved. He had made it to his owner's side.

Without realizing what she was doing Leanza had rushed forward the moment the pup made its first jump. As soon as he'd made the second jump she said enthusiastically "There you go!" while looking directly at the little dog.

Having knelt down to pet and praise his brave pup the young man lifted his head and his eyes met Leanza's. Never losing eye contact he stood up and smiled slightly. He then led his pup off the trail so the two ladies could pass.

"He sure was a brave little guy, wasn't he?" Vonda said. Leanza's eyes turned to Vonda as she answered, "He sure was." As they headed on down the trail it took everything in her not to turn back to look at the man again.

The ladies decided to take a small path over to the water's edge before leaving. As Vonda continued chatting beside her, Leanza thoughts were on the lingering gaze she'd just shared with the pup's owner. It had been instantaneous and intense. She had felt something in those few seconds she'd never felt before, a connection of some sort. She didn't understand it but that didn't matter. She was never going to see him again so she put it out of her mind and turned her attention back to Vonda.

No more than ten minutes later they stepped out of the woods to head toward their parked vehicle. It just so happened there was a white pickup truck approaching so they waited on the berm for it to pass. Just as it reached them the driver looked in their direction. When their eyes met Leanza felt the exact same connection she'd experienced earlier and realized it was the pup's owner. This time the gaze between them was broken quickly when he had to look away to continue driving. Leanza quickly took in his facial features, and as much of his upper body structure as she could see through the truck windows.

And just that quickly he was gone.

Being in law enforcement all of her adult life Leanza had become very observant. She habitually noticed more in such a brief segment of time than ninety percent of other people even could. She could still see him clearly in her mind's eye. His eyes were an intense shade of blue, his skin deeply tanned and his hair a sandy shade of brown just a bit lighter than hers. He was well built as if he worked out or was accustomed to manual labor. As the evening wore on Leanza couldn't seem to stop thinking about him.

CHAPTER 24

Vonda rolled over in bed and glanced at the clock. It was seven-thirty. She yawned and stretched and thought about getting up.

"I'm not ready yet," she said aloud half to herself and half to the Lord. Hearing her, Lilly stirred beside her, stood up and moved closer. Vonda then curled her fingers around the cozy blankets, turned on her side and stuffed her blanket filled hands up under her chin. Lilly nuzzled up to her and began purring loudly, unable to resist, Vonda's hand slid from under the cover and stroked Lilly's soft fur. Shutting her eyes again, Vonda kept to part of her usual morning routine by talking to God.

"Thank you for such a great night of rest, Lord. Thank you for the fun day of hiking with Leanza yesterday. Father, I pray for her and the whole Task Force team as they continue to investigate what happened to all of those people who've gone missing through the years. My heart goes out to the family and friends of each one of the missing. Please comfort them and give them strength. Please prepare them for whatever news they're going to get when the team solves those cases. Thank you Lord, for people like Leanza who care enough to be diligent about bringing missing people home or finding out what happened to them and helping their families find closure. I have no way of knowing what happened, Lord, but you do. You were there with each of them through every moment of whatever they experienced. I'm asking that you help Leanza's team figure this out. Of course, I pray that by some miracle all of those people are safe somewhere, even though that doesn't seem likely. If they're not, please help those they've left behind deal with whatever is discovered. You know their pain and you care for them and love them. You love each of us so much, Lord. We can't even fathom your love for us. So many people are hurting, Father, please comfort them."

Her mind was awake now and her body was ready to follow, so she rolled over. Tossing the covers off, she stretched and got out of bed. After opening the bedroom window dressing to welcome the morning sunshine she chose her clothing and went into the bathroom to get ready for the day.

She prayed for her children and grandchildren, asking God to meet all of their needs and help them in all their circumstances. She prayed for Marshall and his brothers and their families.

Remembering the hospital expansion project, she prayed for the safety of Marshall and all of the construction crew. She thanked God for the medical personnel and all the future patients they would help in that new facility.

Lastly, she prayed for herself. Thanking God for His many blessings in her life and continuous protection over her. She asked that He help her maintain a thankful attitude and set aside the things that really don't mean much in life.

To Vonda's way of thinking most people had it backwards, seeing the things that don't matter at all as the things that matter the most. She prayed for everyone, everywhere, knowing that God loves each one so deeply. She asked God to reveal Himself and draw people into a relationship with Him. She prayed for the entire world to become a kinder, more loving and giving place. She prayed for the President and all those in leadership and for her country's precious freedoms to be protected. She prayed for each person serving in the military, thanking God for their willingness to be away from home and family to protect the freedoms the United States had fought so hard to obtain.

Vonda then asked God for wisdom. She was thinking about going with Leanza to her mother's in Virginia for the Thanksgiving holiday. She had become so very fond of Leanza and was enjoying their friendship so much. She was seriously considering joining her. As she did with all decisions in her life she asked God to guide her to make the right choice.

As was her daily habit, she had prayed all through her morning routine. By this time she'd fed Lilly and made coffee. She stood savoring it while looking out the sliders onto her back patio. The sun looked inviting but she knew it was deceiving. The temperature was cold this morning. Her rocking chair would have to wait for a warmer day.

She hadn't seen Marshall recently and wondered how he was doing. On a whim she decided to invite him to supper. She sent a text asking if he could make it. While waiting for a reply she went into the kitchen to assess what she had available to make. She decided on honey pork chops with sides of corn pudding and mashed potatoes. Getting the pork chops out of the freezer to thaw she heard a text come in.

"I'd love to come for supper tonight, Vonda. That sounds great! With my busy work schedule, I've been missing you."

As she read his text her lips curled upward into a smile. Had he ever said he missed her before?

She replied with a tiny smiley face before adding, "See you at six. I hope you have a good day."

She hadn't said so but she missed him, too. She was very thankful for Marshall. When she'd lost Stanley the thought of a friendship with a man had never crossed her mind at all. She and Marshall had met by accident and their friendship had developed very naturally and simply grown ever since. Truthfully, Vonda could not imagine her life without Marshall in it, nor did she ever want to.

She always kept a clean house so it wouldn't take much to make it presentable. Looking around in anticipation of company she thought she'd sweep the floors and clean the main bathroom. Having that done she decided to go ahead and set the table. It was hours too soon but she'd always been one to do things early so she wouldn't feel rushed at the last minute.

She was reaching for her everyday dishes when she changed her mind and set out her good dishes. I'll just do things up a little bit nicer than usual, she thought. Why not? It'll be festive and fun.

Meanwhile, Marshall was at work trying to stay focused. He'd been surprised and very pleased with Vonda's text inviting him to supper. He found himself re-reading it when he got a few free moments, his anticipation growing as the day went on.

He stayed on top of things to ensure nothing would keep him from leaving the job site on time. He didn't want to feel rushed this evening. He knew it was just dinner between friends but he found himself wishing it was an actual date. What's gotten into you lately? He asked himself.

Vonda almost never bought anything new but last week she'd noticed a pretty dress in fall colors and on a whim she purchased it. This seemed like a good opportunity to wear it. Looking at herself in the mirror she was glad she'd bought the dress. She smiled at her reflection and decided to change her hair just a little for tonight. She did it in a French braid that curved around the side of her head. She left some strands of hair hanging down along her face and neck. It turned out really nice and she felt pretty.

As she went to begin preparing their meal she realized she was hoping that these little extras would be a nice surprise for Marshall. He'd been working so hard lately. Maybe these extra touches at dinner would make him feel special.

Marshall hurried home and showered. He decided to wear a black turtleneck and black jeans. Looking in the mirror he thought he looked too stark. He remembered that he had a V-neck sweater with a splash of color that reminded him of fall leaves. He pulled it over the turtle neck and hoped it matched. He laughed at his reflection and felt a little foolish for going to all this effort. Hopefully he wasn't overdressed since it was just a simple dinner with his friend.

Passing the Food Lion he impulsively pulled in for flowers. Vonda had once told him she sometimes bought herself a bouquet to brighten her life. He chose a colorful mixture he was sure she would like.

Pulling into her driveway Marshall felt a little nervous. What was she going to think when he showed up overdressed and bringing flowers? Little did he know Vonda was feeling the same way he was.

CHAPTER 25

Vonda opened the door and unbeknownst to the other both she and Marshall were instantly taken aback.

Marshall's first thought was: Wow! She's absolutely beautiful! He had always found Vonda attractive but tonight he was completely bowled over.

Vonda's reactions were scattered. She wasn't accustomed to a man bringing her flowers. Beyond that, there was definitely something different about Marshall's countenance this evening. She wasn't used to seeing him dressed up and he looked strikingly handsome in the dark colors he was wearing.

Realizing she was just standing there awkwardly Vonda giggled nervously and said, "Marshall! I'm so glad to see you! Come on now, you get on in here." Backing up she motioned toward the living area as she said, "Lilly, please move out of the way and let Marshall come in."

Stepping over the threshold, he bent down and patted Lilly then stood up and handed the flowers over. Vonda exclaimed, "Oh, these flowers are lovely!"

"I remembered that you sometimes like flowers to brighten the place up," he said, smiling at her. "I thought you might enjoy these."

"I absolutely do!" she gushed, and said again, "They're lovely!"

Not near as lovely as you. Marshall wanted to say but didn't.

"Let's get them into a vase. They'll make a gorgeous centerpiece for the table after we've eaten."

Both of them were thankful for the distraction as Vonda located a vase, placed colored stones in the bottom and went about cutting the flower stems. She instructed Marshall in opening the little pouch and adding the powder to the water. Marshall stood back and watched as Vonda expertly spaced the flowers and poured the water in. He'd had no idea there was so much involved in a floral centerpiece. The flowers looked even more beautiful when she was finished arranging them.

"There!" Vonda said stepping back to admire her work, "This will be perfect on the table. I'll enjoy them all week. Thank you, Marshall! That was so thoughtful and such great timing! I just threw out my last bunch of flowers a few days ago and haven't gotten around to replacing them, yet."

A few moments later Marshall complimented her dress and then her hair style. She reached up and gently touched her hair while telling him how pleased she'd been when the braid turned out so well. She complimented him in return commenting that with the colors in his sweater the two of them almost matched. Chuckling he told her he hadn't known whether or not his sweater looked right with his all black ensemble. She assured him it certainly did and he'd done very well! Their initial nervousness had passed quickly and each of them enjoyed how comfortable they now felt with the other.

When Marshall saw that the meal was about ready he asked Vonda what he could do to help get it to the table. She gave him instructions and they worked together over the next few minutes. Once everything was ready they sat down to eat.

As she looked across the table at Marshall, Vonda relaxed by taking a deep breath and then letting it out slowly.

"Would you like me to pray before we start?" Marshall asked and after her gentle nod they both bowed their heads.

"Thank you, Lord," Marshall's strong voice rang out. "Thank you for life and health and strength. Thank you for the simple joys of each day you bless us with. Thank you for this food and the woman who has prepared it. Please continue to bless her with good health and happiness. Thank you, Lord, for bringing her into my life. What a precious blessing she is to me."

He had said those words with great feeling and Vonda sensed it.

"Now, Lord, we think of our family and friends and we're so thankful you're with them in all of their circumstances and needs. For those who don't know you, and those who have walked away from you, thank you for your patience and love. Thank you for never giving up on any of us. Help us, to love like you do, Lord, and to live our lives as you want us to. Thank you for this time we get to spend together this evening. We love you, Lord and are so thankful that you love us. Amen."

Vonda's heart was full as she lifted her head and looked across the table at Marshall. Overcome with emotion a tear slipped from one eye and gently slid down her cheek. Reaching up to wipe it away she said simply, "That was such a beautiful prayer, Marshall. Thank you."

Watching her closely Marshall felt a stirring inside he'd never felt before. It was a mixture of compassion, awe, thankfulness and attraction. He didn't know what had come over him recently. He only knew one thing in that moment; his feelings for Vonda were changing in a way that felt overwhelming to him.

He was still struggling with how to respond when the moment passed.

Vonda smiled and held her hand out for his plate. As he handed her the plate she placed a honey drenched pork chop on it and handed it back to him.

"Go ahead and dish out your own corn pudding and mashed potatoes since you can reach them. I did set the table with my better dishes just to be more festive but we can still serve ourselves, don't you think?"

"Absolutely," Marshall answered while doing as she had instructed. Soon the two of them were conversing comfortably over the delicious meal.

After they'd eaten, Marshall helped her clear the table. They loaded the dishwasher together and Vonda ran hot sudsy water into the sink for the pans. Marshall grabbed a dish towel and volunteered to dry if she wanted to go ahead and wash. It had been her plan to let them soak but since she had a willing helper she began washing.

Standing beside her as she washed the dishes Marshall was thinking about how lovely she looked with her hair fixed that way. He said something funny and she turned toward him and burst out laughing. Her eyes were shining and her smile was brilliant. The little tendrils of hair hanging loosely were framing her face perfectly. Marshall had never seen her look so lovely. He felt himself fighting an urge to reach out and touch her. He wanted to take her face into his hands and kiss her. In that moment he was thankful she couldn't read his thoughts. He had no idea how she'd react if she could.

Soon the pans were done and everything was wiped down. They went into the living room and sat comfortably on the couch each turned slightly toward the other. Lilly jumped up onto the couch between them and looked from one to the other. They laughed as she tried to decide what to do before finally joining Vonda. They decided it wasn't a reflection of her fondness for one over the other. It was instead most likely her conviction that going to Vonda guaranteed she'd be petted. Proving her right Vonda gathered her pet into her arms and stroked her lovingly as they continued to enjoy their visit.

While talking about the upcoming Holidays Vonda reminded Marshall what a wonderful time they had all had together at Thanksgiving last year. She went on to tell him what her children's plans were and that she wasn't planning to hostess a Thanksgiving meal this year. She wanted to let him know since everyone would be thinking about Thanksgiving and making plans soon.

She told him how surprised she'd been recently when Leanza invited her to fly to her mother's home in Norfolk, Virginia to have Thanksgiving with her family there. She was praying about it and was seriously considering going.

"Well, if you want to go I think you should!" Marshall told her enthusiastically. "The two of you seem to be getting along really well. I'm sure you'd enjoy meeting her family. I haven't even thought about what I'll be doing for the Holidays yet. If nothing else, I'm sure Mason and Stacey will invite me to join them. Whatever I end up doing will be fine by me."

Vonda found herself distracted by how handsome he looked this evening. In all honesty she was having trouble focusing on what he was saying. She loved how comfortable she felt with him, and safe. She always felt so safe when Marshall was around. And he was so funny! She simply loved his wit. No one but Stanley had ever made her laugh as much as Marshall did. Stanley - her mind said to her and she felt a little twinge of emotion. What was that? She wondered, momentarily distracted.

"You know," she heard Marshall saying, "it's not really my place to say but the more I think about it the more I think you taking that trip with Leanza is a great idea. I mean really, when's the last time you flew anywhere to meet someone new? And you love to be adventurous. I get the feeling you wanted to be sure my family wasn't counting on a gathering here and we're not. Last year was great but it's not something you need to fall into doing every Thanksgiving. You don't need to be concerned about me. Most likely I'm only going to take one day off from the hospital expansion project anyway. If you're inclined to go with Leanza I really think you should. I think you'll have an awesome time and if you're worried about Lilly I would be happy to check in on her while you're away."

Vonda thanked him and said she'd let him know what she decided and they ventured off onto other topics of conversation.

Meanwhile Lilly went to the center of the couch and circled a few times before settling in comfortably right between them. She immediately nodded off to sleep.

Just over an hour later Marshall told Vonda he should probably take off. Each of them had enjoyed the evening immensely and Vonda felt a little saddened as she walked him to the door. She had experienced the same thing many times before. It was just loneliness. She had often felt it since losing Stanley so it was easy to recognize now. She knew it would pass soon.

They continued talking right up to the moment of arriving at her front door together. They stood looking at each other and for the first time in their relationship the moment of parting felt a bit awkward. Why was that? Vonda wondered, having no idea Marshall was asking himself the exact same question.

"This was great," Marshall said. "Not to invite myself to another dinner but anytime you want to issue a similar invitation you just go right ahead. Well, maybe that is to actually invite myself to another dinner!" He added while winking mischievously.

"Oh, you!!" Vonda laughed and playfully swatted his arm.

There it is! Marshall thought. Her beautiful smile and that laughter I can't get enough of. Satisfied this was the perfect way to end their evening he turned and headed out the door. Halfway down her front walk he turned back to wave goodbye playfully.

"Good night Marshall!" Vonda called out to him.

He quickly took a mental snapshot of her smiling and waving just before she shut the door.

Little did he know it then, but he'd be savoring that image frequently in the weeks to come.

CHAPTER 26

Leanza hurried down the hallway toward the conference room. She absolutely hated running behind schedule. She wasn't late but was definitely pushing it. Entering the room she rushed over to the table and opened her briefcase. She'd just finished getting her case files out when Jeremy arrived.

"I apologize for holding things up," he said as he hurried over and joined the other agents who were already seated and ready for the meeting to begin.

Leanza called things to order and briefly shared a few items she'd discovered in her own cases. She asked if anyone else had anything to share. A few more issues were discussed before one of the agents said she would like to revisit what Jeremy had mentioned in the last meeting. She pulled out the spreadsheet he had given them and asked if the rest of them had theirs. Everyone shuffled through their folders and produced the spreadsheet. She began to talk about the timeline and locations of the various injuries of the thirteen missing persons.

She had been studying the spread sheet in comparison to her own cases and was now interested in the same information in regard to their cases.

Almost immediately one of the other agents said they'd been thinking about the three medical care treatment facilities; the hospital ER and the two urgent care locations. He had to wonder what the connection between the three places was. Could the disappearances be at the hands of someone who had been employed briefly at each facility?

He reminded them that the disappearances spanned over twenty years. If one person were employed at each place wouldn't that indicate that person was somehow involved, if not directly responsible for the disappearances? Did they have a medical personnel serial killer on their hands?

The energy in the room picked up and kept building. Leanza felt herself getting caught up in the excitement. These were the moments that kept people in this line of work engaged. The agents discussed how they may obtain employee records to make comparisons as to who was at each facility during the past twenty years. If they actually were onto something here, once they knew which person had worked in all three locations they may, for the first time, actually have a suspect.

Jeremy volunteered to go to Human Resources at each facility to begin the process. Leanza agreed, reminding Jeremy they could request the information but if the employers refused they'd have to petition for a court order. They were all hopeful of avoiding that course of action. Jeremy left immediately and the rest of the agents continued to brainstorm on what could possibly be going on.

Over the course of the next few days Jeremy successfully got the employee records they needed. The group reconvened the following Friday to go over it all together. Twenty years of employee records from three separate facilities is quite extensive. Then there's the matter of cross checking to see if employees worked in more than one of the facilities in question. Along with the matter of the twenty year time span this was no simple task.

Having an objective in mind had definitely increased hope and excitement for the team. Momentum was high. Leanza loved the give and take and energetic interaction across the table. There's no question it takes a certain type of person to succeed in investigative work.

After several hours of research a break was obviously needed so Leanza placed a call-in order for lunch to be delivered. She asked everyone to clear a space at the opposite end of the conference room table in preparation for their meal. She saw immediate resistance in their expressions but a few minutes later relief set in. She'd seen this happen often. Detectives who get on a trail have a hard time breaking away despite knowing they need to in order to have a fresh perspective.

Leanza had decided to try an Italian eatery she hadn't been to before. She ordered a variety of dishes including Lasagna, Fettuccine and Chicken Parmesan, along with the salad and breadsticks it made for a delicious meal.

As often happens over a good meal the agents relaxed and ventured into more personal conversation. This was exactly what Leanza hoped for. They needed to clear their minds of casework to gain a fresh perspective. It was good to see them conversing on a more personal level, even laughing together. After almost an hour and a half Leanza asked if they wanted to continue the meeting or reschedule for a different day. Everyone was on board for reconvening so they cleared away the lunch mess and went back to work.

Looking around at the intent expressions on each face Leanza assured herself once more that they would resolve this case before it was all over.

CHAPTER 27

Vonda leaned her head back, turning it slightly to the left so she could see out the small window. She'd forgotten what it felt like to soar through the clouds. How many years had passed since she'd last flown?

Just as she had promised to do, Leanza had taken care of everything. Vonda simply couldn't believe how much had changed. She marveled that a printed ticket was no longer needed prior to arrival at the airport. Leanza had simply pulled something called an e-ticket up on her cell phone and displayed it. A small grin crept to her lips at the thought that Stanley would never believe this. The world just keeps changing Stanley, she thought lazily, while enjoying the view.

"Are you doing alright, Vonda?" Leanza asked quietly.

"I'm doing wonderfully! I cannot tell you how much I'm enjoying this. It's been years since I've flown. Granted, it's not something I ever did often anyway but I've loved it every time. It's such an amazing thing really. I wonder if people even give that any thought. We live in such a busy world now, everyone rushing here and there. Flying has become such a commonality. I mean, we're literally soaring through the clouds and I can't help wondering if anyone marvels that this is even a possibility anymore."

Leanza chuckled, "I'm so glad you're enjoying the trip. My mom's so excited we're coming."

A few hours later the plane touched down. As they headed through the airport terminal Leanza excitedly kept an eye out for her family.

"Oh, there they are!!!" she happily reported to Vonda as she pointed and immediately picked up her pace. Searching the area ahead Vonda spotted the lovely woman who must be Megan. She could definitely see a bit of Leanza in her mother.

Vonda purposefully lagged behind thus allowing the family a private reunion. She happened to be watching Megan when she spotted Leanza. Her face broke out in a huge smile as she rushed forward. She paused and briefly turned to her family to be sure they'd spotted Leanza before rushing ahead to hug her daughter. Leanza was soon engulfed in a group hug, everyone talking all at once and laughing together. The entire scene warmed Vonda's heart.

"Mom, this is my very good friend." Leanza said, extending her arm in Vonda's direction. "Vonda, come and meet my mother, Megan, and my brother, Wade. Here's his wife, Karen and my niece and nephew, Leah and Tyler, aren't they adorable?" Vonda greeted them all and was received warmly by each one.

A short while later they turned into the driveway. The Cape Cod house was exactly what Vonda envisioned a cozy, southern family home to be. The three foot brick base featured five six-feet wide stair steps directly in the center leading up to the front porch which covered the entire length of the house. The rocking chairs and swing there looked inviting. The house itself was sided in country blue which served as a beautiful backdrop to the white porch railing extending from full posts on either side of the front door to full corner posts. The front door was solid white with an oval shaped stained glass inlay. Centered in the walls on either side of the front door were double hung windows framed in white. On the left side of the porch flew an American Flag, which Vonda would soon learn Megan was faithful to put out each morning and bring in each night in honor of her beloved country.

In a large crock pot Megan had prepared meatballs in a thick, sweet and tangy sauce. She served it with cheese cubes, crackers and a variety of breads. Vonda really enjoyed the light meal and made a mental note to ask Megan for the meatball recipe. As everyone enjoyed the refreshments Megan assured them the Thanksgiving meal coming the next day would be much more extensive.

Vonda spent the afternoon getting acquainted with Leanza's family. She especially enjoyed observing their loving interactions. The adults played several board games with the children after sitting on the front porch drinking sweet tea. The afternoon sun was warm and the temperature topped seventy degrees. Megan explained this was a rarity for Thanksgiving weekend in Norfolk.

At her children's prodding, for Vonda's benefit, Megan shared how she and Denvel had come to purchase this particular home. As a struggling young married couple they'd felt particularly blessed to find the right home, in a good neighborhood, at a price they could afford, at the time. Renovations were needed but they could take them one at a time until they'd made it their own. Megan pointed out the many updates she had made to the house throughout the years to fulfill the dreams the two of them had envisioned together.

Vonda loved how naturally Megan spoke of Denvel as if it were just yesterday he'd been there with her. Having lost her own husband - albeit in a very different way - Vonda understood that love and happiness once shared never goes away, even in the face of absence.

As the evening wore on Karen had the children give hugs before she took them to settle in for the night. She encouraged Wade to stay up as late as he may want to enjoy visiting with the others.

Megan told Vonda how thankful she had been to learn from Leanza of their growing friendship. She commented on the demands of her daughter's occupation and her desire that Leanza enjoy life outside of her work. She added that she understood the drive behind Leanza's career choice since her own father had gone missing and his disappearance was never solved.

Looking from Wade to Leanza as she spoke, she turned back to Vonda and said, "I always tried to be honest and open with my children about what happened. That proved not to be so difficult since very little was actually known about Denvel's disappearance. Nothing in what took place was within my control, really. Never knowing exactly what happened has been frustrating, but God has helped us through it. Once I realized he most likely was never coming back, my children's happiness and wellbeing became first priority. Actually, that had always been our first priority together - it just became solely mine when I realized I'd be raising them completely on my own."

Picking up on what his mother had just said, Wade said "Actually mom, I've wondered about this before. I'm not sure why I've never asked until now but was there a certain point when you actually realized he was most likely never coming back? I mean, they never solved his case so I'm curious as to when and what happened that made you decide that?"

A Brick to Remember

Vonda noticed Leanza inching forward in her seat ever so slightly and visibly leaning in the direction of her mother. Her body language spoke of her eagerness to take in every word her mother was about to say.

CHAPTER 28

Marshall couldn't help thinking of Vonda on any given day but that was especially true today since it was the day before Thanksgiving. He felt sure she was having a wonderful time on her trip with Leanza. He was glad she'd gone. He wanted her to enjoy herself, but that didn't mean he wouldn't miss spending the holiday with her.

He'd been pleased to get her text letting him know of their safe arrival, the fun of witnessing Leanza's family reunion and getting acquainted with Megan, and her brother, Wade's family. She ended it with hopes that Marshall wouldn't work too hard and would get to enjoy Thanksgiving.

Marshall still wasn't sure what he was actually going to do on Thanksgiving Day. If nothing else, he would take himself out for a good meal. It wouldn't be the first time he'd eaten out on Thanksgiving. It may be the first time he'd eaten out alone. There was no question Vonda wouldn't want that for him, so he hoped it didn't come to that.

He'd had every intention of mentioning his lack of plans to Mason or Stacey but never got around to making a phone call. Going to the job site daily had kept him occupied. Obviously, it was too late now. He didn't relish the idea of being an add-on in the first place, but certainly not at such late notice. So that option was now off the table.

He truly wasn't concerned about it. He just didn't want Vonda to be disappointed for him and she would be if he did nothing special.

He put that issue aside to focus on the progress of the Myrtle Beach General Hospital expansion. The Genie Company had delivered the big equipment on time and his crew was utilizing it daily to stay on schedule. The outside of the structure was now under roof and fully insulated. It wouldn't be long before the plumbing, electrical and HVAC systems would begin to be laid throughout the internal structure of the building. Walking through the third floor to meet with Saul he found himself looking around in anticipation of seeing the patient rooms and offices take shape. It wouldn't be long now.

He'd be heading to Corporate in Stokesbury for a meeting with Manny about the Residential projects next. He also planned to wish each of his partners and the rest of the staff a good Thanksgiving before the day's end.

Saul gave Marshall a complete update on the scheduling for each of the utility systems including the start dates and projected completion dates. He also presented samples of the color schemes, flooring, countertops and light fixtures for the patient rooms and office areas. Marshall liked what he saw and felt the meeting with Saul couldn't have gone better.

He didn't always enter the main hospital on his way out but today he had one stop to make before heading to corporate. In response to the email invitation he'd received, he was stopping by the cafeteria to take part in the Thanksgiving luncheon being offered to the hospital staff today. This detour was the only reason he came face-to-face with George El in the elevator.

"Hey, Mr. Marshall," George greeted him in his usual friendly manner. "It's been a little while, sir. What's the good word?"

"How about 'thankfulness?'" Marshall responded.

"Ah, I'd call that perfect! And in keeping with the holiday tomorrow! Yes sir, I'd say that's a very good word for the day." George answered with a huge smile.

"I'm on my way to the cafeteria for the holiday luncheon right now. Are you heading there, too?" Marshall asked.

"No, actually I'm not able to stop in for lunch just yet but I plan to after a bit. I'm sure it'll be great. I imagine you'll be belly up to the table with your family tomorrow, am I right, Mr. Marshall?"

The question took Marshall by surprise. He felt a bit awkward about being deceptive so he answered truthfully, "Actually, not this year, George. I've been so absorbed with the project here I haven't touched base with my brother and I'm sure they're assuming I'm spending the day with a dear friend of mine. I've actually encouraged her to take a trip with her friend. She doesn't get those opportunities often and it being something she'd really enjoy I didn't want her to miss out just to spend the day cooking for me.

"I hear you on that one. I'd have done the same thing for Dorma Lee. So now, am I to understand you've got no plans for Thanksgiving tomorrow?"

George asked the question but continued speaking without giving Marshall a chance to answer.

"Well, that just won't do, my friend. We've got to remedy this situation. You're coming to have dinner with the missus, me and our family." George lifted his hand as if he were a traffic cop motioning for a car to stop when he saw Marshall about to protest.

"I'll hear no refusals now, Marshall. You'll join the El family festivities at 1:30 tomorrow, you hear me?" Smiling as they exited the elevator, George pulled a pen and post-it note from his pocket.

"Here let me write down the address for you and we'll be seeing you at 1:30 tomorrow. I know you've got places to be and people to see and so do I, so we'll talk tomorrow. You have a good one now, Marshall." And with that he turned and headed down the hospital corridor.

Marshall could do nothing but chuckle at George's insistence. His first instinct had been to refuse the invitation but he had quickly changed his mind. Having dinner with the El family sounded good.

Entering the cafeteria a few moments later, Marshall spotted the Chief Financial Officer, David Minter. Marshall made his lunch selections and fell in line to pay directly behind David. When the cafeteria clerk went to give David his change, the clerk smiled and handed him a long, thin, rectangular gift wrapped box.

David immediately burst out laughing.

"How *does* she do it?" he asked.

"Don't ask me," the clerk said with a huge smile.

"I'm just the delivery guy today. You never know where they're going to show up though, do you?"

Still laughing David shook his head as the clerk added, "Enjoy your Birthday, sir."

David thanked him and moved along.

Marshall wondered about that exchange as he paid for his lunch. He followed as David headed for a table filled with staff, some Marshall had previously met and others he hadn't. When Marshall arrived, David had just opened his gift and was holding his new pen up for all to see. As Marshall took the empty seat beside him David explained that the Director of Registration was known around the hospital for surprising staff on their birthdays in unexpected ways.

"You never know when or where a card, sign, gift, or some other form of birthday wish will show up around here, but when it does you know it's from Mary!" he said as the others nodded in agreement. Several then spoke up to share the surprise they'd gotten from Mary on their birthdays. It was a fun conversation.

David had previously told Marshall he'd been with Myrtle Beach General for just over twenty years, having come from a small hospital up north. His family had been excited to move to Myrtle Beach at the time and in the long run, it had proven to be an excellent experience. Marshall asked David how his daughters were doing and was given a quick rundown of their school and sports activities.

David then introduced him to the Chief Operating Officer, Mick Fraser, seated to his left, and Marshall fielded questions about the hospital expansion. Finishing his meal, David said he needed to get to a meeting, wished everyone a good afternoon and left.

Interested in getting acquainted with Mick, Marshall asked how long he'd been on staff.

"Oh, I've been around awhile." Mick answered with a huge smile. "Believe it or not I started in the file room right out of high school. I guess it's been about twenty-three years now. Oh man, that *can't be true!*" he added laughing loudly.

"Filing was a strange job for a guy back then but then I've always been a bit strange," he said, laughing again as he turned toward his co-workers whose agreeing nods prompted him on.

"Will you look at that? No one's arguing my point! But seriously, I saw it as a way to get my foot in the door. The job was part-time, which was perfect at the time since I was in high school. I actually envisioned moving away to pursue bigger things later on, you know, see the world and all of that. In the end I couldn't bring myself to leave mom since my dad passed away unexpectedly. As you can imagine, that changed everything. Ah well, you know what they say – all's well that ends well. I've made a good career here at Myrtle Beach General. I've never regretted staying. These people are like family."

After a moment's pause Mick said, "I'm an adventurous kind of guy though. I can make the best of any situation. I can find adventure anywhere.

And let me tell you – there have been times it's been an adventure just working here."

His laugh was loud and inviting. It pulled Marshall in and he found himself laughing too, though he had no idea what was even funny.

Mick seemed to have that effect on people as Marshall wasn't the only one laughing along.

"It's been great working in such a pleasant environment with people I like, especially since they seem to like me well enough."

Looking around the table Mick said, "Either that or y'all are pulling a fast one on me." A few people nodded and laughed prompting Mick to add, "Oh, who knows now? Maybe I'm the one pulling a fast one."

Mick's laughter was infectious and his colleagues seemed to like him. Marshall noted judging from their easy banter.

"I really do work with some of the best people around." Mick continued in a more serious vein, speaking directly to Marshall.

"Everyone's willing to pull their own weight. I try not to overload any one person and I step in when needed and make sure to be encouraging. I try to offer good incentives, too, reward my staff. It keeps morale up. That's important, you know?"

"Yes, I do," Marshall agreed. "We may need to compare notes sometime. I'd like to incorporate more feel-good things with my own staff."

"Sure. Sure!!" Mick said with a smile. "That sounds good. Let's definitely do that."

CHAPTER 29

Megan looked lovingly from one to the other of her grown children for a long moment before she began.

"Actually there was a defining moment," she answered. "But first let me just ask this: do either of you remember my yellow dress?"

Wade's eyes lit up. "Was it a bright yellow with a square neckline and a flowing skirt?"

Megan's head turned toward her son as a huge smile spread across her face.

"Yes!" she said. "It was close fitting to the waist but full and flowing from there. Why do you remember that?"

"I don't know, really. I just have this one clear memory of you in that dress. We were at a park, maybe? The weather was sunny and warm. Dad was playing catch with me and you were pushing Leanza on the swing set. Dad kept looking over at you and I complained. He said something about how beautiful you looked in your favorite dress. And, I think, maybe he said it was his favorite, too?" There was a question in Wade's voice.

"Wow." Megan said in a soft whisper. "Wow, Wade I'm so glad you have that memory of your dad. I had no idea."

Watching Leanza, Vonda saw a profound sadness cross her face.

Megan went on to say money was very tight when she and Denvel were first married. They were very young and it was a struggle trying to find their way in the world. They'd come from extreme poverty and were determined to make a better life. They were wise when it came to not wasting money. They wanted to own a home and were saving for it.

Sometimes just to get out a bit they'd stroll along Main Street looking at the local merchant window displays. They took to playing a game where they'd tell each other what they would buy if money was no object. The main rule of their game was that they always had to name a practical reason for their purchase, at least one.

On one such occasion following a particularly challenging couple of weeks when money was tighter than usual they began to play their game. Denvel chose a lawnmower in the hardware store window saying he'd love to have a mower he didn't constantly have to rig to keep running. Megan went into a comical rendition of the many ways in which he'd already rigged their current mower. They were laughing their troubles away as they strolled along when suddenly Megan looked into the next store window and stopped laughing.

One glance at her expression told Denvel she was completely enthralled. He turned to see a mannequin wearing a bright yellow dress.

"It's so beautiful," Megan whispered, unable to tear her eyes away.

"The dress?" Denvel asked her.

"Yes, the dress...." she answered softly, still staring. "I don't usually like yellow but, wow, it's like a burst of sunshine, isn't it?"

"I can see that." Denvel said. "It sure would be beautiful on you."

Reality hit her square in the face. It *would be* beautiful on you. Her mind replayed. That's what he had said. It would be - knowing she couldn't own such a dress a twinge of sadness pulled at her.

Still in their game mindset Denvel continued, "So it's obvious if money was no object that's what you would buy. Now tell me why."

"Oh," she hesitated turning to look at her husband. "Denvel we both know there's no practical reason to spend money on that."

"No, now wait a minute, Megan. We never said the purchase had to actually be practical. Only that we have to name at least one practical reason. So let's make it a practical purchase. Well, let's see now. You've already said it's like sunshine. So here we are on a grey and overcast day. What does every grey and overcast day need? Why, yes, that's right..." he continued in a sing-song voice "…..every cloudy, overcast day needs a little sunshine or in this case a big ol' burst of sunshine. That's what you said, isn't it?"

Megan couldn't keep from laughing. After all, wasn't the whole point of their game to rise above these financial disappointments by having a little fun?

A Brick to Remember

"You're totally correct, Denvel, and let's not forget it is an item of clothing. I can't be going around unclothed. I'd say that adds practicality. We don't even need to look at how much it costs. Cost is irrelevant once practicality has been established so that's it!!" Stomping her foot she laughed loudly, rushed forward and pretended to grab the dress right through the store window. "I'm buying this dress today!"

Returning to her husband's side Megan hugged him, looped her arm through his and propelled them further along on Main Street. All the while thanking the good Lord for blessing her life with Denvel Williams.

Glancing at her folded hands in her lap Megan was momentarily distracted by the looseness of her skin, wrinkles and a few age spots. When did those get there? Where have the years gone? The questions whispered through her thoughts just before she looked up, smiled and continued with her story.

"That was early spring. We kept working hard, living paycheck-to-paycheck. It wasn't long until we learned I was pregnant with you, Wade." She shot him a smile and winked.

"Truthfully, I thought about that dress only a few more times and it was only when we were walking downtown. Then one day it was gone from the store window and I knew I'd never see it again. By then it was just a fun memory. It wasn't even a wish any longer. It didn't matter. Like so many things we knew we would never have. It truly didn't matter because we were young, in love and happy together.

We knew things were still going to be tight that Christmas so we made a deal to purchase only one gift for each other, something practical. I agonized over what to give Denvel. There was so much we needed. I finally settled on a versatile tool he had mentioned in passing that would allow him to make multiple repairs to our lawn equipment and home appliances. I saved a little bit of the grocery money each week to be able to buy it.

We were renting a little place that didn't have any extra room but I really wanted a Christmas tree. Just two days before Christmas we bought what we teasingly called our Charlie Brown tree. It was the scrawniest little tree, one of the last ones on the lot so we got it at a much lower cost.

On Christmas morning we sat down on the floor near our little tree with our gifts. Your father insisted on opening his first. He made a big show of being curious and excited. When he finally opened it he loved it. He really did love it! I felt so good choosing just the right item. He used it often in years to come and each time I felt that same joy for having chosen the right item.

After thanking me he picked up my gift and placed it in my hands.

"You open yours now, Megan," he said. "And when you see it you remember our deal to only buy practical gifts this year. I gotta tell you, it's very practical but I think you'll like it anyway." He gave me a little kiss and leaned back to watch me open it.

Wanting to prolong our holiday fun I took my time taking the ribbon off the package and removing the pretty paper neatly. I looked at the box for a long moment wondering what kind of practical gift could be inside.

Finally, I opened the lid. Reaching in to lift the white tissue paper I could not believe what I was seeing. I was in shock as I looked up at your father's face. His eyes were filled with such love. He was smiling from ear-to-ear. I don't think I'd ever seen him look happier than he did in that moment. Ever so tenderly I lifted the yellow dress while simultaneously standing to my feet to hold it against me. It wasn't going to fit me until after your birth, Wade, but that didn't matter.

At that moment I felt rich! Looking at Denvel's face again I knew I was the luckiest woman on the face of the earth! Just as your father had intended I remembered the reasons we'd laughingly listed for the practicality of the dress and I determined then and there that I would never feel even one twinge of guilt for owning such a dress. Every time I looked at it I would feel loved and lovely. Your father had chosen to give me something he knew would make me feel beautiful, loved and happy. What could be more practical than that?"

Megan's face was aglow with the joy of reminiscing. She looked at each one of them and joyfully returned their smiles.

"There's more to this story," she said simply. "But it's been a long day and it's getting late. We've got plenty of time yet so instead of rushing through it let's call it a night. I promise to pick this up and finish it while we're all still together. Sound good?"

Everyone nodded their agreement and after hugs all around and goodnight wishes they dispersed to settle in for a restful night.

CHAPTER 30

Arriving at one-twenty-five Marshall's knock was answered by a tall youth in baggy jeans and a head full of shoulder length braids of hair. He flashed a huge smile and said, "You must be Marshall." Stepping back so Marshall could enter he shouted off to his left, "Hey, Grandpa your friend's here!" just as George came up behind him.

"I'm right here, Nathan, there's no need for shouting," George laughingly said reaching up to loving pat his grandson on the shoulder. Turning to Marshall he said, "Come on in here, young man, and meet my family."

While leading him through the house George was throwing names out and nodding in general directions as people glanced up with a smile or wave. George led the way from the front door through the hallway. They passed a dining room where Marshall noticed a long table beautifully set in anticipation of the Thanksgiving meal. Several women were bustling about and Marshall caught a glimpse of a galley kitchen off to the left. George turned a corner and headed down a shorter hallway which led straight into the living room.

Along the way they passed a room with groups of young people playing table games. A small crowd was gathered in another room watching football on a large TV. Folks were sitting together in random locations involved in casual conversation. Women were holding babies, children were playing together - people of all ages seemed to be spread out all through the home. Entering the living room George headed straight to a small, maroon colored recliner. There a woman of George's generation was interacting with a small group of children and young teens gathered beside her chair. As George and Marshall approached, their conversation abruptly stopped.

"I want you to meet my lovely wife, Dorma Lee." George said, smiling toward Marshall. He then turned to look directly into his wife's eyes and continued, "This little lady stole my heart quite a number of years ago and hasn't turned it loose yet. She's pretty special, let me tell you." Gesturing in Marshall's direction he added, "This is my friend, Marshall."

George's wife was lovely. Recent health issues and aging had left her a bit frail but had in no way diminished her natural beauty. Her white hair was cut short and combed to one side in soft layers. She wore just a touch of make-up; a light shade of pink lipstick highlighted her upturned lips. It seemed as if she had to tear her eyes away from George in order to greet Marshall but once she did he had her full attention.

Smiling a sweet smile she reached her hand toward him. Marshall took it as she said, "It's so nice to finally meet you, young man. My George has been telling me about the good work you're doing over at our hospital. Thank you for joining us for Thanksgiving. As you can see the good Lord has blessed us with a large family. You just make yourself at home now and enjoy yourself. My girls are finishing up the cooking and it won't be too long until dinner will be ready. You and George can have a good visit and watch a bit of football after we eat. I myself like to hang out with the young people, as you can see." She turned to wink at her grandchildren.

"Yes, ma'am," Marshall smiled down at her. "I'm so glad to be here with your family today. George was quick to invite me and I sure do appreciate it."

George took his wife's hand in his own and gently patted it before he led Marshall away. Just about then one of George's daughters called for everyone to get seated.

Amid all the chaos everyone seemed to know their place in the dining room. The children separated into groups, obviously based on age, and made their way to various tables around the edges of the room. The adults went to what had to be the longest table Marshall had ever seen in a residential home and began to get seated. If anyone were to ask him later how he knew where to sit Marshall couldn't have answered. He just found himself to the left of George who was seated at the head of the table. Looking directly across the table Marshall sat looking into the smiling face of Dorma Lee. She was seated directly to the right-hand side of her husband. After one of George's daughters explained that it would be a few more minutes before everything was ready several of the young people began asking their Grandpa to share his poem.

As the room slowly filled with the chant, "The Saucer, the Saucer, the Saucer," Marshall heard random voices saying "Come on, Grandpa" and "Please."

George stood to his feet and a hush fell over the room. George smiled and said "I guess I've been nominated to recite. It's been a while since I've done this but I think I've got it."

He cleared his throat, folded his hands in front of him and stood a little taller as he began;
"I've never made a fortune and it's probably too late now.
But I don't worry about that much, I'm happy anyhow.
And as I go along life's way, I'm reaping better than I sowed.
I'm drinking from my saucer, 'cause my cup has overflowed.
I don't have a lot of riches, and sometimes the going's tough.
But I've got a wife and three girls that love me - that makes me rich enough.
I thank God for his blessings, and the mercies He's bestowed.
I'm drinking from my saucer, 'cause my cup has overflowed.
I remember times when things went wrong, my faith wore somewhat thin.
But all at once the dark clouds broke, and the sun peeked through again.
So God, help me not to gripe about the tough rows that I've hoed.
I'm drinking from my saucer, 'cause my cup has overflowed.
If God gives me strength and courage, when the way grows steep and rough.
I'll not ask for other blessings, I'm already blessed enough.
And may I never be too busy, to help others bear their load.
I'll keep drinking from my saucer, 'cause my cup has overflowed."

Looking around the table George said "That's one of my favorite poems. It was written by John Paul Moore – well every line but the one I changed to fit me having a wife and three girls." He said with a wink. "Still, every word of that poem is true for me. I sure have been blessed!"

He turned to smile at his lovely wife as he reached for her hand. Dorma Lee placed her hand into his. Looking around the table at his family again George continued, "Not a day goes by but what we don't thank the good Lord for every one of you in this room: our children, grandchildren and great-grandchildren," Looking over at Marshall he added "and today our friend Marshall. We, each one of us, have so much to be thankful for."

And with that one of the ladies said "I hate to interrupt a good thing but the food's ready! As soon as someone says the prayer we can get started!"

George smiled and turned to ask his oldest son-in-law to lead the family in prayer. At the word 'Amen' the women started bringing the food to the table. Somehow there was calm in the chaos, order to the disorder, and it wasn't long before everyone had a full plate and was savoring the tasty meal and fun conversation.

Licking his lips a bit later, all Marshall could think was that he hadn't eaten that good since the home-cooked meal he'd had at Vonda's.

CHAPTER 31

Opening her eyes on Thanksgiving morning Vonda was thankful to be in a home where the air was thick with love. She couldn't think of a better way to describe it. Now that she'd met Megan she fully understood Leanza's deep devotion and love for her mother.

Not everyone can put words to love the way Megan does, Vonda thought. She has a way of expressing things that makes you actually feel what she's saying. It's a gift really. Thank you Lord, for the blessing of being here with this family, Vonda prayed as she set about getting ready for the day.

Everyone from the children up was involved in the day's arrangements. There were plenty of jobs to go around. Thanksgiving decorations were put out and the table was set. The ongoing preparations became a team effort and before long delicious smells began to waft through the house.

Finally, Megan called everyone to take their places around the table and announced that everything was just about ready. As soon as they were seated everyone lifted and extended their hands toward those on either side of them. Vonda, being the only new person at the table, simply followed along with the rest. After clasping hands everyone turned to look at Megan.

"Leanza, we're going to have you begin this year," she said, smiling at her lastborn. One by one they went around the table, each one naming the thing they were especially thankful for. When it was Vonda's turn she said, simply, "I'm so thankful to be here with each of you today. This is such a blessing!"

After each one had expressed thanks Megan led her family in a prayer in which she thanked God, above all else, for her precious, beautiful family.

The food was beyond delicious. The conversation was uplifting. The entire day was filled with fun and laughter. And never once did Vonda feel like an outsider.

In the afternoon the children were content playing together in another room.

"Wade told me all about the conversation you all had after I took the children to bed last night," Karen told the others as she settled onto the sofa beside her mother-in-law.

"That's good," Megan said putting her arm around Karen and pulling her close for a brief hug. Turning to smile at Wade she picked up right where she'd left off.

"After you were born healthy and safe, life simply went on for our little family. As soon as I was able to fit into the yellow dress, I put it on. I loved it every bit as much as I'd expected to. Every time I wore it your father called me sunshine in human form," she said with a beautiful laugh.

"I knew it wasn't an everyday dress but we weren't extravagant or social people. If I were to wait for special occasions I wasn't going to get much use of that beautiful dress your father had gifted me. So I wore it whenever I wanted to, especially when it seemed we needed an extra dose of sunshine! There were even days your father would ask me to wear it. That's why you remember me wearing it at the park that day, Wade. Your dad said we needed extra sunshine so I wore it for him.

Wade, you continued to grow healthy and strong. God continued to bless us and soon, Leanza, you came along making our little family complete." Megan smiled across the room as she looked directly into her daughter's deep brown eyes that were so like her father's.

"One day while wearing my yellow dress I told your father that because it had brightened our lives so much I now wanted a yellow button up shirt for him to wear. I was just teasing him, of course." Megan laughed out loud.

"But Denvel was such a good and loving man. He wasn't sure whether I was joking or being sincere. At the risk of hurting me he said he wasn't quite sure he could pull that off. I insisted he could, stating that I had every intention of finding such a shirt for him. I'm just a little ashamed to admit it now but I kept him guessing for the better part of that whole day. Finally, he told me he'd never wear yellow for anyone else, but he might for me. He said, 'I'll make you a deal.' She laughed out loud as she added, "We were forever making each other a deal."

He declared, "If we ever find a bright yellow button up shirt I'll definitely wear it." She looked from one to the other of them smiling as she added, "I'm certain he felt fairly safe making that particular deal."

They all laughed.

"He went on to say, "if we don't find one I'll make you a promise. If I happen to die before you do I'll visit you as a butterfly that way you'll know it's me. You won't have a doubt about it, Megan – you won't have a doubt because I'll visit you as a yellow butterfly."

Oh, I can't tell you how we laughed! The mere thought of your father in a yellow button down shirt, or as a yellow butterfly! Well, it was just so funny." They all chuckled. It *really was* just so silly.

Smiling as she looked around the room Megan's eye's met Leanza's.

Her daughter said quietly, "I don't remember the yellow dress at all."

"Well, you wouldn't, Leanza. You were so young then. And after your dad went missing I never wore it again. I guess, it wasn't really my dress at all, it was ours. It was something the two of us shared and without him, wearing that dress just never made sense. I still have it. In fact, there have been a few times through all these years that I've taken it out, looked at it and held it against me just to remember. It always makes me smile. But I could never bring myself to put it on once he was gone.

Now, to answer your question, Wade. Yes, there did come a defining moment. A moment in which I knew your father was never coming back. It was about four years after he went missing.

Turning toward Vonda, Megan said, "Our family has talked a lot about this through the years. There's quite a bit of our story you don't know so I'll share a little with you before I explain.

Denvel loved to fish. When we were children I would often see him fishing in the pond on the property next to ours. He was a good fisherman and his mother regularly fed their family from his catch. We grew up as neighbors. Life was hard back then and we often turned to each other to get through it. Not only did we become best friends but we grew to love each other. It was only natural that we would end up together. We married young and set out to make a better life for ourselves. When we first arrived in Norfolk we would go down to the docks and Denvel would fish from the pier. There were many nights his catch became our supper.

115

We liked watching the cargo ships coming and going. Denvel often struck up a conversation with the workers, and it wasn't long before he landed a job there. Dock work is hard, physical labor but Denvel enjoyed it. He was always telling me stories about interacting with the other men on the job. They were a good crew, always joking around together and talking about their families. Denvel often said their fun made the work day go by faster.

We were happy living here, especially once we'd bought this house. I was so glad Denvel enjoyed his work. About a month before he went missing I noticed he wasn't talking about his work days much anymore. When I asked about it he said there had been some changes in the crew. A few of the guys had moved on and there for a while the work load was heavier. It made for harder days. Then they hired a new man but Denvel didn't like him. He wouldn't say exactly what it was he didn't like, just that he didn't fit in with the rest of the crew. He told me not to worry. He was sure things would improve. It made my heart heavy that he wasn't as happy at his job but I thought things would get better.

The first time he came home late I was really worried. He apologized saying they were shorthanded and he'd had to work late. He said this might happen sometimes and for me not to worry when he ran late. That's why I didn't think much about it the day he went missing. He'd been late about three times over that last month so I just thought they were working him late again. As the evening wore on I got more concerned. When he wasn't home by eleven I was really worried. He'd never come home later than nine. The only phone number I had was for the dock office. I called it repeatedly with no answer. I didn't know what to do. It was late and I was frantic. Finally, I called the police.

That was a long night, let me tell you.

He still wasn't home by the next morning and his car wasn't at the dock. Neither of his co-workers nor his boss knew anything about where he was.

That was when the nightmare began.

Those first months, well, that entire first year really, I was diligent to stay on the police about finding him. They got tired of seeing me and my children. I can tell you that. I went in often asking what they knew and what they were doing about finding my husband. By the end of the year they told me quite forcefully that I needed to accept the fact that he had left us. Well, you already know how I felt about that! I continued to call the detective in charge every six months, if I didn't actually visit the station. A couple of years later I hired a private detective myself. He didn't find anything either.

It was hard staying here in this house without him. He loved it so much. He'd been so excited about the changes we were planning and the life we were going to have here as a family.

There were days I wanted to leave this house so badly! Just to escape the memories and being faced with the fact that our dreams weren't going to come true. It always came down to my belief, my hope, that one day he would come walking through the door. How could I leave when this was the one place he could find us?

You can all imagine how hard it was holding onto that hope while time kept passing and there was nothing to feed it.

As I said earlier, four years had passed. I'm not sure what made me break that day. Our wedding anniversary was approaching so maybe that had something to do with it. Maybe it was just the culmination of no answers after so much time without him. I was weary, emotionally exhausted really. I so wanted to believe he was still out there somewhere. But so much time had passed. Knowing how deeply he loved us, I just couldn't find any justification for him staying away. The only explanation that made sense was that he was gone. I mean *really gone*. I had held onto hope for so long but that day I was wrestling with it. I'd wrestled through that entire week and I just couldn't do it anymore.

I broke. I finally just *completely* broke.

I told the Lord I couldn't do it anymore. I had to know, one way or the other. I just had to know. I asked God - is he still out there trying to come back to us or has he gone on to be with you?"

Looking from one to the other of her children Megan said, "I talked to your father, too. I told him how deeply I loved him. How much I missed him. That I was taking care of our children every day and I was making the changes we'd planned to our sweet little house. I told him I would wait for him forever. I just needed to know he actually *would* return to me someday.

I was crying when I finally broke down and begged him to give me a sign. Then I begged God to give me a sign. Exhausted and emotionally spent I fell across the bed and cried myself to sleep.

I woke up about an hour later. You children were in school and weren't due home for another hour.

I needed to get out of the house so I decided to walk down to the park. You know the one," she nodded her head toward her children.

"I felt better having rested. I got to the park and sat on one of the swings just gently swaying a bit, feeling the warmth of the sun and the breeze in my hair. It was therapeutic. In a bit I closed my eyes and leaned my head back. I pushed off from the ground and started to swing. It was freeing and I felt as though my burdens were falling away. I knew it didn't mean anything in the grand scheme of things but I needed it at that moment.

After a bit I stopped pumping my legs so I'd slow down. I came to a slower pace and the swing was coming to a stop. I was lazily looking around the park.

You kids will remember that not far from the swing set, over to the right side, there are some flowering trees and bushes, just a beautiful setting of foliage. My eyes drifted over that way and I was taking in the beauty of the various colored newly opened blossoms. As I looked from one to the other I noticed a slow flash of movement off to one side. Looking more closely I realized it was a butterfly, just sitting there gently opening and closing its wings. As I stood up and started walking in that direction it lifted off the leaves and floated toward me. I was walking toward it at the same time. It kept getting closer and I expected it to just fly away but it didn't. Instead it gently rose and continued fluttering eye-level towards me. It seemed like it was looking right at me.

"What are you doing?" I asked softly, intrigued, laughing a little as I stopped walking and stood to watch it.

It fluttered there a few more times. On impulse I lifted my hand and opened my palm directly in front of the butterfly. Without hesitation it flew over and gently lit upon my uplifted palm. Again, it seemed to look right into my eyes. Ever so slowly it began to open and close its wings drawing my attention to them. As I watched those movements your father came to mind and the deal he had made came back to my memory. I heard him speaking in my thoughts. "If we ever find a bright yellow button up shirt I'll definitely wear it." In my memory he went on to say, 'if we don't find one I'll make you a promise. If I happen to die before you do I'll visit you as a butterfly that way you'll know it's me. You won't have a doubt about it,

Megan – you won't have a doubt because I'll visit you as a yellow butterfly."

You already know what I'm about to say, don't you? The butterfly in the palm of my hand was yellow."

CHAPTER 32

Thankfully, I never had another teacher like Mr. Strong. It was my misfortune to have had even *one* such teacher. I've sometimes wondered if every student has had such a teacher during their academic career. I think not and the part of me that still feels compassion hopes not. The part of me that's become most like him doesn't really care.

I'm not sure how much of me is a result of these two separate parts. One thing I do know - the part that's most like him has led me to where I am and that can never be changed.

I can only assume my life would've been happier if that part didn't exist, but alas, it does.

I've done the best I know how to be happy, admittedly it's usually come at the expense of others. I didn't know how else to achieve it. Like I said, though, I've done the best I know how; perhaps, therein lies the problem. I just don't know how. I've never really figured that part out.

I've thought about that a lot.

I'm not sure I've ever truly been happy: a result of not doing what's right along the way? Maybe...

I was a quiet child prior to entering the sixth grade. Of course, I remained quiet afterward, perhaps even quieter. Considering the beating my self-confidence took that year it's no wonder. After Mr. Strong entered my life, I wasn't just quiet, I was withdrawn.

Truth be told, by the end of my seventh grade school year, I had lost all hope of ever having a friend.

But we all know life is unpredictable....

A Brick to Remember

By some strange twist of fate my family and the family of a classmate set up camp at the exact same campground that very summer. Our parents became camping buddies which basically forced us together. They told us to go play together - so we did.

The camping facility had a game room, a lake for swimming and fishing and access to several free paddle boats. We took advantage of all of it. There were no other kids our age so we stuck together and it went great.

I was surprised to find my classmate accepting, fun and very funny. We had a great time hanging out together and we laughed a lot. Looking back now I may actually say that summer was the happiest I've ever been. I was elated to finally have a friend. It was like a dream come true. My life was so much better and it was going to get better and better from then on. I just knew it.

On the first day of eighth grade, as we passed in the hall, I smiled and loudly greeted that particular classmate. A few seconds later, unnoticed in a hallway filled with students changing classes, my classmate, my summer friend, pressed in against me. Our faces mere inches apart these words were hissed into my ear, "We're back in school now and *I don't even know you*!" Immediately, I found myself alone and reeling from shock.

What had just happened? What about the last three months of gaming, fishing, swimming, boating and laughing? We'd done all of that together - especially the laughing, was none of that real?

It literally took everything in me to hold back the tears as I stumbled to my next class.

By the end of that day I'd processed what had happened. The reality of my life had slapped me in the face. I had to accept the fact that this was just another eye-opening experience in my ongoing miserable childhood. I made up my mind this would be the last time I was ever humiliated by anyone. If I had to play head games to get by in life without being hurt then so be it. Bring it on!

Thus began my education in self-protection through manipulation.

I never again trusted anyone. What's more - no one even realized it. I learned to pretend everything was fine, literally everything. It didn't matter what anyone said or did. I was never shaken. I developed a very thick skin which nothing could penetrate, at least not visibly. Interestingly enough, once I displayed no reaction those few classmates who, with Mr. Strong's subtle encouragement, had continued to torment me - stopped. Without a reaction they simply lost interest.

Finally, the years of mistreatment ended.

Unfortunately, the damage was already done. True to what I've come to consider my own personal rotten luck, I'd figured it out too late.

Once I'd made the decision there was no turning back. I never opened my heart to another human being. Other than my mother, I never truly cared about anyone ever again. I looked out for me and only me. No matter what it took, I made sure I would never feel that kind of humiliation and pain again.

I tolerated the remaining years of my formal education while honing what I inwardly labeled my 'fooled you' skills. By the time I entered the workforce I had a pretty good handle on that. Most people, dare I say all people, now perceive me as positive and caring. They don't realize the extent to which I have manipulated and used them to my own advantage. Having blocked the ability to truly care I got very good at skimming off the top in order to fulfil my own desires. Nowadays I take what I want and leave the rest wanting.

A person can only be beat down so many times and I passed my personal limit pretty early in life. Sure, at times I may feel a twinge of compassion. But I always measure it against what I'm getting out of the situation. When push comes to shove, I make sure I land on top. I've perfected getting what I want without people realizing I'm the one making it all happen.

Obviously, my early social and educational life experiences left a lot to be desired.

My home life, although not stellar, wasn't that bad. My mother was mild-mannered and socially awkward. Right out of high school she landed a job working in the file room of the local healthcare system. She spent her days filing in the basement and seldom actually interacted with others. Being detail oriented and a dependable employee who literally never made mistakes and rarely missed work made her a real asset to her employer. I'm not sure you could call what my mother accomplished a career but she did hold the same job her entire working life. Surely there's something to be said for that.

My father was an over-the-road semi-truck driver so he basically came and went during my childhood. He was gone for days at a time but generally no longer than a week. He was a good man and for the most part life at home was pleasant when he wasn't on the road and tolerable when he was. By the time I reached high school he had landed a job that allowed him to be home every evening.

The company then offered him a position which would have him making occasional long-distance runs. Those jobs paid significantly more and only came along every three or four months. Since being on the road would be infrequent he and my mother agreed he should take advantage of the offer.

For reasons unknown to me my parents never had any other children so I was raised without siblings.

As if my life hadn't held enough torment already, I arrived home from school one day during my freshman year to find my mother crying at the kitchen table.

She said, "Sit down, I've got terrible news.'

I sat down and she proceeded to tell me my father had died in a tragic vehicular accident while driving through Tallahassee earlier that afternoon.

That was the first time I ever heard of Tallahassee. Now it's forever burned into my mind. I like the sound of the word, Tallahassee. Tal~la~has~see… I like to say it in a musical way, almost singing the word.

Tal~la~has~seeeee….

I think that's got the ring of a country song, especially when I add how the place affected my life. There's definitely a country song there.

When I sing it I can really hear it; Tal~la~has~see~ee~ee you took my father from me~eeee.

Sure is a sad crooning.

CHAPTER 33

Prior to arriving at the El residence Marshall's plan was not to stay long after they'd eaten. Once he was inside and had been warmly welcomed and included it became difficult to stick to the plan. The longer he stayed and the more he got to know them, the more impressed he was with the El family.

Clearing away the mess after such a large meal proved to be a joint effort. George and Dorma Lee's oldest daughter assigned a task to each person and everyone cheerfully pitched in making the huge job quick and easy. Afterward everyone dispersed to socialize and relax. Some went back to watching football while others played games. The rest gathered together going through family photographs. Dorma Lee was reminiscing and the children were enjoying her stories.

Over the next few hours many remained scattered throughout the house while some said their goodbyes and headed home. When Dorma Lee went to rest George made himself and Marshall a cup of coffee. Each man got a slice of pie and the two sat down at the now normal-sized dining room table. George shared that as their family had continued to grow he had crafted extra leaves to be inserted into the table. In this way he was able to fulfill his wife's wish that the family always gather around the table for holiday meals.

After the men had talked about the progress on the hospital expansion Marshall complimented George on his large and loving family. This prompted George to share a bit about his youth. Marshall sat listening as George spoke of young love and marrying Dorma Lee.

"You've got quite the story there, George," Marshall told him. "Being on the outside looking in it's easy to see that this young love you talk about can last a lifetime. Here you two are still together and surrounded by family all these many years later."

"You're right about that," George agreed wholeheartedly. "God sure has blessed us. He's seen us through the hard times, and there have been some.

On the other hand He's also given us some really good times. I've had a great life. I hope I don't, but I could die tomorrow and go out a happy man."

"I hope you don't either but that's wonderful," Marshall answered wondering if he could say the same.

The two men sat in silence enjoying their coffee for a few minutes before Marshall spoke again.

"I don't know if you know this about me, George, but I've never been married. My parents died when I was twenty-five. I took custody of my two younger brothers and finished raising them. I was just getting the construction company going and was focusing on building a successful business at the time. With that and taking the boys in, things got really busy. I always assumed I'd marry and have a family one day but the years kept rolling by and it just never happened."

"I didn't know," George replied and went on to say, "I don't know why these things come together for some of us and don't for others. Life's unpredictable and there's so much we're just not meant to know until it happens. Having been blessed with such a large family I don't know what it's been like for you not to have that. I would imagine there's been loneliness along the way though. When you told me you had no plans for today you mentioned a special friend. I've been thinking that there might be a lady you care for in your life."

"Well, yes. There's that," Marshall answered a bit hesitantly.

Not sure what his response meant and not wanting to pry George wasn't sure what to say next. It didn't matter as it wasn't long before Marshall spoke again.

"I'll be honest, George. I'm not really sure where to go from here. I met Vonda a couple of years ago quite by accident. She had just lost her husband the year before and was still grieving deeply.

Circumstances kept bringing us together and that resulted in us becoming good friends. Our friendship has just gotten stronger. We have a lot in common. We talk easily with one another. I'm very comfortable with her and I believe she is with me. When we met I never even considered anything beyond friendship although I have to admit I was immediately attracted to her. I guess I put those thoughts aside out of respect for her grief.

Here recently I find myself thinking and feeling differently towards her. I'm not really sure what to do with that. She's become very important to me and I want her in my life. I mean, I *really* want her in my life. I find myself thinking about her almost constantly. And sometimes my thoughts surprise me." Marshall looked, and felt, a little embarrassed as he said those words. "Truthfully, I simply don't know what any of this means."

Marshall couldn't believe he'd just said all of that to George. He'd never told anyone his true feelings toward Vonda. What's gotten into you lately? He asked himself. He seemed to be asking himself that frequently these days.

George was just sitting there smiling.

"What?" Marshall asked, "Why are you just smiling like that?"

"Well, Marshall," George replied. "It's been a long time since I've seen young love but I'm pretty sure what you're describing and what I'm witnessing is exactly that. You, my young man, are in the throes of young love."

"What?!?" Marshall said a little louder than he'd intended. "George, you've been calling me young man all day today but I'm not young anymore. I mean, I know I'm a bit younger than you but still, I'm not young."

George chuckled, "That's not what I mean at all. Love has nothing to do with age. What I'm telling you is that your love for Vonda is just beginning. It's the love itself that's young not the person feeling it. It's been a lot of years but I still remember how it feels. Even when you know you've been struck and you're sure it's love you're not really sure what to do with it. I hear that in what you're telling me.

I'll give you this; your situation is complicated by the fact that you two have been good friends for quite some time. How do you make the switch to something more now? I'm sure you're right in thinking you reserved your emotions because of her grief but time has passed. You must sense that much of her grief has lifted. That's not to say she won't always grieve for him. She will. That'll never change, so don't expect it to. But that doesn't mean she can't love you."

"Whoa. Now, *whoa!*" Marshall said, putting his hands up between the two of them. "Slow down George. I don't think I'm ready for all this."

George laughed out loud.

126

"Well, okay Marshall. You may not be ready but I'm just gonna go ahead and tell you it's here anyway. I believe you're already in love."

And with that George picked up his coffee mug and took a long slow sip giving Marshall sufficient time to process the information.

Marshall felt like he'd been bowled over. It reminded him of the way he'd felt when Vonda first opened the door the night she invited him to supper. Come to think of it, he'd been feeling this way fairly often when he was with her these days. He clearly remembered wanting to take her face into his hands and kiss her that night. Was George right? Had he fallen in love with Vonda Graham without even realizing what was happening?

Watching Marshall's face, George could see the emotional struggle just below the surface. He felt a little sympathetic toward his friend. He'd spoken truthfully earlier. He hadn't forgotten what young love felt like. People only like to focus on the good things but George remembered the feelings of confusion, fear, uncertainty and just generally not knowing what was happening or what you were supposed to do about it. And especially that fear that she wouldn't love you in return.

George prayed silently for his friend. He hoped Vonda was already in love with Marshall. What a blessing that would be for a man whose early life circumstances had cost him the chance to have a family of his own.

I sure hope this is from you, Lord, and you're about to bless this man big time. George prayed. Whatever's in store for Marshall, Lord, please guide me in how to be there for him.

George then silently sat waiting as his friend tried to digest the words he'd just spoken to him.

CHAPTER 34

Leanza woke up before the rest of the family. She made herself a cup of coffee and went back upstairs to pack her things. She might as well get ready so she could spend as much time as possible with her mom and Wade's family before she and Vonda flew out that evening.

When she went back downstairs a bit later there was a bustle of activity in the kitchen. It seemed everyone was up and about. Looking around she didn't see Megan anywhere.

"Where's mom?" she asked Wade as he poured his coffee. "Isn't she up yet?"

"Yeah, she's downstairs switching the laundry over," he answered.

Leanza went to the basement door, opened it and went down the stairs. Sure enough she could see her mother moving the clothing from the washer to the dryer in the back corner of the room. She hadn't been downstairs in years and glanced around the room on her way over to Megan. She wished her mother a good morning and gave her a little hug.

"Oh, Leanza, you didn't need to come down. I'd have been back up in just a few minutes," her mother said.

"It's not a problem, mom. In fact, I'm kind of glad you're down here. Last week I was remembering how Wade and I used to roller skate down here in the winter since we couldn't go outside. We had so much fun!" She laughed as she looked around the room.

"Oh, yes, that's true!" her mother said. "I forgot you kids did that. I doubt if you remember this, but you used to ride your tricycle down here. You loved going in a loop around the support posts and the furnace there in the middle of the room. You got pretty fast at it, too. Your dad and I used to call you The Streak." She laughed at that. "Of course, you didn't go that fast but for a three-year-old you were really moving!"

"Really? I rode my tricycle down here?" she asked.

"You did more than that. We had an entire play area set up. We hadn't finished renovating the main level yet. Of course, we almost always had laundry going with you and Wade being such active children. We even brought an overstuffed easy chair down here so whichever one of us was doing laundry could sit comfortably and watch you kids playing.

"I wish I could remember that," Leanza said and Megan saw a look of sadness cross her daughter's face. "Why don't I remember, mom?"

Megan slid her hand gently along one side of Leanza's face lovingly. Looking into her daughter's eyes she answered; "You were very young then. And after your father disappeared our lives changed drastically. In those first months I was at the police station more than here. I tried to make them keep the investigation going. I was grieving the loss of your father while learning to care for you children alone. I was confused and I missed him every waking moment. Our lives changed quickly.

Your dad was the only one working so I had to figure out how to keep us afloat. There was a lot going on and we just didn't come down here for you kids to play anymore. When the weather got warmer I took your tricycle outside and eventually you outgrew it. I guess you were just too young to remember riding and playing here with your dad. Do you remember him at all?" she asked gently.

"I wish I could say I do, mom, but I don't think so. I mean, I know what he looked like but maybe that's just from the pictures you've shown me and have sitting around. No. I can't honestly say I have even one memory of him. I can't see his face in my mind or remember anything specific we did together. I guess I was just too young when he went missing. I just hate that. I really would love it if I had even just one memory to hold onto."

"I'm so sorry." Megan said as she drew her daughter into her arms and held her tenderly. "He was truly a wonderful man. And he loved you so much! That's why he dubbed you his Little Dove."

Leanza's body suddenly jerked back from her mother as her eyes sought her mother's face, "What did you say? Mom! *What* did you *just say*?"

Megan was startled by her daughter's aggressive tone and behavior.

"I said you were his Little Dove. Why? *What's wrong?* You already know that. I don't understand this reaction?"

Leanza's eyes were brimming over and a tear rolled out of her right eye and slid silently down her check. She quickly reached up and wiped it away.

"No, mom, I *don't* know that. Dad called me that? Mom, you've *never* told me this before. I didn't know dad called me that! I don't know how to explain this but I know the name 'Little Dove'. I've written it hundreds of times through the years but I've *never known why*. I didn't know where it came from. I never knew my father called me that. Don't you see what this means?"

Megan was confused. Had she never told her daughter Denvel's pet name for her? *Really?* In all these years she had never told Leanza her dad called her Little Dove? She felt her heart tighten in her chest.

"Don't you see mom? This means that maybe I do remember him after all." A small sob caught in Leanza's throat. "I've had that phrase Little Dove in my mind my entire life, but until now I had no idea where it came from. Why did he call me that, mom?"

Megan was still standing very close to her daughter so she stepped back a few steps and looked deeply into Leanza's face.

"As you know your father and I both had a very difficult upbringing. The one light in your father's childhood was his grandmother. She was a lovely woman who loved your father very much. If she could've taken him in and raised him there's no doubt she would have. But times were different back then. She never got to keep him but every time she could do something good for him she did it. Every time he visited her he felt loved and wanted. Despite the difficulties he faced she made sure he knew he was loved. That's why we gave you her name Leanza Clementine." Megan smiled and stroked Leanza's cheek again.

"Yes, I know that part, mom. I already knew all of that but it doesn't explain why he called me Little Dove."

"Oh, yes, no, you're right. Her name was Leanza Clementine just like yours. But all of her family and most of her friends, everyone close to her called her by her nickname: Dove. I guess it was only natural then that your father adapted her nickname to you. From the moment you were born you became his Little Dove."

Leanza felt a warmth envelope her body from head to toe. Her heart was happy and for the first time in a long time, maybe even in her entire life she felt a sense of total peace.

CHAPTER 35

Marshall was seated in his high back leather chair in the sitting area of his corporate office. Having spent most of the morning going through contracts and supply requisitions for the hospital, he was taking a much needed coffee break. He needed to clear his head of work for a bit so he turned his thoughts to his conversation with George on Thanksgiving.

Yesterday, had it really been just yesterday?

Vonda had sent Marshall a text that morning wishing him a Happy Thanksgiving and hoping he would have a good day. Marshall hadn't found it until he'd returned home from George's. Of course, he had answered telling her where he'd gone and that it had been a wonderful day with kind and welcoming people. The two of them texted back and forth a few times and Vonda told him she and Leanza would be flying home the next day.

Today! He thought happily. Vonda's coming home today! Marshall found himself smiling. He would soon be seeing her again.

George had drawn an interesting conclusion concerning Marshall's recent confusions. Once over the initial shock of George saying he was in love with Vonda, he began to see the possible truth of it. As the two men continued to talk, George asked Marshall if he would consider letting Vonda know how he now felt about her.

Marshall had conflicting feelings about that. If she was open to a deeper relationship with him he definitely wanted to tell her. If she wasn't open to something more than friendship he didn't want to risk losing what they now shared.

Vonda had become a very important part of his life and he absolutely did not want to lose her. He didn't know if he'd be able to continue having just a friendship feeling the way he now knew he did. But he was pretty sure he couldn't handle Vonda not being part of his life at all.

George saw his point and the two men began to brainstorm as to the best way for Marshall to handle the situation. In the end they decided a verbal announcement of his feelings might not be the best course of action.

Marshall confessed that he often found himself wanting to do special things for Vonda. He shared having taken flowers to her most recent dinner invitation. He had also dressed nicer than he would have in the past. While telling George about that evening Marshall remembered that Vonda had worn a new dress and fixed her hair in a braided style he'd never seen her wear before. She had also set the table with her best dishes. George told Marshall he had to wonder if those things might indicate that Vonda's feelings for Marshal were changing, too. Perhaps just as had been the case with Marshall, she wasn't even fully aware of it. There was no easy way to be sure.

George shared his lifelong observation that most women respond to how they're treated more than to what's said to them. That's not to say it's not important for a man to voice his love but at this early stage of things it might be better for Marshall to do instead of say.

Perhaps Marshall needed to continue spending more time with Vonda just letting his love show when they were together. Both men were of the mind that this would give her feelings for Marshall a chance to grow, too.

Marshall wasn't in a hurry to change things. More than anything else he just wanted to be near her. He loved listening to her, seeing her smile, hearing her laughter and knowing she was safe and happy.

George told Marshall that was exactly what a man in love would say. He then just sat there smiling again.

As the day ended, George assured his friend he would be praying for Marshall to have wisdom and for Vonda to be receptive to Marshall's love. Unbeknownst to Marshall, before he had even gotten to his car, George was already asking God to bless their relationship.

Marshall finished his coffee and stood up. Walking toward his desk he thought about how anxious he was to see Vonda now that she was returning from Virginia. Even as he returned his attention to work, he was trying to think of a way to see her again.

CHAPTER 36

At the exact same time Marshall was brainstorming about how and when to see Vonda again she and Leanza were arriving at the airport to catch their flight home. After hugs and goodbyes with all of Leanza's family the two ladies went through the airport security check.

Vonda noticed Leanza seemed preoccupied and unusually quiet as they sat together waiting to board. Vonda assumed it might've been difficult saying goodbye to her family. She decided not to press for conversation in case Leanza needed time to adjust to the separation.

Half an hour later after they had boarded the plane and taken off Vonda was getting a little concerned about her friend.

"Are you doing alright with leaving your family, Leanza?" she asked gently.

"What? Oh, sure. Sure I am." Leanza answered, still seeming a bit distracted. "That's just part of my line of work, you know? It was wonderful seeing them again and we had a great time. It's been a good trip but goodbyes can't be avoided. That's alright. We'll be together again soon."

"Yes, that's true." Vonda answered. "Thank you so much for inviting me. I had a wonderful time. I absolutely loved meeting your mom and your brother and his family."

"Thanks so much for coming along. Everyone loves you and they were so glad to meet you. I told you how welcoming mom would be. I wasn't wrong, was I!?"

"Not at all," Vonda answered as Leanza turned away to look out the window again. Feeling as though she'd been dismissed, Vonda left her friend alone. She wasn't sure what was going on but felt something definitely was. She leaned her head back and silently asked God to help Leanza with whatever she was dealing with.

About an hour later Leanza turned to Vonda and said, "I think I'm ready to talk now."

Vonda immediately sat up straighter in her seat and turned to face Leanza with a smile. "Ok then. I'm definitely ready to listen."

"I know you've seen that I've had something on my mind today. Thanks for giving me the space and time to process it."

"Of course," Vonda answered.

"I don't think I've mentioned this to you before but I keep a daily journal. It's something I started at a very young age, probably in my pre-teen years. It just helps me categorize my thoughts and process life events. It's very therapeutic, really.

I don't know when but at some point along the way I would sometimes fall asleep while making my journal entries. Since I type the entries into my computer I always check what I was typing the next time I make an entry. This is how I've discovered that at times I keep typing even though I'm falling asleep. Those entries make no sense at all. Sometimes they're quite funny, as you can imagine. Anyway, I've begun calling them my sleep-typing entries. Instead of deleting them I highlight them in yellow.

So here's the thing. There are certain phrases I've noticed that are regularly repeated in my sleep-typing. They often refer to my dad or at least contain the word daddy. Something about bricks or a brick shows up often. And there's a phrase – Little Dove. I have no idea how often these things show up and I've never known what any of this means. I save my sleep-typing but other than a quick read through I really haven't given it much thought and I've never audited it in any way at all.

This morning when I was in the basement with mom she told me something she's never told me before. She thought she had but she hadn't. She told me my father used to call me his Little Dove. I don't know if you can even imagine my reaction. I mean the phrase Little Dove has been in my sleep-typing literally for years! In all this time I've had no idea why or what it's meant. As far as my rational mind is concerned I have no memories of my father at all. When my mother told me Little Dove was his affectionate nickname for me it knocked me off center. I felt like she was telling me I actually do have memories of my dad. I was in shock! But I'm also very happy with this news."

"Oh, Leanza, that's wonderful! I'm so happy for you!" Vonda said, relieved to hear what had been affecting her friend wasn't bad news as she'd earlier feared.

"Thanks, I think so, too. But now that I know that phrase means something it's got me wondering if the other recurring phrases in my sleep-typing mean something, too.

Truthfully, I don't even know what all the repetitive words or phrases are. I'm finding myself a bit frustrated now. I mean, I don't have time to delve into this. I'm committed to the A413TF team. I can't get distracted with a personal situation right now. I've got to stay focused until we solve these cases. Can you see my frustration? I've got new information, a new clue to an old mystery, if you will, but I can't devote myself to solving it."

"Yes," Vonda said "I can see what you're saying. That *would* be frustrating!"

The two women sat back in their seats again, each woman mulling over the information and considering the situation.

After about ten minutes Vonda leaned forward and looked at Leanza.

"I'm having an idea, Leanza," she said softly.

Leanza turned her head and looked at Vonda.

"Yes?" Leanza answered simply.

"Well, I'm not sure how we could do this, or how you'll feel about it. But I'm retired now and I live alone. I have plenty of time and I'm more than willing to take on a new project. I'm just wondering how you would feel about giving me access to your typed journals. I mean, I have no interest or purpose in reading your daily entries. What I could do instead would be to copy and paste all of the yellow highlighted sections onto another individual document. I could then study those entries for repeated similarities or phrases, essentially doing - as you've mentioned - an audit of some sort. This would give you more condensed accumulated information. Perhaps allowing you to see what you might not be seeing now." Vonda shrugged her shoulders as if to say 'I don't know' and leaned back in her seat again.

"Wow," Leanza said softly. "That's an idea alright. I'm going to have to give that some thought. If you're sure that's something you'd be willing to take on I might just have to let you do it. Let's see. How could we make this work? Well, I guess, I could look back and see if I can find the first yellow highlight. I could then copy/paste my entire journal entries from that point

135

on into a new document. That way we don't risk losing any of my original entries or personal information. I could put that document onto a flash drive you could plug into your computer and you could take it from there.

It would just be a matter of you deleting all the entry information except the yellow highlighted sections. Once you did that you could begin to inventory the frequency with which each repeated phrase appears.

Wow, the more I talk this through the better I like the idea. You might be onto something here, Vonda."

CHAPTER 37

For the past three hours the A413TF team had been going through the extensive employee list and each person's history for each of the three facilities in question: Myrtle Beach General Hospital Emergency Room, Urgent Care of Myrtle Beach and Doctor's Care of Stokesbury. They now realized the search was going to be a considerable process. They were looking for one particular employee who had been employed in all three facilities during the past twenty-two years since the first disappearance. There was a lot of cross-checking involved.

Having thus far failed in finding the elusive employee Leanza was beginning to sense a spirit of discouragement. In truth she was feeling discouraged herself. How perfect would it have been to have quickly found one person tied to all thirteen disappearances? Talk about tying things up in a pretty little bow.

Experience had taught her it just doesn't happen that easily in most cases.

Not wanting the morale and momentum of the team to drop, Leanza began talking about the benefits of the research they were doing. Even if they didn't make an obvious connection they were learning valuable information about past and present employees. Although their long sought after answer wasn't as obvious as they had hoped, it may still be in this information.

"We all know how case work goes," she said simply. "It's in the redundant, repetitive and seemingly unending search that the answer is finally revealed. Would it have been simpler to immediately see one employee who transferred between the three facilities? Sure it would. Does our not having seen that yet mean nothing's here? Certainly not! We all agreed this was a worthwhile search so we've just got to keep at it. Any minute now the answer may come to light."

Several agents were nodding their heads in agreement. This spurred her on so Leanza began to verbally list the information they'd gathered thus far. The more she talked the more the others began to chime in. This process led them to the decision to compile two lists.

One list would consist of employees who had worked at only one of the three facilities before leaving the healthcare system completely. Since they had accepted a position elsewhere it was likely they were never to return again. The other list would consist of employees who stayed within the system taking positions in one or more of the other departments. These people were worth another look. Over time they could have feasibly served in one capacity or another in the other two facilities since they were constantly transferring between departments.

The plan was to do a quick follow up of the names on the first list to be certain no one from that list was rehired at a later date. Once that was established the names on that list could be removed. The team would then be free to do more research into those on the second list.

As they continued to compile this information they saw that some employees had made a career of moving through the healthcare system in a wide variety of positions. It was as though their single most important mission in life was to remain employed within the system. In order to achieve this some people appeared to have accepted any position they could, at some points even regressing instead of advancing. If one position ended, didn't work out or just didn't suit them, they simply moved on to another position.

One such woman had started out in the file room. When the healthcare system decided to go paperless she accepted a temporary position scanning files into the computer system. Once that was completed she moved to housekeeping. During her time in housekeeping she worked in both the Myrtle Beach General Hospital ER and the Stokesbury Urgent Care facility. For a while it seemed to the agents as though they might have gotten lucky. They were disappointed once they realized she had never worked at Doctor's Care. At one point she moved to a low-level administrative position back at Myrtle Beach General Hospital. After that she moved into registration. Her final move was into the finance department where she currently worked as a Medical Billing Coder. They were left to conclude she'd taken professional classes to become a billing coder at that point.

Having been around that long and in so many various positions she was sure to have seen and heard a lot through the years. For this reason the agents made note of her name. She may be willing to talk about the place if they needed clarification.

As it turned out she wasn't the only employee to have such a wide range of positions within the healthcare system. This wasn't going to be an easy or fast process. However, since they were each convinced it was a worthwhile pursuit they diligently worked on.

Occasionally, someone would say "I think I've got something."

Immediately, the others would join them until the possible lead had been exhausted.

At the end of the session they had acquired quite a bit of new information. But the coveted missing piece still eluded them.

CHAPTER 38

Vonda had sent Marshall a text that the return flight was to arrive in Myrtle Beach at ten-fifty the night before. Since it was arriving late, she promised to let Marshall know once she'd arrived safely at home. When her text came he had to keep himself from jumping into his car and going to see her right then. Instead, he replied by wishing her a good night's sleep and adding that he was looking forward to seeing her soon.

The next day Marshall called during his lunch break. After acknowledging the late notice he mentioned the possibility of having dinner together. Vonda assured him it would be lovely not to have to think about cooking on her first evening home and they arranged to meet.

Vonda was now waiting for Marshall to arrive at the Back Alley Cafe. She hadn't seen him since before her trip to Virginia and was anxious to hear all about his Thanksgiving and tell him about hers.

When the restaurant door opened and Vonda saw Marshall she quickly got up from her table and rushed to meet him. He was almost halfway across the dining room area when she reached him. Each of them was smiling broadly as Marshall opened his arms. Vonda walked into his embrace and pressed her head into his shoulder and he tightened his arms around her.

"Oh Marshall, it's so good to see you!" she said, smiling up at him. "It feels like I've been gone forever."

Marshall squeezed her close and held her for just a few seconds longer than usual. When she didn't pull away his smile grew and he gave her another gentle squeeze. Releasing her they both turned and walked to the booth along the back wall where she'd been seated. As he slid into the seat across from her he said, "You're right. It does seem like you've been gone forever. Did you have a good time?"

"I did," she answered, "and I have so much to tell you I don't even know where to start."

"Well, we've got all evening so just jump right in." He invited, with a chuckle.

"I will, just as soon as we place our order." Vonda said as she handed him the menu.

Their server, Melanie, shared the evening's specials and left them to talk over their preferences. By the time she returned with their sweet tea they had made up their minds. After placing their order Vonda went into a detailed description of Leanza's family. Marshall sat smiling as he listened to her animated version of the events of the past several days. Her laughter was music to his ears and he truly believed he would never grow tired of listening to her happy voice.

When Vonda saw Melanie approaching with their food she was surprised. "Marshall!" she said, "I've barely let you get a word in edgewise! I am so embarrassed."

"Oh no, you don't," he said with genuine feeling. "You never need to be embarrassed by talking with me. I enjoy it! Besides, I've been looking forward to this so don't leave a thing out! Now what was it you were saying?"

Melanie arrived and placed Marshall's Pork Chop Platter and Vonda's Hawaiian Mahi Mahi meal on the table. She made sure that they had all they needed before going to seat some new arrivals. Vonda smiled at Marshall and reached both of her hands across the booth toward him. Unsure of what was happening Marshall reached out and gently took her hands into his.

Vonda bowed her head and said simply, "Thank you Father for such a wonderful Thanksgiving this year. Thank you for giving both of us the chance to celebrate with new friends and for bringing us back together now to share it all with each other. Please use this food to nourish and strengthen us. We are so very blessed and we love you, Lord."

Marshall said "Amen" along with her and they began to eat. They weren't in the habit of holding hands during prayer. It was just something Vonda had wanted to do. She then picked up right where she'd left off telling him all about her visit, even relaying Megan's story about the yellow butterfly.

As he had known she would be, Vonda was very happy to hear about Marshall's Thanksgiving dinner with George and his family.

Of course, Marshall didn't share the conversation he'd had with George about his feelings for Vonda. Some things are just better left unsaid. The two of them talked and laughed often as the evening passed. When they later looked around it was to realize they were the only two left in the cafe. Feeling badly for keeping the servers from completing their end-of-the-night duties they quickly paid leaving Melanie a generous tip. Joey, the Café's owner, thanked them for coming in and wished them a good night. While walking to the car they talked about the good folks who ran so many of the businesses in Logan.

Marshall found himself wishing the evening didn't have to end. After getting settled in the driver's seat Vonda smiled up at him. Wanting to postpone the inevitable he placed his folded arms on the car outside her window and leaned down long enough to tell her to drive carefully and wish her a goodnight. It was all he could do not to lean in and plant a soft kiss on her shapely lips.

CHAPTER 39

Although the night air was cool Leanza's body was drenched in sweat. She had yet to awaken from the dream that held her captive. It had started out pleasantly but was now becoming troublesome. In its beginning she was a happy little girl riding her tricycle in a large circle in the basement of her childhood home.

In her dream-state she watched herself and somehow knew this scene was taking place in her mother's basement and she was no longer a child. Though she couldn't see his face she knew someone she loved was nearby. She was smiling and calling out for him to watch. She sensed his smile and knew he was proud of her. She felt loved and so very happy until suddenly the dream changed. The room grew cold and dark and was enclosed in a thick fog and the air felt damp.

On some level she knew this wasn't real either. It was only a dream; but she was powerless to wake herself or escape its grip.

Though no one was there to see it, she began to thrash about in her bed.

She was no longer riding her tricycle. Now she was staring at a brick wall. Everything around her was shrouded in darkness. She felt alone and was afraid. She had the sense of pending disaster.

She wanted to move away but there was nowhere to go. Now she was surrounded by brick walls on every side. There was no escape and she couldn't find her toys. She wanted her daddy. He had been there just a moment ago but now he was gone. He had given her his toy. Where was his toy now? Wanting to run to him she turned aside but bricks were all around her. Thinking he was nearby she turned and reached her arms out in front of her stretching out as far as possible.

She called out to him, "Daddy come and play with me. Please daddy, I'm scared! I can't find my baby! Her bed is gone. Where are you? Help me, daddy!"

Turning back in the other direction again she watched as the brick wall in front of her suddenly parted. A sliver of light shone through. It was a very small opening at first but became larger and continued to grow. She could see it opening into a gaping area. The lighted area began to turn dark. She felt as if it would swallow her up.

"Little Dove!" her daddy shouted with great alarm in his voice. "Don't go in there! Come back!"

She heard a different voice now. "You must keep daddy's toy safe," it said. Not knowing who had spoken she turned again to look at her father but all she saw was fog and darkness stretching out before her. Suddenly she felt something grab her. It was trying to pull her into the dark chasm. She jerked away with all her strength.

"Nooooo!!!" she screamed.

Leanza's body thrashed and she awoke with a start. She was sitting straight upright in her bed, her hair was wet and sticking to her skin along her face and neckline. Her heart raced.

A soft glow of moonlight shone through the window blinds illuminating the room. Her eyes began to focus as her mind slowly registered where she was. This was her bedroom in the condo, her current, temporary home. With this realization Leanza understood she'd just awoken.

It was a dream. It was all just a very bad dream.

She walked into the bathroom and turned on the shower. Dropping her night shirt, thick with perspiration, she let it lay in a heap on the bathroom floor and stepped in. Letting the water cascade over her, she began to assess the contents of her dream. She'd never had such a dream before. What had brought this on? Was it from being in her mother's basement? What was all of that about brick walls and her daddy's toy?

By the time she finished showering Leanza had made a decision.

Since it was still in the wee hours and she was going back to bed at some point she put on a fresh nightshirt. She then went to her makeshift office area and retrieved an empty flash drive from her briefcase. She sat down with her computer and opened her personal journal document and began to search for the first yellow highlighted entry. Finding it, she began at that journal entry and copied the entries through the end of that year which she then pasted into a new document.

She went on to copy each year's journal entries right up to the present into the document she had created. Having all the journal entries since the sleep-typing had started in a document on the flash drive she set her computer aside and put the flash drive on the table.

She would call Vonda first thing in the morning. Perhaps they could meet for lunch. Leanza would tell her about the dream and give her the flash drive so Vonda could delete the journal entries, keeping only the yellow highlighted sleep-typing entries. She could then begin to audit the sleep-typing. Leanza didn't know if she'd be able to sleep any more or not but she went back to bed to try.

Obviously, the little girl she once was had tucked away some significant memories of her father. Had something happened in that basement, something that had to do with her toys and her dad? Leanza now believed her mind had been sending messages from her younger self to her present self for a very long time. Specifically what those messages were and what they meant was a mystery Vonda was willing to help her with. It was time for Leanza to solve this.

More accurately, it was *well past* time.

CHAPTER 40

It wasn't easy for Leanza to drag herself out of bed the next morning. The long night had left her feeling as if she'd been drugged. Unfortunately, she had a full schedule and couldn't just hide under the covers hoping to capture the sleep her restless night had stolen.

After sending Vonda a text requesting a lunch date she pushed through getting dressed. She pulled her hair back and was clipping it loosely at the nape of her neck when Vonda's text reply came in. She felt relieved seeing that Vonda had asked when and where to meet her before promising to be there.

Vonda arrived early at The Coffee Grind, Logan's coffee, tea and sandwich shop. When Leanza joined her she couldn't help noticing her friend's tired features and eyes. She understood a few minutes later as Leanza told her about her dream and handed her the flash drive. Sipping their flavored coffees the two women discussed what needed done and how Vonda may best outline her findings.

This was the first they'd been together since their return from Virginia so there was a bit to catch up on. As Vonda shared that she and Marshall had met for dinner Leanza noticed a distinct sparkle in Vonda's countenance she hadn't seen before. Whether she'd simply overlooked it, or it was something new, she wasn't sure.

Leanza had been a little curious about their relationship when she first met Marshall but they didn't seem to be a couple, just a couple of dear friends. Watching and listening to Vonda as she spoke of him now Leanza found herself wondering if she'd been mistaken or if something had recently changed.

When Vonda finished talking Leanza said, "I might have asked you this before, I'm not sure, but exactly how is it that you know Marshall?"

"Oh," Vonda laughed lightly. "That's a funny story actually. I met him at the little league ball field near the concession stand. I'd ordered myself a full meal with a large soda and was trying to make it back to the bleachers with it precariously balanced in my hands. Marshall stepped out in front of me and needless to say, I proceeded to lose control and started dropping everything. The worst part was when the soda tipped forward. It spilled all over Marshall starting at his shoulder and poured all down his arm. It was a terrible sticky mess! You can probably imagine how embarrassed I was. To make matters worse I had nothing to wipe him off with! Thankfully, some kind stranger held out a handful of napkins. Oh, you should've heard me apologizing! I was absolutely mortified!

But then I heard Marshall's kind voice telling me it was alright and not to worry about it. When I looked at his face I found him smiling. The best thing being that his smile came from his eyes not just his lips. That's how I knew he really meant it. He put me at ease from that moment on. He helped me clean the mess up off the ground and then insisted on replacing my meal. We ended up laughing over the whole matter. He invited me to sit with him and introduced me to his brother, Mason, whom you've met now as well. So that was the beginning of our friendship." Vonda smiled while adding, "And as they say the rest is history."

Leanza had been smiling throughout Vonda's entire rendition of the event. Now she leaned forward just a tiny bit, looked Vonda deeply in the eyes, winked and asked "Soooo what exactly is the rest?"

"What?" Vonda said as her cheeks turned a slight shade of pink.

"You're blushing!" Leanza laughed.

"I'm not!!" Vonda argued, looking totally out of sorts. "I don't know what you're insinuating but Marshall has always been just a dear, dear friend to me."

Feeling as though she was being a bit naughty making her friend feel uncomfortable Leanza backed down a bit.

"Okay," she answered. "I'm sorry if my teasing upset you. I just felt like maybe there was a bit more to the story."

"Well, there's not." Vonda answered, glancing down at the table to avoid eye contact.

"At least, I don't think there is," she added before lifting her eyes to meet Leanza's.

Realizing Vonda may be feeling a bit sensitive on this subject Leanza set all teasing aside. She was Vonda's friend and this seemed like a moment in which Vonda may actually need another woman's input.

"Do you want to talk about this?" Leanza asked Vonda gently.

"I don't know if there's anything to talk about, really." Vonda answered.

Leanza nodded and sat waiting.

"I mean, Marshall's the closest friend I have here in Logan. Am I surprised that my best friend is a man? Yes, I am. Stanley was my closest friend, my husband, the father of my children and the love of my life for many wonderful years. When I lost him I was devastated. The thought of another man in my life, even just as a friend, never even crossed my mind. But life is unpredictable, we all know that. Life is also funny. I've found that to be true so many times. I can't tell you how often I've laughed about the way I met Marshall. I mean, it's funny, right?"

"Yes. Absolutely! It's very funny," Leanza answered, laughing over the story again.

"It just seemed that from the moment Marshall told me it was all right and no harm had been done our friendship was established. Of course, everything that followed solidified it. I mean, we were both so concerned about his missing co-worker. Once we realized my life was in danger Marshall became very protective. He made me feel so safe. He still does. He called me every evening back then. Just to be sure I was in my home, safe and well. He was so concerned about me. It just became natural for me to lean on him, to share everything with him. I grew to trust him completely. With all that was going on it simply wasn't possible that we weren't going to be close friends."

"Of course, that all makes total sense," Leanza said. "So is that still where you stand with each other or has something changed?"

For the first time since Leanza had met her Vonda looked unsure. Leanza could see confusion playing itself out across Vonda's face, whether it was confusion about her own feelings, or confusion about what to say, Leanza wasn't sure.

Finally, Vonda lifted her eyelids and looked directly into Leanza's eyes. "I don't know the answer to that question. I simply don't. I know I'm Marshall's dear friend. Beyond that I don't know what he feels for me."

She shifted in the booth for a few seconds, picked up her coffee and took a sip before sitting it down again.

Finally, she looked at Leanza and said, "The only thing I can tell you for certain is that I care for Marshall Davidson in a way that is much more than someone caring for a dear friend."

CHAPTER 41

After my father's death I tried to step up and be there for my mother. I made grocery runs and learned to cook a few simple meals so I could make dinner a couple of nights each week. I didn't really know her but I could tell it made her happy that I was trying to be helpful.

Sometimes she would ask for my input on financial decisions which, in turn, helped me learn about budgeting and running a household. Thankfully my father had invested in a small life insurance policy which allowed her to keep our home and meet the normal monthly expenses. My mother continued to work to provide health insurance for the two of us. I'm sure it was good for her to stay with her usual routine and have something to keep her busy.

As I got to know her better, I realized mom was a recluse. At the very least she was socially awkward, a fact that left me wondering how she ever managed to get married at all. I decided that perhaps I could be there for her on a social level. After all, I was a bit of a recluse, too.

It turned out that we were birds of a feather in that way. Friendships had eluded me my entire life, at least true and real friendships. Since I'd honed my 'fooled you' skills a handful of students now spoke to me on a regular basis. These were people who had moved into our school district after middle school. Not having witnessed my sixth grade humiliation their view of me had never been tarnished.

I still wasn't invited to participate socially outside of school but at least my days weren't pure torture anymore. It felt good to fit in at least enough to get through the day without wanting to disappear.

Since she was now a widow, I didn't want my mother to become dependent on me. I was careful not to spend too much time with her and went out of my way to establish my independence. I needed to make sure she realized I wasn't staying to permanently take care of her. To that end, I got a part-time job, filing for the local healthcare system. It was in no way the kind of work I wanted to do but it got me away from the house. Mom seemed good with it. I think she was even a little proud that I had taken the initiative to get a job, not to mention that I was doing what she had done. It gave us something to talk about anyway.

Since the job gave me spending money, I mentioned maybe going to a movie together sometimes. We enjoyed searching the movie ads in the newspaper for something we'd both want to see. We had very different interests so that wasn't an easy find. Our first outing together went well so we repeated it the following month. This time we went out to a local eatery before the movie. Since neither of us had a social circle this soon became part of our monthly routine. We both looked forward to it.

I got to know my mother better through those outings. She was awkward and could come across as not being especially bright but she certainly wasn't dumb. She had a sharp mind but didn't seem to possess what's known as common sense. I got the feeling it had made her the butt of childhood teasing. That's probably why she was socially stunted. I could surely relate. I never told her about my experiences with Mr. Strong. I didn't see the point since none of that could be changed. I knew she missed my dad and I wanted her to be happy so I made the decision to only talk positively when we were on our outings.

My mother may be the only living person whose happiness I've ever considered besides my own. Looking back over my life now I've come to realize my most loving relationship was with my mother.

Without the resources to attend college, and having already lost one parent, I loaded my high school schedule with business and administrative classes. I hoped those efforts would help me land in the business field once I graduated. It wasn't quite the same, but I did eventually advance from filing to an actual full-time office position after high school.

When I decided to get my own place, mom handled it well. She even let me take my bedroom furniture since she didn't have a need for a guest room. She surprised us both by deciding to buy herself a new living room suite so she could give me the old one. She also seemed to enjoy picking things up for me. Things like bath and kitchen towels and small everyday household items. I appreciated the help since it was my first time on my own and I didn't really know what was needed.

Since we no longer lived together I decided to increase our monthly outings to weekly. She was my mother so I figured I should touch base with her regularly. To give her something to look forward to I suggested we branch out from just going to the movies. Sometimes we went to a museum or a play or some other local event. If nothing else, we always got a meal together. Admittedly we were both socially awkward but we enjoyed those evenings out. Having a friendship with my mother met what little need I had for social interaction.

Mr. Strong and the bad treatment from my peers left me with a lot of pent-up anger. By the time I entered high school things had died down though and for the most part I was simply ignored. Still, I continued to hold a strong distrust of people in general. Since I had never been in a good one, I imagined most relationships to be phony, with one or both parties having ulterior motives. I believed most partners would hurt the other person should they get in their way. I certainly knew I would.

It's an indisputable fact that bad relationships are everywhere. I've actually had a front row seat to some of them. Hearing students and co-workers talk gave me a bystander's view of the way people use and hurt each other. This only served to increase my sense of paranoia and isolation. As a result, I continued to purposefully use people to my own advantage. I simply didn't care that I didn't have friends. I learned to appear as if I truly cared for people, when in all actuality, I didn't. Truthfully, if my colleagues were to be asked, they would probably classify me as one of their friends. They would be mistaken.

I was twenty-five when mom had her first heart attack landing us at Myrtle Beach General Hospital's emergency room. She was admitted for what turned out to be the first of many such occasions. As a result, I got to know my way around the facility. One day while sitting in the waiting room, yet again, I decided to check out the job listings. There were openings right there at the hospital that my background would serve well for. I figured with mom's problems my life would be a lot easier if I worked there, so I applied.

It was a good day when I got hired at the hospital. The convenience of being near mom was one of the best things about it. I've changed jobs frequently since but it's always been in the healthcare system. Eventually I advanced to a management position and have stayed in my current department ever since.

I've never told anyone this but it makes me proud that despite life's setbacks and my lack of financial resources early in life I've managed to have a good career.

It just goes to show that even in the hardest life things do fall into place sometimes.

CHAPTER 42

While driving toward the hospital Marshall looked the facilities over closely. Even after an intense inspection he couldn't deny being impressed with how nicely the outside of the new expansion was blending with the original structure.

It's almost identical to the 'old girl' he thought as he applied George's affectionate nickname for the hospital. Each entrance on the new addition replicated the entrances on the original structure. Every entrance stood out from the rest of the building in the same way, which was what he had hoped for. The main feature was a large round window on the upper section above the double doored entrance. Marshall had been certain to include that feature in the design of the new facility thinking it would tie the two buildings together perfectly. He was absolutely right!

CEO Daniel Travis always had the Christmas celebratory luncheon scheduled for the first Friday of December. It was his way of kicking off the holiday season and encouraging the staff to enjoy this time of year. Today was that day and everyone was in high spirits. Most of the staff looked forward to this event all year. The chef prepared many seasonal favorites and everyone loved his Christmas cut-out cookies in the shape of stockings, Santa Clauses, reindeer, Christmas trees and stars. Of course, there was an abundance of delicious foods along with alcohol free egg-nog and hot chocolate.

The luncheon began with a holiday speech and the unveiling of the cafeteria's Christmas tree. It lasted the entire afternoon and everyone stayed, enjoying the festivities as long as their schedule would allow. Marshall's entire construction crew had been invited and he encouraged them to spend as much time as they chose. His team had been working hard and they deserved this break.

Marshall had come to enjoy the monthly staff luncheons and greatly anticipated today's event. He looked forward to the food as well as the opportunity to socialize with hospital staff. Having already met a number of quality people there he looked forward to the chance to meet more.

When he fell in line with Director of Registration Mary McCoy the two began talking right away. Before long, several members of her department joined them. The entire group was chatting and laughing as they inched closer to the layout of awesome food choices. Looking ahead to the table several commented on the various dishes and desserts they recognized from years past. When they got close enough to make their choices a lot of comparisons and recommendations took place. His plate filled, Marshall turned to see how Mary's was coming along.

"Let's find a round table large enough for all of us," she said looking around the cafeteria. "My staff will want to sit with us and take advantage of the opportunity to meet you. I've got one of the best teams here. They're dedicated, hard workers who are always willing to step up when extra shifts are needed. I've worked diligently to create an atmosphere of teamwork and keep a good rapport with my staff. Nothing makes the work day better than getting along with your co-worker s."

"That's very true," Marshall agreed. "And it's a wise manager who knows it."

"Oh, go on now!" Mary said, making a gesture with her hand as if to brush him away. "Every manager knows it takes a good working atmosphere to keep a great team."

"No, actually that's not true. I think you'd be surprised at the number of managers who don't make that a priority," Marshall said sadly. "I've seen it time-and-again. When the morale of a team is low, it's usually due to management failing their staff. An uncaring manager can cost a company many good employees. But that doesn't seem to be the case within this healthcare system."

"That's good to hear," Mary responded. "I can't speak for other department heads, but I sure want my team to be happy. A happy team functions more efficiently. Yes sir. That's why I've focused on teamwork and collaboration from the day I became manager. When I hire I'm looking for long-termers. I've been here almost twenty-five years myself. Obviously, I value commitment. It's a drain on a department constantly having new staff to train. That's not to say I begrudge anyone moving forward ~ I just don't want quitters on my team. Having quitters is costly, in time, training and resources. My parents were very loyal to their employers. They set a great example for me when it came to work ethic and loyalty. That's one reason I'm always looking to provide a welcoming and steady atmosphere for our staff. I'm trying to keep them." She laughed at herself as she told him she'd had no intention of going on so long.

Everyone was seated by this point and they were soon interacting across the table while enjoying their meals.

As it turned out, Mary had to leave early to attend an afternoon meeting. Marshall was curious whether anyone's tune would change once she had departed. He found himself pleasantly surprised when they all continued in a positive vein. In fact, once they started talking about it Marshall pieced together that Mary was the sender of the birthday gift he'd seen the COO open at lunch on an earlier occasion. He then made the realization that she was *the* Mary who was well known for remembering everyone's birthday. Not only those in her department but staff throughout the entire healthcare system. She was known for popping in with a birthday cupcake, leaving a small gift on an office chair; at times she may enlist other staff to make surprise deliveries as well. At the very least, a brightly colored birthday email card would pop in or a card would show up under a car windshield wiper at the end of the work shift. It was said that very few people on staff got through their birthday without a surprise from Mary. It was obvious those in her department genuinely respected her and enjoyed being on her team. Without question the efforts Mary put forth to keep her staff happy were paying off.

CHAPTER 43

Vonda was quick to begin her work on the flash drive Leanza had given her. Upon returning from their lunch date she set about to delete the actual daily personal journal entries from the document. This left only the yellow highlighted sleep-typing entries in each one-year document.

Vonda then created a new document in which she listed titled sections by which to organize the entries. Leanza had given her a list of key words and phrases to search for. She would use those to title each section. She would then work between the two documents by copy/pasting sentences with the key words into the correct section. Once this was done she could more closely audit how often each key word or phrase had been typed as Leanza was entering sleep mode. Perhaps Leanza could then discover what the words and phrases may signify.

At a young age Leanza had begun journaling in spiral notebooks. In her teen years she saved her money and purchased a typewriter. She then began typing her journal entries and put the pages into a three-ring binder. As a young person entering college she'd gotten her first computer and her journaling document was kept in a folder there. Five years prior to meeting Vonda she'd occasionally fallen asleep while typing and started noticing the sleep-typing entries. Those were the journal entries Leanza wanted Vonda to audit. This meant Vonda had five years of sleep-typing entries to comb through. The frequency of Leanza falling asleep while typing varied, which in turn meant the number of sleep-typed entries varied. While deleting the actual journal entries, Leanza saved the sleep-typing entries by date. At the end of each year she began a new section, thus keeping everything in one year documented format. It wasn't long into the process before she was able to calculate that the sleep-typing entries averaged once to twice and occasionally three times monthly. Over a five-year span this meant she was looking to analyze, categorize and audit sixty to one hundred sleep-typing entries.

Having read through a good portion of the sleep-typed comments while she was deleting and condensing the original document she now understood what Leanza meant in saying most of it made no sense. In all actuality almost none of it made sense. Each entry was basically a series of incoherent sentences strung together. Even when the sentences made sense none of it seemed to mean anything in particular.

One entry simply said, "I'm not sure how many people will be comfortable with me but that's alright. Here I am. She basically told us she doesn't know how to be friends so she'll do what she did in Virginia. That's to cover her eyes. So yeah, it's not a good plan."

Another entry said, "This meant those involved would be there already. She saw no reason why the Supreme Court may decline that effort. She asked if we had a cell phone and said she'd get back to me."

There was nothing significant to anything Leanza had shared with Vonda or asked her to be mindful of in either of those two entries.

Other entries did include the specific words Leanza wanted to know about. One of those words was *brick*. Vonda opened a new document she named <u>Sleep-typing Audit</u> and titled the first section <u>Brick</u>.

She read the next sleep-typing entry which said; "Later I called a cab for her but we left together. I could feel it and the brick pulled out. She knew what she saw but no one else knew."

From that entry she copy/pasted into the Brick section these words "I could feel it and the brick pulled out."

She then created another section and titled it <u>Secrets</u>. She copy/pasted into that section these words, "She knew what she saw but no one else knew." This was not one of the phrases Leanza had asked her to audit. She didn't know if it was pertinent or not. She just felt the secret nature of the phrase begged for follow-up.

She went on to read the next sleep-typing entry which said; "The agents are searching. The brick lay beside a pink tennis shoe. Her shirt was green Interviews are completed but nothing is clear. The toy is covered but the inside is hard."

From that entry she copy/pasted into the Brick section these words "the brick lay beside a pink tennis shoe".

She then created another section and titled it <u>Toy</u>. She copy/pasted these words into that section, "The toy is covered but the inside is hard."

By the end of that first day Vonda was well organized and had actively begun the auditing process. She had no idea what all of this would uncover, if anything at all, she just hoped it would somehow be helpful to her friend.

CHAPTER 44

Along with the rest of the A413TF team, Jeremy was fighting discouragement. Despite the fact that he was constantly tying up loose ends and the team had continued to scour through their case file notes, compare information, and go over every word of the past, as well as most recent interviews, nothing new had been discovered.

They had even decided to interview those people the missing had interacted with in the three months between their vacations and the day of their disappearances. Despite all these efforts, they could locate no one who served as a common denominator between all the victims. The best connection was still that of the medical situations which had sent each person for treatment. However, they weren't finding a specific person that seemed to connect the three emergency care facilities.

As often happens in FBI case work the entire process was getting tiresome and most definitely discouraging. Weary from watching the team get more and more disheartened, Leanza decided to change tactics for the month of December. She told them they needed to lighten things up. Of course, they would all continue to devote time and energy to the case but in an attempt to gain renewed clarity and new focus she wanted them to take a bit of a holiday break. In this vein, the most important assignment the agents now had was to choose an event, the rest would join them in, during December; ideally, a Christmas event.

Like Leanza, the other agents had temporarily relocated into the area to work this case. They were out of their usual life routines and living environments. They were now entering the biggest Holiday season of the year away from friends and family. If Leanza wasn't careful, that could play against them. Focus is a large part of success and it was clear to Leanza her team was losing focus.

A Brick to Remember

After explaining the assignment Leanza announced she would be the first to choose an event. She shared a little about the town she was living in during this assignment and told them about Logan's Christmas Festival. The festivities included music, a tree lighting ceremony, Santa's arrival by parade and all around Holiday cheer. They were each invited to join her and her friends in walking to town at three-forty-five. She'd been excited for the Christmas season in Logan ever since her friend Vonda shared her love of hearing Christmas music streaming on Main Street while shopping. The Logan Christmas Festival was the kick-off of the holiday season. It was all happening this Friday. Her friends, Vonda and Marshall had invited Leanza to walk to town for the festivities with them, and she was now inviting the A413TF agents to join in the fun.

Being in South Carolina the weather wasn't very cold when Friday rolled around. They were warm enough in light coats. Still Vonda stashed a pair of mittens in her coat pocket just in case they were needed. She and Marshall chatted comfortably with Leanza as they waited for the other agents to arrive. Once everyone was gathered and introductions had been made they all walked along together.

Leanza exclaimed happily when lighted trees came into view along Main Street. Logan really does their decorations up big. Lighted shapes representing each of the twelve days of Christmas line the train tracks in the old train depot area. The street lights feature lighted Christmas wreaths and a canopy of white lighting overhangs Main Street. It's really something to see. Each person in the group felt their spirit lifting as they looked everything over and conversed lightly with their companions.

Not far from the main intersection in town a huge Christmas tree awaited the main tree-lighting ceremony. Local musical students were taking turns performing Christmas music on a small stage nearby. Main Street was filled with townsfolk singing along and applauding after each performance. Many were drinking hot chocolate and everyone greeted each other happily while waiting for the tree lighting countdown.

At twenty minutes after the hour the mayor took the microphone and announced the performance of the last song of the evening, Silent Night. He explained that as soon as the song ended the countdown would begin and the Christmas tree lights would be turned on.

People had continued to talk and wander about during the singing for the past half an hour, but not this time. The crowd grew silent as a very talented young lady stepped onto the stage and began a reverent rendition. When her voice grew quiet the mayor stepped up to the microphone and began the countdown.

Excitement filled the air as the crowd counted along. Leanza and her team of agents were all smiling as they glanced at each other and shouted the countdown in unison with the crowd. When the number one was shouted the tree lights came on. Everyone applauded at the beautiful colors lighting the Christmas tree! It was absolutely stunning!

Standing in front of Marshall, Vonda turned her face slightly back to look up at him and smiled warmly. This prompted him to slide his arms around her waist from behind for a soft embrace. She placed her own arms over his and patted his hands with hers as she leaned back. They both smiled contentedly. Having witnessed their private moment Leanza smiled. Her heart felt warm and her spirit light.

It was in that happy moment that she just happened to glance up to make direct eye contact with a very familiar set of eyes. Taken by surprise she was held in the exact same instantaneous and intense gaze she'd experienced on the day she and Vonda went hiking. Instinctively, she knew. It was him, the young man whose young pup had hesitated before jumping over the fallen tree trunk. It was the man she had assumed she would never see again. Breaking eye contact, she took in his entire face, only to find him smiling warmly in her direction. It felt as if everyone around her slowly disappeared until they were the only two people present. She truly had never experienced such a phenomenon, except with this man.

Leanza wanted to meet him. Not only that, she felt compelled to meet him. He had crossed her mind fairly often since their first encounter. Seeing him again now, it seemed as if meeting him was meant to happen. She felt herself returning his smile as her eyes met and locked with his again. In that instant she made a decision. She would go to him right then. She would introduce herself and see where things went from there.

It was in that exact moment that the crowd around her came to life. Apparently someone was working their way through and people were parting to let them by. A woman fell forward, jostling her from the side. Almost immediately Leanza was knocked forward. She was fortunate her fall was broken and she didn't actually go completely down. She turned instantly as the man behind her began profusely apologizing.

When she was finally able to look in his direction again, he was gone. Vonda and Marshall had seen what happened and came over to check on her. After assuring everyone she was fine Leanza excused herself and went to the spot where he had been standing. She searched the entire area but he was nowhere to be found.

After her fifteen minute search proved futile she returned to her friends and watched the Christmas parade. Throughout the evening she continued searching the crowd for those eyes, those unmistakable eyes. Walking home later she decided it may not be meant for her to actually meet this mystery man after all. She determined once again to put him out of her thoughts and went back to focusing on the here and now.

CHAPTER 45

Waking to Lilly nuzzling her neck, Vonda reached up to gently stroke her soft fur.

"You're such a sweet girl," she said softly as Lilly began to purr and snuggled closer in contentment.

Her own feelings of contentment reminded her of the night before. Filled with the joy of the Christmas season and the happiness of the evening, she had turned to look behind her at Marshall. Meeting her smile with his own he had gently slipped his arms around her waist. Ever so slightly, he'd pulled her against him. She had simply relaxed into him as if it were the most natural thing in the world. It was obvious things were taking a more personal turn between them. Vonda was ready. Perhaps he was, too.

Losing Stanley had been one of the hardest things Vonda had ever experienced. He was a wonderful man who was not only her husband but her best friend. While raising their beautiful family together, they'd leaned on each other through the hard times and made happy memories during the good times. She would never forget him or the love they shared. He was forever a part of her.

Vonda had since learned that although it doesn't seem like it at the time, life does go on after loss. God is true to His word. He never leaves us alone. God was with her at the moment of Stanley's death, in the very next moment when the numbness set in, and still later when it wore off and the heart wrenching pain of loneliness came. God stayed with her through the hours, days and months that followed. He was with her again in each moment as she wandered through their quiet home feeling so alone. He comforted her and gave her strength. He was there when time began to bring healing and when each day finally seemed easier. God was still there with her when her memories finally brought smiles instead of tears.

That was about the time she met Marshall and in the following months their friendship had grown.

"Thank you, Lord," Vonda prayed as she got out of bed and began to get ready for the day. "Thank you for bringing not one, but two wonderful men into my life. Stanley and I were so happy together. I will always be thankful for the life we shared. When I lost him you saw me through. You helped me heal and begin again. And now you've given me the wonderful blessing of my friendship with Marshall. I don't know what the future holds for us but I trust you, Lord, and I trust him. That's enough for me right now. I'm just trying to take life a day at a time. I know you're with me and you'll stay with me through whatever comes and that's all I need to know."

Meowing loudly, Lilly looked up at Vonda.

"I know," Vonda said as she lifted Lilly into her arms and sat up in the bed. "It's time to get up. I'm sure you're ready for breakfast by now." Walking to the kitchen she sat Lilly down and filled her food dish, checked her water dispenser and patted her head gently.

As Lilly began to eat, Vonda went to set a K-cup to brew and returned to her bedroom to get ready for the day. Still talking with God, she asked Him to help her friend, Leanza, and the agents discover what happened to those missing people. She asked that He help Leanza open her mind to the deeply hidden memories of her father and for clarity to decipher the clues in her sleep-typing. She thanked God for seeing her family through the many challenges of dealing with Denvel's disappearance. She asked God to lead them to learn whatever had happened to him all those many years ago.

Vonda got her coffee and sat down. Having finished breakfast Lilly pounced up into her lap.

"I know you know what's best for each of us," Vonda said, finishing her prayer. "You're there for us through the worst times of our lives. You love us so deeply and you hurt for us when we hurt. Thank you for going through the deep waters with us, for keeping us afloat when we feel as if we're drowning. Thank you so much for giving us people to listen to us, help us and love us through life's struggles. You are such a good Father!"

She had been absentmindedly petting Lilly as she prayed. Now, looking down at her beautiful cat she smiled. She told God how thankful she felt for Lilly, too, Such a sweet companion.

CHAPTER 46

Since nothing was breaking in the case, Leanza encouraged the A413TF agents to take a few days off and go see their families. She decided to do the same and was excited to be with her mom and Wade's family over Christmas.

Vonda's children and grandchildren came to visit her the week before Christmas when the children first got off school for winter break. This allowed them to celebrate with their grandma and still have Christmas at home the following week.

Vonda baked her famous sour cream cut-out cookies prior to their arrival. As Christmas music filled the house they all had a wonderful time decorating the cookies together. Sending a container of cookies home with each family warmed her heart and made them all happy.

Stacy, Vonda's friend and Mason's wife, invited Vonda to the Davidson's Christmas Eve dinner. Of course, Marshall was going too since it was his family's Christmas celebration. Vonda loved Marshall's family. She felt as if they were her own. They were definitely the family that made Logan feel like home for her. Knowing them so well helped her choose just the right gifts for each one and she was looking forward to spending Christmas Eve with them. Even though Vonda assured him it wasn't necessary, Marshall insisted he would pick her up and take her back home after the festivities.

Unbeknownst to her, Marshall had an ulterior motive for insisting on being her chauffeur. He'd been putting a lot of thought into what to give her for Christmas. He wanted it to be something extra special since his feelings for her were extra special now. He hoped his gift would be something so thoughtful and unique she would realize how much he had come to care for her.

As he puzzled over what to get for her Vonda herself gave him the answer. She was in the passenger's seat of Marshall's car and they were stopped at a red light when Vonda exclaimed excitedly, "Look Marshall! Isn't it beautiful?"

Looking past her Marshall realized he was looking at the perfect gift. Ever since he'd known her she'd been pointing these out. She had even frequently expressed the desire to have one of her own.

"I could look at those forever," she added. "They're just so fascinating!"

Marshall couldn't believe he hadn't thought of this before and set out on a search for the most unique and beautiful wind spinner he could find. The one he ultimately chose had a solar light in the center of three artistic spinners which rotated in various directions when the wind blew across them.

The plan was for her to see it on Christmas morning when she opened the blinds to the sliders leading to her back patio. Marshall would love to be there with her when she first saw it. He was now trying to figure out how he could get it into her yard without her knowing. He wasn't sure just yet how to make that happen but he was going to try.

When Christmas Eve arrived Vonda was glad Marshall was giving her a ride. She hadn't realized how many gifts she'd purchased and wrapped for the Davidson family until she began to pile them on her dining room table. She was relieved Marshall would be there to help her carry them to his car and into the house. She had to chuckle at his reaction when she pointed them out after his arrival. Always the good sport, Marshall helped her get the job done. They both laughed when they finally placed the last of them under Mason and Stacy's tree. She'd definitely gone a little overboard. She told Marshall it was just the result of being in the Christmas spirit.

Christmas music and the savory scents of dinner filled the house. Vonda volunteered her help in the kitchen and the two women put the finishing touches on the meal. Everyone got seated around the table. Mason stood to say a few things about the miracle of Christmas: the birth of Jesus, God's only son, born of a virgin, part man-part God, who came to give the gift of eternal life to those who chose to receive it.

The entire day was filled with the spirit of the season, fun conversation and wonderful companionship.

After their Christmas dinner everyone moved to the living room. The boys played an instrumental duet of <u>Oh, Little Town of Bethlehem,</u> Caleb on the piano and Declan on the trumpet. They'd been practicing for weeks and did an excellent job. Mason opened the Bible and handed it to Mitch asking him to read the story of Jesus' birth from Luke chapter two. Everyone was then given the chance to share and many mentioned being thankful to be part of such a loving family.

The boys were excited to get on to the fun of exchanging gifts. Lots of laughter and the words 'thank you' could be heard over the next hour until every last gift was opened. The boys hurried off to play while the adults enjoyed coffee, eggnog and dessert.

After the goodbye hugs shouts of "Merry Christmas" echoed across the front lawn as Marshall and Vonda got into the car. On the way home they chatted happily about how much they'd enjoyed the day.

"I'm not planning to come in for a visit this evening," Marshall said to Vonda as he drove along. She felt a twinge of sadness until he added, "I'm hoping you'll allow me to come back early in the morning instead. I'd like to give you my gift on Christmas morning instead of tonight. Would that be alright?"

"It's a lovely idea," she answered him feeling very pleased with the suggestion. "How early did you want to come? I'd be happy to have you join me for breakfast."

"I'd like to be here first thing actually. What time do you usually get up?"

"Well, let's see. I usually wake up at about seven-thirty. I'm up and dressed by eight-fifteen or so. I feed Lilly, make a cup of coffee and open the back blinds to welcome the day." She laughed lightly at herself for reciting her morning routine.

"That sounds perfect," Marshall told her. "How about if I arrive at eight fifteen and join you for coffee. I'd really like to spend Christmas morning with you this year."

"I'd like that, too," Vonda said as her heart warmed with happiness.

"I'm sorry if you thought I'd stay longer this evening. What will you do with yourself now?" Marshall asked.

"Actually, I'm close to finishing a good book I've been reading. I think I'll run a hot bath right away and finish it before going to bed tonight."

"That sounds relaxing," Marshall said as he walked her to the door. "The perfect ending to a wonderful evening," Vonda answered.

Stepping inside she entered the security code into her alarm system before turning to give Marshall a hug.

"I'll see you in the morning," Marshall said as he released her.

Looking down into her upturned face he winked and added "Let's open the back blinds and welcome Christmas day together, okay?"

"Oh, I love that idea!" Vonda agreed. "Sleep well tonight, Marshall."

Marshall got into his car and backed out of the driveway. Feeling a bit sneaky he passed the next three houses and pulled into the driveway of Vonda's friend and neighbor, Kay Lynn. He had contacted Kay earlier letting her know of his plan. Kay was excited to be part of Vonda's Christmas surprise.

Hoping Vonda was in the bathroom with the water running for her bath by now he quickly got the wind spinner from the trunk of his car and briskly walked the distance back to her house. Hurriedly and quietly he walked to the corner of her back patio where he inserted the two posts of the spinner's support system into the ground.

Having previously thought this through he had decided this was the perfect spot for it. Vonda would be able to see the spinner from inside the house as well as when she was seated outside on the patio. Once it was firmly in place he retreated quickly, got into his car, waved goodbye to Kay and headed home.

Mission accomplished! He thought, feeling quite proud and excited. He couldn't wait to see her face when she first spotted her very own wind spinner in the morning.

CHAPTER 47

Marshall woke up smiling on Christmas morning. For just a moment he thought he could smell the enticing aroma of his mom's homemade cinnamon rolls. It had been her tradition to bake them every Christmas morning. The memory tugged on his heart as he headed to the shower.

On the drive to Vonda's Marshall asked God to be with them this morning and bless them with a good day together. He admitted he wasn't sure what Vonda felt for him. Vonda and Stanley had shared a deep love and happy life together and he would never want to diminish that. He didn't know how these things worked for someone who had loved and lost. He only knew he loved Vonda. His love for her filled him with the hope that she could find a place in her heart and life for him. As he had often done over the past four weeks, he asked God to help Vonda open her heart to him. He chuckled lightly while admitting he had no idea what he was doing. He asked God to give him the words he needed to say when he needed to say them.

Despite how inept he felt, he was encouraged as he remembered meeting her for dinner at the Back Alley Café after her return from Virginia. She seemed to have missed him. He was sure she was genuinely happy to be with him as she hugged him longer and tighter than usual. Then more recently at the Christmas tree lighting ceremony when she turned and looked at him so lovingly.

Was that what it was - lovingly? It seemed so at the time which was why he'd reached out and put his arms around her. Having her lean back against him - welcoming his embrace - had made his heart skip a beat or two. Holding her had felt so natural to him. It seemed as if it did for her, as well.

Though he was in unchartered territory Marshall was certain of one thing, he wanted today to be happy for both of them.

He felt very blessed as he approached Vonda's front door. It opened the moment he rang the bell, as if she'd been standing right there waiting for him. She was wearing a long sleeved red dress with a flowing skirt. She looked beautiful! Laughing as she reached up and touched a necklace made of small Christmas lights she asked him if she looked festive.

"You do," Marshall answered with a huge smile, "You look very festive!"

"Merry Christmas!" she said motioning for him to come inside. As soon as he did she opened her arms and stepped toward him. Taking her into his arms Marshall felt as if his heart would burst from happiness. After their embrace they moved apart and he looked toward the kitchen asking "Is that cinnamon rolls I smell?"

She laughed again. "Yes! I've made fresh cinnamon rolls to go with our coffee. Come on and get one. They're ready."

After Marshall took a moment to greet the waiting Lilly she tagged along with their every step toward the kitchen. Vonda had set two coffee mugs next to a plate of warm cinnamon rolls. Having made a pot of coffee earlier she filled their mugs as Marshall placed a cinnamon roll for each of them onto two small plates. Moving to the dining room table Marshall noticed the window blinds were still closed. Before Vonda could sit down he pointed to the blinds and said, "You waited for me."

She followed his gaze and answered, "Of course I did. We'll welcome Christmas day together just as you said last night. Are you ready?"

Filled with anticipation he nodded. He watched her closely as she walked over and reached for the handle to the blinds covering the sliders. She lifted and pressed the bar to move the blinds toward the far side of the sliders. With each step Vonda took the blinds opened wider and sunshine flooded the room. She was looking at Marshall so it wasn't until the blinds were fully opened that she turned toward the sliders to look outside. Keeping his eyes on her face Marshall caught the moment she saw the wind spinner. Her smiling lips parted and her mouth opened slightly in a look of surprise and wonder. Her hands went up to her mouth as she took two small steps closer to the sliders.

"What?" she almost whispered the word. "It's a wind spinner. Oh! It's so beautiful! I love it! I absolutely love it!"

171

Tears filled her eyes as she turned to look at Marshall. "Did you do this? Marshall? Did you do this for me?"

The look of joy on his face was all the answer she needed. Her body and eyes turned back to look at the wind spinner again as she wiped the tears from her cheeks and said softly, "It's perfect! Marshall, oh, I can't believe you did this. It's just so absolutely perfect."

Turning away from the sliders again she walked straight to Marshall and put her arms around him. She laid her head on his shoulder and hugged him tightly.

"I love it, Marshall!! I love it so much! Thank you!! I don't know how you knew but it's the most perfect gift. I shall never tire of looking at it!"

Marshall's heart was full.

Her reaction simply could not have been any better.

CHAPTER 48

Marshall invited Vonda to take the seat at her dining room table that faced the sliders so she could enjoy watching her new wind spinner. She agreed even as she told him she was excited to give him his gift. He smiled and said she could do that after they enjoyed their coffee and cinnamon rolls. Nodding in agreement she commented that they would taste better while still warm.

As they ate she continued to marvel over her wind spinner. She asked questions about how he knew what she would want and how he chose this particular one. He, on the other hand, was intent on the cinnamon rolls which amazingly tasted exactly as he remembered his mom's.

Neither of them could keep from smiling.

He was so happy with her reaction. He truly didn't care if she gave him a gift at all. He'd already gotten the best gift he could get today - seeing her happy.

After they had finished eating and cleared everything away Vonda got a gift box from under her Christmas tree. She placed it on the dining room table and told Marshall she wanted him to open it there. She stood nearby smiling as she watched him.

Marshall removed the wrapping and opened the box. When he lifted the tissue paper he saw a book in the form of a three ring binder. The words on the cover read "The Davidson Family."

Glancing at Vonda curiously he lifted it from the box and placed it on the table in front of him. Opening it, he saw that each page was enclosed in a clear sheet protector. The first was a title page which said "The Davidson Family Story". Below that he read 'Designed and compiled as a gift to Marshall Davidson by Vonda Graham.'

"What is this?" Marshall asked with great interest, looking up at Vonda.

"Just keep going," Vonda urged.

173

He looked back down and turned the page. The next page read: "This book is dedicated to Marshall Davidson who stepped in to parent and be a mentor to his two younger brothers, Mitch and Mason Davidson upon the death of their parents, Maria and Marcus Davidson."

Turning the page Marshall found himself looking at a wedding photo of his parents. The caption below it contained the date and location. It was followed by a brief summary of where the two had met, how they came to be a couple, a brief dating history and the story of his father's proposal to his mother.

Flipping ahead through the pages Marshall caught glimpses of snapshots of the young couple, their first home, his birth announcement, more childhood photographs, the birth of Mitch and of Mason. In between the photograph pages were typed pages containing stories about his parents and their family.

Looking up at Vonda Marshall asked in awe, "How did you do this?"

"With the help of your brothers and your extended family, your mom's sister was very helpful. She's the reason my cinnamon rolls taste so much like your mom's this morning," she said with a twinkle in her eyes. Her quick wink made Marshall laugh out loud.

"She gave me your mother's recipe. Some of your cousins helped as well. Mason was invaluable in the process. He visited Mitch quite frequently and the two of them shared memories. I think that was quite healing for them. It's been in the making for quite a while. Do you like it?"

"Do I like it?" Marshall echoed her, "Do I like it? I'm in shock!! I can't believe you did this for me. I want to devour every word of it. Vonda, this is incredible! I love it!! I absolutely love it!"

A shadow of sadness crossed over his face as he said, "I've felt so badly for the way I neglected my parents after they died. I didn't tell the boys about them. I didn't even talk with the boys about them or encourage keeping them close. I let their memories die. Do you realize how guilty I've felt for that?"

Looking down at the book and then lifting his eyes to hers he said quietly, "I guess you do."

Vonda crossed the short distance between them pulling a chair close to his and sitting down. "You did a wonderful thing all those years ago Marshall. Something not everyone would do. It was an overwhelming task for a young man making his way in the world and building a career. Of course, you weren't going to do it perfectly. None of us does anything perfectly. That's why we must always remember God's promise in Romans 8:28 that when we love Him and follow his calling on our lives He will work all things together for good. He's done that for you and your brothers, especially over these past several years. Through the grief counseling Mason's taken and the help Mitch has gotten with Dr. Rossman and through the three of you talking about your parents again. I'm hoping this book will help you forgive yourself and give you and your brothers back the sense of family Satan took from you when your parents died. Your brothers have their own version of this book now too, by the way."

"Oh that's wonderful," Marshall said to her. "I don't know how to thank you for the time and effort you've put into this. I'm so excited to read it. This is in an incredible gift! Thank you, Vonda."

Smiling her sweet smile Vonda looked him in the eyes. "I'm so glad you like it Marshall. I love your family. You know that, right?"

"I do," he said softly. "And we love you."

"I know that," she answered.

Marshall looked down at the book on the table for a few seconds. He then looked up into her face and said "Is it okay with you if I set this aside now and continue to read it later at my own pace?"

"Of course," she said.

"Good," he replied, standing up and reaching up for her hand.

She placed her hand in his and stood up. He led her to the sliders and lifted his right arm as if to invite her in. Without hesitation she stepped into his embrace. The two of them stood looking out the slider at the wind spinner and the back of Vonda's property.

"I'd say we've had quite the Christmas morning together, wouldn't you Vonda?" Marshall asked.

"Yes I would, Marshall," she answered as she laid her head over onto him and he gently tightened his grip around her shoulders. "I'd say it's been absolutely perfect."

Marshall tilted his head and planted a soft kiss on her hair. Lifting her head and turning her face upward Vonda looked into his eyes.

Marshall felt a stirring in his heart he'd never felt before. He felt vulnerable and afraid and yet, at the same time, his heart was filled with hope. Mustering every ounce of courage he had Marshall said softly, "You don't have to say anything right now Vonda, I just think you should know that I love you."

He waited breathlessly as he watched her beautiful smile widen.

"I know you do, Marshall," she said sweetly "and I'm so glad you do since I love you."

To his surprise she stretched her neck ever so slightly lifting her face toward him. As if it were the most natural thing in the world he lowered his face to hers so their lips could meet.

CHAPTER 49

Spending Christmas in Norfolk with her family had refreshed Leanza and she was counting on the same being true for the rest of the agents. Now it was time to get back to solving these missing person cases.

Being with her mom and brother always did her good. From the day she'd entered Wade's life, his wife Karen understood that the bond he shared with his mother and sister went beyond the norm. She also seemed to realize spending years as a team after losing Denvel had created a unique relationship between Megan and her children. It had never been a threat to Karen. She felt secure in Wade's love and his devotion to their family. She recognized that Wade, Leanza and Megan had an inherent need for time with the other two. She would never deprive them of being together. Her heart went out to them for all they'd been through. Karen realized, where perhaps they themselves didn't, that their connection gave them the strength they needed to get through whatever life threw at them. It made each of them stronger and Karen would never interfere with that.

Leanza didn't understand how or why, she just knew the time she spent with Megan and Wade strengthened her. It was almost as if their mere presence in her life served as a reinforcement. This visit had been no different from so many others. It had left her feeling stronger.

With the Holiday ended she flew back to Logan feeling ready to take the world on again.

It was a little disheartening then, only three nights later, to awaken in a cold sweat. Again she had dreamed of being only four-years-old and back in her mother's basement. The dream had no rhyme or reason. It was a jumbled sequence of random scenes which seemed to center on brick walls, tiny toys and her daddy. She distinctly remembered seeing a lone brick on the basement floor. It made no sense. She also heard her daddy refer to the hideaway again. What was he talking about?

During her time with Megan, Leanza had told her mother of her recent dreams and the repeated references in her sleep-typing. Leanza pointedly asked if any of these things meant anything to her mother. Megan assured her daughter she had no memory of there ever being a pile of bricks or even one brick in the basement of their home. The only brick wall she was aware of was the wall under the stairs. She remembered nothing significant about Leanza's toys either. They kept toys in a play area down stairs but nothing out of the ordinary. And she was totally confused about the reference to her daddy's toy. Wade had no explanation for any of these things either.

The three of them had even gone to the basement together and looked around. Megan now used the area under the stairs as a small storage space. She stored her Christmas decorations in clear tubs which were piled in front of the brick wall waiting to be filled and put away after the holiday season ended. They didn't move the tubs away. They just looked closely at the entire area for any clues that might mean something. Finding nothing they had gone back upstairs.

So here she was again clueless as to what her dreams might mean. At this point Leanza was hopeful something would come to light once Vonda finished the sleep-typing audit.

Less than a week later, she sent a text to Vonda asking to meet so they could go over the progress she had made. When they met Leanza was impressed with Vonda's efforts. She had created a Microsoft document in which she detailed her findings. The audit covered five years of Leanza's journal sleep-typing. The phrases which appeared repeatedly included the words 'hide, hideaway, brick, bricks, toy, toys, my toys, daddy's toy, daddy, and Little Dove'. Leanza was frustrated nothing had immediately occurred to her to offer an explanation for anything in her dreams.

Still, she appreciated all Vonda had done for her and told her so very clearly. Vonda said she would continue asking God to open Leanza's mind and memories to whatever all of this meant. She was praying for a resolution of this mystery in her friend's life. Leanza responded that she could use all the prayers she could get.

A couple of nights later Leanza dreamed again. The dream was another mixture of the same things she'd previously dreamt. This time, however, the dream contained a scene in which she, her mother and Wade were in the basement looking at the tubs lining the front of the brick wall just as they had been during their Christmas visit. And then in the weird way dreams so often do, her dream changed. Suddenly, there was another person with them. It was a shadowy figure but Leanza had no doubt upon waking that it was her father. He'd been standing there with them as they all looked at the wall.

In a strange way Leanza felt encouraged. It was almost as if the past was trying to join the present.

It gave her hope.

CHAPTER 50

Despite her heart issues mom did pretty well living on her own for a good number of years after I moved out. She was grateful my job kept me close by during her extended stays at Myrtle Beach General Hospital. We both were, really. Being able to visit her before and after my work shifts or during my lunch break definitely made life easier.

When she was home I only saw her once a week but we usually talked more frequently. I guess that's why I knew her well enough to notice when she started slipping. It was little things at first like forgetting appointments and being confused. She wasn't that old at the time but I figured these things were a normal part of aging. I'm sure at least some of it probably was.

But then she started doing things that just didn't make sense. I noticed she was using the wrong words without ever realizing it. Sometimes she'd say things that made absolutely no sense and not understand why I couldn't comprehend her meaning. She got argumentative and was even confrontational which wasn't like her at all.

I finally realized something was seriously wrong when I arrived for our weekly outing and found her wearing a sandal on one foot and a loafer on the other. I laughed while saying she must've been choosing between the two when I arrived.

She looked annoyed at my laughter and perplexed. Not at her own behavior but at me. She very rationally explained she simply wasn't sure what the weather was going to do. She reasoned she'd be comfortable having one sandaled foot if it was warm and sunny and equally as comfortable with one dry foot if it rained. She was very sincere. It actually took a bit of persuasion to get her to put her other sandal on since it actually was a very warm and sunny day.

I called her doctor the very next morning and set up an assessment appointment.

A Brick to Remember

It was a sad day for both of us when we heard the diagnosis. My mother was experiencing an early onset of dementia. Through mom's doctor and my own professional contacts I was able to line up an excellent in-home care provider.

Things went along well for a while and I was thankful. It was important to me that my mom's life continue as consistently as possible. My mother had been through a lot: not having much family to start with, becoming a young widow left to finish raising me alone and then being fraught with health issues. I didn't want her life disrupted more than it had to be. She was my only friend and I loved her but I wasn't equipped to take care of her. I had to work, I couldn't bring her to live with me and I wasn't about to move back in with her.

Sadly mom's dementia progressed more quickly than projected. As her condition worsened costs began to add up. She was diagnosed with sugar diabetes and had to be given insulin shots. She needed to follow a regimented diet. This along with her long-term heart disease made her a candidate for more extensive health care. The only facility I could find to provide everything she needed was three hours away and very costly. I didn't know what I was going to do.

I'd been under a tremendous strain both mentally and financially for several months and was just about at my wit's end. Added to that stress was the fact that my only social outlet was quickly disappearing along with the only loving relationship I'd ever known. Mom barely remembered who I was most of the time. She could no longer have even the most basic conversation. It took everything I had to carry on my normal persona during work hours so that no one saw the strain I was under. I found myself utilizing my 'fooled you' tactics more often. I was presenting myself as a caring, attentive colleague when truthfully all I cared about was finding a way to provide for my mother, no matter what it took.

I had never done anything like this before but I went to one of those cash advance places for money. Of course, I had to pay it back at a high interest rate but it got me through a financial tight spot. I ended up going back several times. It was a temporary fix that ended up being a long-term burden. I was able to get my mother placed in the facility she needed but in the meantime I was digging a financial hole I might never climb out of.

And then something unexpected happened. I returned to make the payment after taking the third cash advance. While waiting in line I talked with the person standing nearest me about my situation. I had never done that before either but I was just so upset. I said I couldn't keep doing this as the interest rates were making my situation worse.

As I left the building after making my payment, a man approached me. I was leery of him but he assured me he only wanted to help. He'd been inside and overheard my story. He said he was sure he had an answer for my situation.

We went to a nearby coffee shop and he shared a story very similar to mine. Not that long ago but for different reasons he found himself desperate for money. He too began using the cash advance place. But then something happened that changed his life. He had come today to pay back the last cash advance he would ever need. He gave me a phone number, assuring me it was a legitimate way to make extra money.

I was skeptical but desperate. I called the number that afternoon. The man I spoke with said he was in the business of finding people who could help businesses. He seemed very knowledgeable and was very reassuring while I expressed my concerns. He then asked a few questions about my line of work. Not long into the conversation he said he had very good news. There was a company that did medical surveys and was always looking for people to contact. He asked if they could give me a call as he thought I could be helpful to them. Based on his experience he assured me I would be nicely compensated.

I gave permission and about an hour later I got the call. By the time I hung up I had been hired. I was so relieved. My instructions were simple. I was to copy the Emergency Room/Urgent Care Intake forms of healthy patients who came in for emergency medical care. At the end of each week I was to put the copied forms in an interoffice envelope, take them to the hospital mailroom on the bottom floor and put them in the first mail slot on the bottom row just inside the entrance door. I would be paid by automatic deposit into the bank account of my choice.

I was a little suspicious that this was some kind of scam to get what little money I had. Always looking out for myself, I set up a new savings account for this express purpose. Although I had been cautioned to be discreet, the representative I spoke with assured me that was only because there were a limited number of these positions open. Of course the hospital was well aware of the arrangement so there was no one I needed to speak directly with and they themselves would contact HR. I have to admit I briefly wondered about that but I needed the money so I went with it.

The representative told me it was better to submit too many forms than not enough. The medical survey team would weed through the candidates and only contact those fitting their criteria. I would be paid a set amount per intake form but significantly more for the ones they chose to contact.

While placing my first envelope into the mail slot I figured I'd never see a dime for my time and effort. I had a hard time believing it could really be that easy to make extra money. I was very surprised, but pleased, when I actually saw a deposit come into my new account a few days later.

Things don't always go in my favor so it was a nice surprise when this actually worked out. Having the extra income took a lot of worry off my mind. Once I started getting those regular deposits, it didn't take long for me to count on that money. It relieved the pressure I'd been under from the added costs of my mother's situation. Having the money I needed was all I really cared about so I gave no thought to what the contact information was being used for.

CHAPTER 51

Every January the healthcare system holds an annual pinning ceremony to acknowledge their employees for consecutive years of service. They're given a five-year pin, ten-year pin and so on, to commemorate their loyalty.

Patient care is a twenty-four-hour commitment, so staff is needed around the clock, making it impossible to get all the staff together at one time. For this reason the cafeteria has proven to be the best location for ceremonies and staff events such as the pinning ceremony. Staff event lunches always span three hours, from eleven until two. This provides ample time for staff to have lunch and learn about the event they were unable to attend.

Daniel, the CEO is a big believer in giving credit where credit is due. Not only does he feel strongly that employees deserve to be valued, but it's been his personal experience that acknowledgement leads the staff to see their own value. It's a win/win situation. What could be more beneficial? Treating staff with respect, appreciation and honor also leads to minimal turnover. When there's no reason to leave and plenty of reason to stay that only makes sense.

While the healthcare system still gave an actual pin displaying the number of years of service Daniel has made sure a cash amount gift card is given as well. To his thinking, no matter who you are, or how loyal you feel, money talks. His employees were hardworking and loyal. They had earned and they deserved a monetary bonus and he was all about making sure they got that.

There were a significant amount of pins being awarded this year. Each of the various departments had at least one employee reaching the twenty-year mark. In fact, Daniel had been there twenty-five years himself and would be pinned as well. As he looked back over his tenure he was amazed at how many staff members had been along for most of his journey.

While preparing for today's event, Daniel realized the head of seven departments were being honored for twenty years or more. He was certain this was why so much of the staff considered Myrtle Beach General Hospital their home. Working with the same co-workers that long was bound to foster a sense of familiarity and family. Daniel considered it outstanding! He was thankful to be part of it.

Keeping in mind that an all staff gathering was impossible Daniel had ordered a large banner listing in bold letters the names of the seven department heads being pinned. All others being pinned were listed as well. The banner would be hung on the cafeteria wall. In this way the names of all of those being pinned could be seen by the remaining staff as they utilized the cafeteria.

Daniel had arrived early to check out the banner. He was admiring it when Amanda and Janet arrived together. Daniel wasn't surprised. The two women had grown up in the area and coincidentally, had joined the staff at Myrtle Beach General Hospital in the same year. During the twenty-two years since then each had advanced to the position of director over their respective departments; Amanda in Human Resources and Janet in Housekeeping.

Being mere acquaintances during childhood, it wasn't until they were on staff together that they really got to know one another. Since they were both movie buffs they could often be heard discussing the most recent showings. On many occasions they went to the movies together. It wasn't uncommon to see them deep in conversation in the cafeteria or while walking through the hospital corridors and today was no exception.

While complimenting the banner they were joined by Debra, the Director of Nurses. She and the CFO, David, were the youngest in terms of years of service. Each would be pinned for twenty years in today's ceremony.

Within half an hour the cafeteria was filled and Daniel walked to the front to begin the ceremony.

"Welcome to our Annual Pinning Ceremony!" he announced while standing directly below the banner. "I hope you'll all take a close look at our banner honoring the directors and all other staff being pinned today. This year we have seven directors, among the other honorees, so we had this beautiful banner printed. Please remind your co-workers to stop by and check it out. I wish there was a way to get everyone here at once but we all know our patients need constant care so that's just not possible. I'm hopeful every staff member will be able to come through today. As usual, I know you'll cover for each other to give everyone equal opportunity. As always, the chef has prepared a wonderful spread in celebration of today's event! Be sure to enjoy it.

Without further ado, we'll get started. It's not often an organization has so many long-term staff and I'm honored it's true of us. I am so pleased! Actually I feel blessed to be part of such an organization. I truly believe it's a result of so many of us having been here for the duration that we get along so well and keep things running so smoothly. Having various departments working well together doesn't always happen in organizations as large as ours. It's truly something to be proud of!

I've even had other CEO's ask me how to get what we've got. I wish I had a magic formula to give them. All I can say is that we treat each other with mutual respect and we've become a family. That's not something a CEO can make happen, it takes each and every one of you! So thank you for that. Won't you please give yourselves a hand?!"

He stood smiling until the applause started to die down, at which point he continued.

"As most of you know, I myself, along with our Director of Registration: Mary McCoy – Mary, come on up here and join me – celebrate twenty-five years this year!"

Daniel had extended his arm toward Mary as she approached. He picked up her pin and the small envelope containing the gift card and handed them to Mary. In lieu of his hand Mary moved in to hug him and Daniel laughed.

"That's right, Mary," he said good-naturedly, "a handshake just isn't gonna do it today!" Everyone applauded again. Mary walked over to the table, picked up the pin and envelope for Daniel and returned to hand them to him as she offered congratulations.

"Thank you, Mary. We're a mutual admiration society right here!" Daniel said smiling broadly as he accepted the items. Everyone applauded as they hugged again.

Daniel went on to make the following pin presentations: Chief Operating Officer Mick Fraser – twenty-three years, Human Resource Director Amanda Brookes and Director of Housekeeping Janet Kay – twenty-two years, Chief Financial Officer David Minter and Director of Nurses Debra Monique - twenty years.

Other staff received twenty-year pins as well. A good number were pinned for fifteen, ten and five years of service. Being the first time so many staff had been pinned it was quite the ceremony. Without question it was a red letter day for the Myrtle Beach and Stokesbury area healthcare systems. Daniel enjoyed seeing so many smiles and was feeling quite pleased as he made his final comments.

Unbeknownst to him and everyone else, with Daniel's birthday being only three days away, Mary had seized the opportunity to surprise him at the close of today's pinning ceremony. Everyone in attendance began to smile when she came out of the kitchen rolling a cart on which sat a beautiful birthday cake she had asked the chef to prepare. Daniel was facing the crowd and enjoying all the smiling faces when Mary stepped up beside him and began to sing happy birthday. Turning toward her his face registered his surprise. He began to laugh when he saw her standing there with the cake. When the singing died down he said, "Now this one takes the cake, Mary! You really got me this time! This may be your best birthday surprise yet."

"I believe it is!" Mary said as she laughed along with him and everyone else.

Inviting everyone to come up and join them for a piece of cake Daniel stated that this was the perfect ending to their celebratory ceremony.

CHAPTER 52

Having finally voiced their love for one another, Vonda and Marshall began spending more time together. Those who knew and loved them were very happy to learn they were now officially a couple. Leanza was extremely happy when Vonda shared the news and soon began to enjoy more time with Marshall as a result.

The three of them often did things together and sometimes Vonda invited both of them to dinner. On one such occasion Vonda asked Leanza how things were going for the A413TF team. This prompted Leanza to update Marshall that her team was trying to solve thirteen missing person cases with ties to the Myrtle Beach area. The agents were feeling a bit frustrated they hadn't found the connection they needed. Although it was out of character for her to do so, Leanza talked at length about the case with her two friends.

At one point she explained that the team had suspected a connection between a healthcare employee and the three emergency care facilities but nothing had panned out. This piqued Marshall's interest and he asked her how long ago the first person went missing. Leanza told him it was just short of twenty years ago. This was, of course, one of the reasons the team had suspected employee involvement.

Marshall shared that through the hospital expansion project he had become acquainted with several people on the hospital staff. He specifically mentioned his friend George El. Since George was approaching thirty years on staff Marshall was thinking he may be a good person for the team to speak with. Leanza made a note to share this with the agents at their upcoming meeting.

When Marshall and George bumped into each other a few days later they went to the cafeteria for lunch. Marshall had previously told George about spending Christmas morning with Vonda. George was happy to learn Vonda returned Marshall's love and the two of them had happily moved from friendship to being a couple. The two men praised God for answered prayers since He was obviously working in that relationship.

Noticing the banner in the cafeteria, the men fell into a conversation about the staff. Marshall took the opportunity to ask George about the two urgent care facilities. He was impressed with George's recall of events as he shared that the Urgent Care in Stokesbury was one of the first such facilities in all of South Carolina. If memory served him correctly, George added, it was about ten years later when Doctors Care opened in Myrtle Beach.

Remembering what Leanza had shared, Marshall was impressed with the accuracy of George's information. He took the opportunity to pick George's brain by asking if he remembered any staff members who had worked at all three facilities. George was intrigued with the question and began to verbally run it down. Marshall sat listening intently. In the end George was unable to pinpoint anyone who had worked at all three locations over the course of the past twenty-one years. George noticed that Marshall seemed frustrated and asked what any of this had to do with his construction project. Marshall admitted the two weren't actually connected.

"Then why are you frustrated with my answer?" George asked pointedly.

Marshall chuckled lightly, remarking on George's keen observation skills before admitting his curiosity wasn't self-motivated.

"I know you're a man of integrity, George. That's the only reason I'm sharing this since it isn't public information." He then added, "A good friend of Vonda's, who is now becoming my friend as well, is on a special Task Force that's investigating a number of missing person cases in this area. The one thing they all have in common is that they all visited one of those three emergency care facilities close to the time they went missing."

"You don't say." George responded looking incredulously at Marshall.

"Yes." Marshall answered quietly. "I was actually hoping your knowledge of the staff might help but since no one worked at all three facilities over that length of time it's a dead end."

"Huh, Hummm," George said quietly.

"What does that mean?" Marshall asked.

"Well, I'm just thinking that may not actually be the case." George answered. "I mean, a person might not have had to physically work at all three locations to be involved."

189

"What do you mean?" Marshall asked with great interest.

"Well, it's not something I know much about," George answered, "but it seems to me technology has changed a lot over the past twenty years. I imagine having access to patient information doesn't require being in the same place as the actual patient anymore. Isn't there a possibility this person could've accessed the patient's information regardless of which facility they worked at?"

"That's true enough," Marshall agreed. "Actually, now that I think about it, you make a very good point, George. They may not have ever even worked at the urgent care location the patient visited. Now that's something to pass on, for sure. Maybe this will help the investigating team. I knew you'd be a good person to talk to about this! Thank you, George."

"Well, we don't know yet if I've actually helped but this should give them another angle to look at it from."

CHAPTER 53

Leanza could hardly wait for the A413TF agents to arrive so she could get their January meeting started. As soon as everyone was present she stood up and thanked them all for coming.

She touched briefly on appreciating everyone's participation in the December activities. She added that it had appeared as if everyone enjoyed them. Sharing how refreshing it was to spend the holidays with her family, she expressed her personal hope that each of them felt the same. Seeing their heads nodding affirmatively made her smile.

Finally able to get to the point she told them she was excited to bring something new to the table. Leanza then made a full explanation of the healthcare system's annual pinning ceremony. A picture Marshall had taken and sent to Leanza appeared on the screen. It showed the banner listing department director's names in bold letters with more names in regular print. Leanza pointed to the list as she told them these seven directors and the other staff members had just been pinned for an excess of twenty years of employment. There were ten altogether.

Leanza immediately began to feel the energy in the room change.

When it came to new information these agents were like bloodhounds. She sensed that they could hardly wait for her to stop talking so they could get on the trail. She concluded her remarks and within minutes the names of each person was listed on the dry erase board with off-shoots of information being written in.

Feeling very pleased, Leanza was confident there would be not a dull moment for the duration of the meeting. They may even go into the evening hours on this one. In fact, she fully expected they would.

She found herself not only hoping but praying this was the break they had all been waiting for.

Leanza had forged ahead prior to today's meeting gaining clearance for the team to access personal information they would need to track down. Putting their innovative system and clearance to work, the agents were pulling pertinent information instantaneously. Before long the room was abuzz as more and more information came flooding in.

A digital file as well as a hard file was started for each of the ten people in question. The agents huddled around their computer screens as employee personnel files were looked into, phone records studied and bank accounts assessed. The printer was constantly humming as hardcopies of anything that seemed remotely questionable were printed for further scrutiny.

Documents were studied and placed into the files for future reference as needed. There was no question about it, this team worked together like a well-oiled machine. What one didn't notice, another one did. If anyone made even the slightest questioning sound the others took notice and were quick to join in a question and answer session if not a downright search, whatever was needed to get the job done! Once a resolution was located everyone went back to their own work.

It was one of the most productive meetings the team had held thus far. But of course, ten people's lives couldn't be dissected in such a short time span. Soon it was growing late and everyone was hungry and getting tired.

Although the entire team was willing to stay late into the evening, Leanza vetoed the idea.

"No, now we all need to get home and unwind. I know you all feel as I do - that the answer is just outside our grasp. Hopefully we're right. If so, it'll still be there tomorrow. Let's decide how to divide these files up and call it a night."

Knowing she was right, everyone nodded their agreement and went to work discussing which cases each agent would continue to pursue. Half an hour later, the information organized and divided, they were heading home.

Leaving the building Leanza noticed it was unusually warm for this early in the year. She chose a nearby drive through and grabbed something to eat on the drive. Pulling onto Anderson Avenue twenty minutes later she spotted Vonda and Marshall sitting out front at Vonda's. As she got out of the Impala they called out and waved her over. She couldn't resist the opportunity to thank Marshall for his input with the investigation. Excited to tell him how it had added to the meeting, she headed toward them.

A Brick to Remember

"Y'all look pretty relaxed sitting out here," she said as she approached.

"We are that." Marshall answered with a contented smile.

"Pull up a chair and join us." Vonda said motioning to the extra chairs she kept at the side of the house.

"I do believe I will." Leanza answered heading in that direction. "I don't mind telling you it's been a loooong day!"

"Judging from the time, I'd say it must've been." Marshall said, looking at his watch. "I'm glad you aren't too beat to join us."

"Since all you're doing is sitting I thought I could manage," she laughed. "Besides that though, you, Marshall, are a huge part of why I came over. I wanted to thank you for the information and picture from the pinning ceremony. I shared them with the agents earlier today and we've been hard at it for hours. There's a new level of energy in the team right now. It really feels like we're onto something and I truly believe the answer lies with these folks we're looking into. If it does, you'll be a huge part of these missing person cases being solved."

Vonda was smiling at Marshall as Leanza spoke.

"No thanks necessary." Marshall answered. "I just passed on public information. The digging and finding answers falls to your team. If there's something to be found I have no doubt you'll get the job done. I sure hope you're right and this thing can be put to rest and whoever's responsible can be held accountable and stopped!"

"Amen to that." Vonda added solemnly. "Heaven knows that needs to happen. These families need to know what happened to their loved ones once and for all."

Vonda offered Leanza some iced tea and the two ladies headed toward the house to get her a tall glass and refill Vonda and Marshall's glasses. Seeing Lilly peering out through the front door window gave them a chuckle. Lilly was very protective of Vonda and was always watching over her. Being strictly a house cat it was a little hard for her whenever Vonda sat outside. Vonda scooped her up as soon as they got inside.

"It's alright girl," she said as she cradled Lilly in her arms. "I'm safe out there with Marshall and Leanza. There's no need for you to worry. How about a treat since you watch over me so well?"

After giving Lilly one of her favorite treats and getting their tea they returned to the front yard. Vonda handed Marshall his glass and sat down beside him.

Sinking into her chair, Leanza let out a huge sigh. It sure felt good to relax.

Marshall shared that the Myrtle Beach General Hospital expansion was almost complete. They could hear the pride in his voice as he talked about what a good job his crew had done on the building.

"I can't begin to tell you how pleased I was as I stood looking down the hallway this afternoon. The rooms are completed and the beds will be delivered this week. It won't be long before the place is ready for patient admittance. It's a good feeling knowing what we've done will provide a place for people to heal and return to good health. I really don't know how to describe it. It just gives me a sense of great accomplishment, I guess."

"Of course it does," Vonda said, "and it should! Your company has done something wonderful for Horry County. I imagine you're going to have similar feelings of accomplishment when your team solves the case you've been working so hard on, Leanza. Both of you have been involved in such important work."

The three of them sat quietly after that, just feeling the gentle breeze and watching dusk fall. As often happens with close friends there was no need for words. It was the perfect ending to a long day of work for Marshall and Leanza. For Vonda it was simply a perfect evening with close friends.

Reaching out to take Marshall's hand and smiling at Leanza Vonda said softly, "We sure are blessed."

"We sure are." Marshall and Leanza agreed simultaneously.

CHAPTER 54

Feeling impatient, Jeremy Alan looked at the clock again. It was seven-thirty a.m. Still pretty early but he wasn't sure he had it in him to wait any longer. He'd been working on his case files until well after two. He was onto something. He was sure of it!

It had taken everything in him to keep from calling his boss in the wee hours of the morning. He was anxious to tell her about the trail he'd been following. Exhausted, he had finally slept, but fitfully. His mind was too geared up to actually settle down.

He had no idea what time Leanza's day normally started. He was pretty sure it was socially acceptable to call people after eight a.m. but not before. He looked at the clock again and decided he wasn't up to waiting another twenty-five minutes.

Speaking her name into his phone he hoped and prayed she would agree with his logic once she heard what he had to say.

"Hello," Leanza said, answering the call on the second ring.

"Hey, it's Jeremy. I'm sorry to call so early but I really think I'm onto something important here."

"It's okay Jeremy, I was awake. It's a rare morning I sleep past seven."

"Okay, good to know. I'm not in the habit of calling early. But I'm not kidding - I really think I'm onto something. I was up 'til after two tracking this down and I need you to take a look at it. If I'm seeing what I think I am, we may have finally found the person we need to talk to."

"Ok Jeremy. I hope you're right. Do you want to get into it over the phone or would it be better to show me?" Leanza asked.

"I'd love to just blurt it out, but I don't think you can verify accuracy unless you're seeing what I am."

"Enough said. Tell me where you want to meet and I'll be there as soon as I can. If you're right we'll fill the rest of the team in at this afternoon's meeting and determine our next steps. Either way, great work Jeremy! I'm proud to have you on the team."

They worked out the details and hung up. As he laid his phone down Jeremy was surprised to realize his hands were actually trembling from anticipation. A glance at his watch verified he had time to get a quick shower. Thinking that might settle him down and clear his mind for the meeting he headed to the bathroom.

Leanza had been up awhile and had already enjoyed her first cup of coffee. She drank a protein shake as she was getting dressed. After filling her tumbler with another cup of hot java she headed out the door. She could feel the adrenaline kicking in as she anticipated finally solving this case.

Twenty minutes later Jeremy and Leanza sat together looking over hardcopies of three separate bank statements, all three belonging to the same person, a department director. There was a checking account and two savings accounts with the past five years of transactions listed. One savings account and the checking account appeared totally normal and were tied together. The other savings account had been getting direct deposit payments either monthly or quarterly, in various amounts from an unknown depositor. The deposits were called out with the initials SMBF. Jeremy asked Leanza if she had any idea what type of payments these would be. After looking everything over together, neither of them had any idea why the payments were being made. Jeremy had been theorizing. He'd come up with a number of scenarios. Without further information there was no way of knowing if he was onto anything or not.

"First of all," Leanza said, "we've got to get into these accounts to see how long this has been going on beyond the five years we're looking at. If we've established at least a twenty year time frame, we'll have to track down the source of the payments. Until then we're not really sure what we're looking at. But, yes, Jeremy I'm in full agreement with your thinking that something very suspicious is going on here."

CHAPTER 55

Vonda reached out and took Marshall's hand as they walked along the boardwalk at Vereen Memorial Garden in Little River. It was a South Carolina day through and through; the beautiful big sun was bright, and yes, hot! But a gentle breeze rose up and swept across their skin so frequently it provided steady relief from the heat of the day. The overhead sky was rich in blues with a few fluffy white clouds lazily hanging in place. It was the kind of day every true South Carolinian loves.

Looking out across the salt marsh Vonda spotted several herons standing in the reeds. The couple approached a little too closely causing one of them to quickly take half a dozen steps on its long skinny legs and spread its wings. It swiftly lifted off the ground and took flight.

"Look at him go!" Vonda said, turning to Marshall with a smile.

"It never gets old, does it?" he asked, thinking of more than just the heron as he squeezed her hand gently.

"Never!" Vonda answered, enraptured by the sight.

A few seconds later while glancing down to watch her steps she chuckled and added, "Neither do they!" She was pointing a few steps ahead on the path at the little crabs dashing away and quickly dipping into tiny holes in the dirt.

"There are so many of them!" she laughed. "And they're so quick!"

Marshall was smiling happily and it wasn't just because of the crabs. It was for the joy on Vonda's face and in his own heart.

He was still astonished that this woman he'd grown to love so deeply actually loved him in return. He couldn't believe that after spending a lifetime alone he could be so blessed. He felt thankful - so very, very thankful.

"Shall we?" he asked as he lifted his arm and motioned toward the swing just ahead.

"Absolutely," Vonda answered as they made their way over and sat down together. Immediately they began to gently sway and their eyes sought the beautiful view stretching out before them.

A few moments passed in silence.

"I've been thinking a lot about Leanza these past few days," Vonda said as she turned to Marshall. "She's got so much going on right now. I've been praying for her and the entire A413 Task Force. They're about to solve the case, which is great, but I'm very concerned about what exactly they'll discover. I hope I'm wrong, Marshall, but I'm expecting it to be something sinister. I keep asking God to help them deal with whatever has happened to those thirteen missing people. I'm hoping for the best, but so much time has gone by with some of them that I can't help but expect the worst."

"I know exactly what you're saying," Marshall said somberly. "It'll be nothing short of a miracle if any of them are still alive. I have no idea what's become of them but it doesn't seem likely they've survived after all this time. I've said quite a few prayers for the team and the families of those who are missing, too."

"Not just that," Vonda continued, "but Leanza has carried the burden of her father's mysterious disappearance her entire life. Leanza, Wade and their mother, they're all such precious people, Marshall. I wish you could've met Megan and Wade. My heart just goes out to them so much! Ever since I spent Thanksgiving with that family I've been asking God to let them learn what happened to Denvel. I mean, Marshall, can you even imagine what it's been like for them?"

"No, I really can't. I can't even fathom it. I mean, my parents died when I was twenty-five. The night of the accident they were both suddenly gone from my life. It was beyond tragic, but at least my brothers and I knew what happened to them. I absolutely cannot imagine losing a family member and never knowing what happened."

They sat together silently just swaying gently for a few more moments.

"I just want them to have closure," Vonda said, "especially Leanza. I've gotten to know her these past five months. I've really come to care for her. She's such a lovely young woman. She's got so much of her life ahead yet. I want her to be freed of the burden of the unknown. I want so badly for Leanza to understand the meaning of her dreams. I've actually come to believe they're memories. She was only four-years-old when he went missing. I cannot imagine how it's possible, but it just seems as though she knows something. Will you pray about this with me Marshall? Will you join me in asking God to reveal to her whatever it is she actually knows?"

"Of course I will." Marshall said lovingly. Lifting his arm he slid closer toward her as she moved into the shelter of his embrace. Vonda hadn't meant right then at that moment. She had just meant in his personal prayer times. But when she saw him lowering his head with his face close to hers she realized he was going to pray with her right then and she loved him all the more for it.

"Father," he said just loudly enough for Vonda to hear him "we're coming to you together right now. You've heard our entire conversation, Lord. You know our thoughts and you see our hearts. You've blessed our lives with the friendship we share with Leanza. We don't know why these things have to happen in life, God: pain, death, tragic loss of loved ones, such hurtful times we must live through. We'll never understand it, but we're so thankful we don't have to go through any of it alone. You love us so deeply, Lord, that you go through every hurtful moment with us. Thank you, Father! Thank you for giving us others to care and be there and to pray for us as well. We're praying for our friend right now, Lord, and for her brother, Wade and her mother, Megan. We're thinking that maybe somewhere deep in her mind Leanza knows something about what happened to her father so many years ago, or maybe just something that could help find out what happened. We don't know, Lord, but you do. You see all and you know all.

Knowing nothing else, we know you love them. They're your children and you only want what's best for them. So we ask now, if it's your will and if it will be good for them, please help Leanza regain her memories. Please help them find what they need to find in order to know what happened to Denvel. But Lord, if that's not to be, we simply ask that you give Leanza, Wade and Megan peace: your peace, not this world's but yours, Lord, since that's the only peace that passes all understanding."

"Amen." Vonda whispered softly.

Opening her eyes she lifted her face and looked at Marshall. A sense of great calm and tranquility had come over her as he prayed and she told him so. She couldn't help thinking of John 14:27 where Jesus said "Peace I leave with you; my peace I give you. I do not give as the world gives. Do not let yourselves be troubled and do not be afraid."

Her heart was overflowing with love and thankfulness. After sharing such a happy life with Stanley, Vonda was thankful to now have Marshall in her life. She knew without question she had been doubly blessed and she didn't, for even one second, take it for granted.

CHAPTER 56

"What's going on?" I asked as I was escorted down the corridor by a woman who had identified herself as an FBI liaison. What does that even mean? Is she an FBI agent or not? And what in the world do they want with me?

I had been quite startled when she entered my office and told me I needed to come with her to the FBI headquarters in Stokesbury. Talking fast and acting like it was urgent she'd said something about some missing people they thought I might have information about. I told her I knew nothing about any missing people but, of course, I was willing to help if they thought I could.

After introducing me to a man she called Jeremy, the two of them rushed me to a vehicle. He drove us to this tall building in downtown Stokesbury and we took the elevator to the eighteenth floor. Reaching the end of the corridor, we entered a large conference room where several people were working at separate workstations. Everyone stopped and looked up when we entered the room but then they went back to what they were doing. I was directed to take a seat and the woman and Jeremy went to speak with the others. After huddling together for a bit they separated and those two finally returned. Jeremy told me they needed information and hoped I would willingly comply.

A foreboding feeling rose up in my chest but I said, "Of course."

The woman who had called herself a liaison sat directly across from me and looked me in the eye.

"As a part of our investigation we've been looking into the actions of hospital staff. Obviously, that includes you, and we have some questions about your sources of income. Would you mind explaining the source of the deposits being made into your secondary savings account?"

"What?" I said, astonished that they were asking about my personal income. "Why is that a concern of the FBI?"

"I'll explain that. Of course, I will." The woman whose name I'd missed said. "We just need to clear up where the income is coming from and what service you're providing for it since it's obviously not from the healthcare system you work for."

"Well, not directly," I said looking from one to the other of them, "but they're aware of it. The two organizations work in collaboration with each other so technically, it does come from the same place."

"Oh?" She said questioningly. I noticed her eyebrows arching a bit. "Well that could explain a lot. Would you care to tell us about that?"

"I guess not," I said, still confused as to what this was about. "I don't really have all the details. The organization pays me by direct deposit for information I provide them. It's all based on an agreement with the healthcare system. Certain staff members provide them with patient contact information which they then sift through to find patients who fit the criteria for surveys in their research programs. HR is fully aware of this arrangement. That's as much as I know about it, really."

"Okay," the young man, Jeremy, said thoughtfully, "and how long have you been providing this organization with patient contact information?"

"How long? Oh, well, I'm not exactly sure, a long time, somewhere around seventeen to eighteen years?"

The woman shook her head oddly, almost as if to try to clear her brain. She had a look of disbelief on her face. Like this didn't make any sense.

Jeremy was looking at her as if he was waiting for her to speak. When she didn't say anything Jeremy asked, "That long?" He paused looking at her again before asking me, "And you've been being paid by direct deposit into this account all that time? You didn't find that strange? In the beginning, I mean. The healthcare system wasn't paying by direct deposit that many years ago, was it?"

"No, you're right," I said, smiling since I understood his confusion. "It *was* strange in the beginning but the representative explained that all employers were moving in that direction and it wouldn't be long before everyone would be paid by direct deposit. It took longer than she'd said it would but in the end she was right, eventually the hospital made the change and as you know everyone's paid that way now."

"What about tax information?" Seeming to have finally cleared her head the liaison woman asked. Immediately following up with, "Have you been filing taxes on this income? We didn't find any W2's on it."

"Is that the problem?" I asked, feeling alarmed, "They assured me that was all being done through the healthcare system since the two organizations work in collaboration with each other. I remember asking that question at tax time the first year I worked for them."

"Oh? How did you contact them to ask that question?" she asked, seeming very interested.

"I just wrote the question out and included it with the intake forms I always submit. A representative called a few days later and assured me it was being handled through the healthcare system," I answered, being careful to remain calm as the feeling that they believed I'd done something wrong rose up inside me.

"What phone number called you?" I was then asked.

"What?" I asked, feeling confused and annoyed, "Oh, I have no idea. I don't have a number for them. Anytime I have a question they call me within a day or two and we talk. I'm sorry if that's not helpful, I'm just telling you how it is. I still don't understand why any of this is of concern to the FBI."

CHAPTER 57

Leanza felt as if she were in an episode of the Twilight Zone. Could anyone actually be this naïve, especially a professional, intelligent, educated person who'd been a hospital employee more than twenty years and had advanced to the position of department director?

Was this person naïve or was this just a really good acting job? What were they actually dealing with here?

Her eyes met Jeremy's and she could swear he was thinking the same things she was.

They continued the interview but it never revealed the questionable income's source. They were stunned to realize communication had never advanced beyond hand written-notes transported in an envelope of patient intake forms through the basement's mailroom slot. They may ultimately have to get a subpoena, forcing the bank to reveal the source of those deposits.

With no proof or admission of anything illegal taking place they had no choice but to end the interview. After their return to the hospital and before leaving the director's office, Leanza and Jeremy expressed their thanks for the cooperative interchange. What else could they do?

Returning to the conference room, the two met with the team and discussed their overall impression of the suspect. They all agreed it was difficult to believe anyone could be this clueless that something illegal was going on.

A subpoena would be a last resort as the team collectively felt there had to be an easier way to get to the bottom of this. After much debate they decided the best course of action would be to follow the envelope and use the information at the end of the trail to flush out the truth.

At this point they agreed that the hospital CEO Daniel Travis must be contacted. The team also agreed that Jeremy should go with Leanza for that meeting as well and the two of them headed back to the hospital.

After stressing the importance of speaking with him and promising to respect his busy schedule, Daniel agreed to a meeting. Leanza gave him a short version of what had been said during the earlier interrogation.

"Do you mean to tell me HIPPA laws have been broken by a member of my staff, a department director, no less?" The CEO asked, obviously alarmed.

"We believe so, sir." Leanza answered. "You should know we stumbled upon this information in the course of an entirely different investigation. We're here today because we're loath to continue without your knowledge and involvement."

"Well, thank you for that! I appreciate it. I surely do, but I'm quite alarmed by these allegations. I'm going to need to know what proof you have so I can handle this thing on my end. When it comes to patient information we have a zero tolerance policy here, let me assure you."

"Oh, sir, please don't misunderstand me. We are in no way accusing you of being party to what's taken place." Leanza assured him.

"That's good and I appreciate it but that doesn't change the fact that I have to deal with whatever happens in this healthcare system under my watch!"

"We understand that, sir, but in this matter we're asking for your help in solving our case. That being said, our case needs to take precedent over anything else. What I'm saying is that we may need to resolve that before you deal with what's taken place on your watch. Could we discuss that please?"

"We can discuss it but I'm not willing to sit on this for long," Daniel answered.

"Understood, completely understood, sir," Leanza said before filling him in on the details.

Daniel was appalled to learn patient intake forms were basically being sold from the facility under the guise of some kind of collaboration. And this had been going on for over twenty years! How was this even possible? He was not only livid, he was shocked, at exactly who was suspected of being involved. Further discussion revealed an uncertainty within the Task

Force team as to the intent of the suspect. Was this a blatant betrayal or some kind of innocent ignorance? Either way there had to be accountability.

A plan was devised and immediately set in motion beginning with a trip to the mail room to locate the mail slot in question. Unbeknownst to whoever was heading up this operation the envelope in question would be closely monitored until its final destination was known to the A413TF team. At which point this entire case may be blown wide open. That was the hope anyway, it remained to be seen how it would actually play out.

CHAPTER 58

Though she was sleeping deeply, Leanza's lips curved into a smile and a small childish laugh escaped them. In her dream she was a vibrant, happy, little girl of only four-years-old.

"Watch me daddy!" she called out as her little legs peddled the tricycle as fast as they could. Turning her head toward the corner of the room as she sped past she saw him seated in the easy chair. He was smiling. The next time she rode by he leaned toward her craning his neck to see her better and clasping his hands together.

Her heart felt light and happy.

In the strange way of dreams she was suddenly no longer on her tricycle. She was under the stairway now placing her baby doll into the toy baby bed. Chattering happily she covered the baby doll with a blanket.

"Hey, Little Dove," she heard her dad say "do you remember what we found when we played down here before?"

She cocked her head to one side and thought but the dream suddenly changed again.

She was now standing in front of the brick wall lifting her hands and placing them flat against the bricks. Looking down she saw her pink tennis shoes. Sensing him behind her now she turned and threw her arms around his neck.

"Oh, daddy! What fun!" she said excitedly.

Again childish laughter escaped from the sleeping adult as she turned on her side and snuggled into her pillow.

In the dream there were now four very small toys lined up on a little ledge.

She felt something strange in her hand. She opened her little fist and looked down to see what she was holding. And it was in that precise moment that Leanza awoke.

After stretching, she rolled over and looked at the clock. Seven fifteen. Time to get up, she thought even as she resisted and rolled in the other direction and closed her eyes again. Lying there peacefully she began to remember her dream. No wonder I feel so happy this morning, she thought remembering the happy child she'd been just a few seconds before.

Wait. She'd actually seen her father this time. Sitting up on the edge of the bed she felt a sense of wonder. That hadn't happened in her previous dreams. She'd heard his voice and felt his hug before but this was the first time she had awakened to a memory of looking directly at him. The glances were quick - as she rode past him on her tricycle - but they were there. What does this mean? She asked herself in a whisper.

What else was in this dream?

Nothing else mattered in that moment. Her only thought was to try to remember whatever she'd dreamt. Knowing if she concentrated too hard it would escape her, she gently lay back onto the mattress, drew her pillow into her arms and settled in on her side. Closing her eyes she willed herself not to stress, not to try too hard. Just lay here, she thought, just lay here and think through the dream.

She'd never tried this before but it seemed as if it was working.

Slowly she thought back and remembered the fragmented pieces of her dream. She had no idea if she remembered it in the right sequence or if she remembered all of it but she didn't let that matter. She only knew she was getting some of it back. It had been a pleasant dream of a happy child playing while her daddy watched. She remembered him calling her 'Little Dove'. Wait, what was this? He asked her if she remembered something they'd found before. What did that mean? She needed to write that down, didn't she?

Not yet, she thought, just keep thinking through the dream. What else was there? But now nothing else was coming. After another minute she got up, got the notepad she kept on her night stand and wrote down as much as she remembered. Reading over it a few minutes later she was satisfied. There was more there than usual. What does this mean? She asked herself again as she got out of bed and began her morning routine.

CHAPTER 59

I was completely unnerved after being questioned by that FBI liaison woman and her agent Jeremy. I didn't like the way they had rushed into my office, made me feel as if everything was urgent and then rushed me away for questioning.

I wouldn't be so easily manipulated again.

They came back the very next day but that time I was ready. I told them firmly I had work to do and I wasn't going to be whisked away from my job without explanation. I politely demanded more information. In response I learned the liaison woman's name is Leanza Williams. She's a police detective/advocate for missing persons heading up a special Task Force on an important case out of Stokesbury. Jeremy's an FBI agent on that task force.

They told me they believe the information I've been providing is tied to a missing person. Next they demanded a list of patient names from the forms I've submitted. I told them I wasn't giving them any information without my employer's consent. Not to mention the fact that I've never kept such a list. I've simply done what I've been instructed to do. They wanted me to explain the process but I wouldn't be bullied. I said I wasn't obliged to give them a description of my job and had no intention of doing so.

To my relief, they left. I thought the whole thing was over but I was wrong. They returned with the hospital CEO, my boss. He said he'd been briefed and was granting me permission to explain my job duties. Having no other choice, I told them I had been instructed to keep an eye out for overall healthy people who come into the emergency room or urgent care for treatment. I work from patient intake forms the patient fills out at the time of the visit so I just watch those closely. When I see treatment sought for an injury or short term illness on an otherwise healthy individual I copy the form. I put those into a file folder in my top desk drawer. On the last

Thursday of the month I put the copies into a large manila envelope and seal it. I write the number of intakes included on the front. At close to two o'clock I take the envelope downstairs to the mail room and place it into the first slot in the bottom section closest to the door. The timing is important since the inner office mail gets picked up around three.

If the envelope isn't there on time my pay will be docked. That's never happened to me though. I do my job correctly so it's never been late.

This prompted them to ask about my pay. I explained getting paid a set amount monthly if none of the patients match the criteria for the current research project. I get significantly more pay when there's a match who is successfully contacted and enters into a research program.

I had a hard time believing Daniel was willingly participating in this interrogation. You get to know someone when you work closely together for such a long time. I could tell he was angry the entire time I was talking. It was obvious he had been strong-armed into submitting to this Task Force interrogation. I felt for him because I wasn't participating willingly either.

I couldn't believe it when the agents insisted we all walk down to the mailroom. They made me show them the mail slot I dropped the envelope into. I heard one of them say, as I've often thought, that the slot isn't quite as thick as all the others, almost as if it's not actually a mail slot at all.

At the end of the meeting Daniel stood up, walked over to me and told me I was in violation of the healthcare HIPPA policy. He then said there was no collaboration with another organization and that I was being used for some kind of criminal activity. I didn't say anything. I was intent on remaining totally calm. Although I'd had my suspicions through the years, they had no way of knowing that and I had no intention of ever admitting it. I did what I had to do to take care of my mom. That was it. It was up to them to prove it if anything was amiss.

Daniel emphasized that I had to give my full cooperation to the agents since they were simply trying to get to the bottom of whatever's been going on.

Ms. Williams then told me they'd be putting some kind of undetectable marker on the next envelope I submitted so they could track it.

I can't believe any of this is real! But then, looking back over my early life this is just the kind of thing I should've expected to have happen. It feels like my childhood string of bad luck has returned. All I know is that I did what I had to do and I'd do it again. No one is going to make me admit to anything. As far as any of them know now, or will ever know, I had no idea what was going on.

I'm just an innocent pawn in a bigger game.

CHAPTER 60

"Is it true?" Amanda asked Janet. "It can't be true, can it?"

Janet looked as confused as Amanda felt.

"I don't know," she said. "As usual, when something happens around here the rumors are running rampant. If it's true - it's unbelievable! I mean, we're talking about a breach of protocol that spans over twenty years. And look *who* we're talking about! I'll say it again, it's *unbelievable!*

It sounds like this FBI group has traced it down to someone outside the healthcare system though, someone who had access to the mailroom. How that was ever managed, let alone for so long, is beyond me. But it's better than if someone in-house was behind it all. I'm just glad the hospital won't be held liable." Amanda said. "Just think of it! We could be in terrible legal trouble if this had actually happened through proper channels."

Seeing Debra enter the cafeteria Janet caught her eye and motioned for her to join them. She hurried to their table and sat down.

"I feel so badly for our CEO," Debra said immediately. "Can you imagine learning a staff member is involved in such a thing? It's even more than that though, a long standing member of his team, a department director I'm sure he considers a friend. He's got to be beside himself over this." She looked genuinely concerned.

One of the women noticed their COO and CFO huddled together at another table. Pointing them out to the others she said, "Let's go talk to Mick and David. We've got to stick together through this."

"I've only got a short break and I've got to have something in my stomach." Debra said. "I'm going to grab something to eat, but I'll be right over."

She hurried away as the other two picked up their trays and moved to join the men at their table.

Mick saw the women coming.

"It looks like we're about to have company," he said to David who turned and watched the women approach.

"Have any of you heard how Daniel's taking it?" he asked immediately out of concern for their leader.

"I heard he was irate. But wouldn't you be?" Janet asked.

"I heard he showed great restraint," Amanda said. "Apparently the FBI has already told him all the charges that will be brought."

"I just can't wrap my head around any of this." It was the first time Mick had spoken. "I mean, we've all had hard times when money was tight, but how does someone do such a thing? Especially knowing what was happening to those people. I'd never sleep a wink for the rest of my life!"

"That's just it." Debra said having rejoined the group. "According to what I heard it was presented as if it was just some kind of medical research project."

"So it wasn't deliberate?" Mick asked, looking relieved.

"That's what I'm saying." Debra answered him.

"Well, that makes me feel a little better. I mean, it's hard to believe HIPPA protocol has been being broken by the *one person* whose position requires confidentiality more than anything else. But what makes all of this so unbelievable is that we're talking about one of the kindest, most thoughtful people on staff here. I've been asking myself all day how this could've been done by our Director of Registration. It just doesn't seem possible! I mean, come on! We're talking about Mary McCoy here!"

CHAPTER 61

Stepping out of the Chevy Impala in the parking garage felt reminiscent of her first day in Stokesbury some six months before. Needing to keep her professional focus Leanza took a few moments to smooth her pencil skirt, re-tuck her blouse, put on her suit jacket, run a comb through her hair and touch-up her lipstick. She then picked up her purse and briefcase, shut the car door and walked across the parking garage to the elevator. Exiting onto the eighteenth floor, she looked down the long corridor toward the conference room. Again she couldn't help remembering the first day she'd walked the length of the extensive hallway stretched out in front of her.

Mentally preparing for the meeting about to take place, she straightened her shoulders, focused her mind and took those first few steps. She wasn't sure she was emotionally prepared since she wasn't about to meet her new team for the first time today, she was instead about to say goodbye.

The past six months had been some of the most grueling work of her career. It had also been the most rewarding. She was proud of herself and she was proud of her team. She only hoped she could make them understand exactly how proud she was before the day was done.

Inside the conference room the Task Force members were waiting anxiously for Leanza. They had arrived almost an hour earlier and been hard at it decorating the room and laying out quite a celebratory spread.

"She's coming!" Jeremy told the others after a quick peek out the door. "What should we do?"

"Just sit down as if it's just another day," was the quick reply, followed by the entire team's laughter. "After all, she told us in no uncertain terms that's how this meeting was to go."

They all hurried to their seats and sat down.

The door opened and Leanza stepped into the room.

Her eyes immediately went to the decorations. She purposely resisted the smile that played at the corners of her lips but when she saw the table of food and the cake she couldn't keep from laughing out loud.

"What did y'all do!?!" she asked as the entire team burst out laughing. "*I told you* we were treating today like any other day."

Jeremy stood up and said, "Oh, come on! You didn't really expect us to do that, did you? I mean, come on boss! We did it!!! We solved the case! You gotta admit that deserves a celebration!!"

They had all stood up and gathered around her while she and Jeremy were speaking. As Leanza looked from one smiling face to the other she couldn't keep from smiling herself.

"Yes, Jeremy, we did!!" she finally conceded. "Well, okay then. Yes, you're right! A celebration is in order but we've got to have an actual meeting first so everyone sit back down and let's do this."

For the next forty-five minutes they went over every detail of how the case had been solved. In the process they made sure the final report missed nothing.

As soon as Jeremy discovered the secondary savings account they set their sights on Mary McCoy and everything started to fall into place. Once their interrogations confirmed their suspicions they brought the healthcare CEO into the loop. He was totally shocked to hear Mary talk about what she had been doing. Hearing that her actions were in direct violation of HIPPA protocol Mary gave her full cooperation. By the time it was all over she had told them the entire story.

Mary's professional life had begun to unravel when the decline in her mother's health resulted in added financial strain. Wanting to believe she was providing valuable and needed services she simply didn't question the legitimacy of the program. She needed the money and the representatives she had spoken with assured her everything was above board. She insisted that she honestly had *no idea* what was happening with the information she was passing on.

Mary was a long time member of the hospital staff. She was respected, well liked, known for her kindness and birthday surprises to almost everyone within the hospital staff family. The news of her involvement hit a lot of people pretty hard. Whether she realized what she was doing or not Mary was legally accountable for her actions. This case would definitely prove the truth of the old adage "ignorance is no excuse". There would be consequences for Mary's behavior but exactly what those were remained to be seen.

Once the Task Force confronted Mary and found no question of her involvement, they placed an undetectable tracer on the next envelope she submitted. The tracer uncovered a system through which the patient names and addresses were being sold to a human organ trafficking operation. Those targeted were studied, followed and taken at their most vulnerable moments, never to be heard from again. When the FBI raided the operation a list of victim names was recovered. The names of all thirteen of the missing people the A413 Task Force was investigating were on the list.

It had fallen to Leanza and her team to deliver the news to the families of the missing. While their hearts were broken to learn their loved ones had met with such a cruel end they were grateful to the team for giving them closure.

At the conclusion of today's meeting Leanza gave a speech. It wasn't the most professional speech of her career but it was definitely the most heartfelt. She made it abundantly clear how proud she was of the work of each and every one of these agents. So proud, in fact, that she had already made advancement recommendations to each of their superiors based on their performances on her team. She wished all of them every success both professionally and personally. She also made it clear that she expected them to stay in touch.

She commended them for their dedication to finding the truth and their compassion in dealing with the victim's families. She proudly announced that the Task Force had been nominated to receive a Commendation in the field of Missing Persons Advocacy. She fully expected each of them to be notified at some future date to receive that honor.

At the close of her speech she told them that while they were no longer a team they would forever be connected through this experience. Each had made an impact in the lives of the families of those who were missing, in each other's lives and within the human race. They had taken down an underground organ trafficking operation and through that action the lives of countless people who would've become victims had been saved. Those people would continue to enjoy healthy, safe and productive lives because of the work the team had done.

She stated that she had never been as proud of any group she'd worked with as she was of this team. She thanked them, she commended them and she challenged them to continue the good work they had just proven themselves capable of.

It was one of the most inspiring speeches Jeremy had ever heard.

Leanza then spent the rest of the afternoon enjoying delicious foods, celebration cake and wonderful conversation with her team.

CHAPTER 62

As Vonda reached for the sundress she was thinking of wearing today her mind drifted back to past Davidson Construction Picnic's. It was always a fun day and she was certain today would be as well.

Leanza was to be her guest today which was bittersweet since it would be their last outing together. Leanza was leaving the next morning. The two had become quite good friends over the past six months. Vonda couldn't help smiling at the memory of the day they first met at the <u>Down at the Barbershop</u> concert in downtown Logan. There was no doubt about it, she was going to miss her friend.

Life sure is funny, she thought, as she dressed and braided her hair. Some people come into our lives for just a season but they sure make an impact. Leanza was one of those people for her. Of course, they would promise to stay in touch. And they really would try but Vonda had lived long enough to know some such relationships don't make it. She would just have to see what life held in store for this one.

As so often happened in Vonda's mind her thinking very naturally flowed from her own thoughts into a conversation with God, "Thank you Lord that I crossed paths with that lovely young woman and for the time we've spent together. Thank you for answering my prayers that you help her team solve the mystery of those missing people. Thank you that they've exposed that terrible operation and put a stop to it. Thank you that those families have gotten some closure. I know you'll continue to be with them as they adjust to what they've learned.

Oh, that reminds me, though I know you haven't forgotten, especially since we've talk about this so often. I just want to ask again that you help Leanza remember whatever she knows but has forgotten. Please help her figure out what her dreams and those sleep-typing clues mean. Please give

A Brick to Remember

Leanza, Wade and Megan the comfort, strength and peace they need and a resolution to Denvel's disappearance."

Ending her prayer Vonda glanced in the mirror one last time, set the security code, said goodbye to Lilly and headed out her front door.

Across the street Leanza was just closing the condo door behind her. She smiled, waved and walked across the yard to join her friend. The two got into Vonda's car and headed to the fairgrounds.

Just like he did each year Marshall had told Vonda he'd be busy most of the day making sure everything went smoothly and interacting with his employees. Hoping they could have lunch together he had promised to try to meet her at the lunch tents at one o'clock.

The women had thoroughly enjoyed themselves over the past several hours. They had watched the children make their choices and sit for their face paintings. They spent time in the animal petting area and played a few games. Walking down the midway Vonda turned to Leanza and said, "It's almost one we'd better head toward the lunch tents. Since they've used the same caterers again this year I imagine we're in for a real treat."

"That's good to hear because I'm starving." Leanza answered as they entered the tent.

As Marshall came rushing up to join them he said "I was afraid I wasn't going to be able to make it! Something went wrong with the power in one of the game booths. I've got one of my guys working on it. He saw how anxious I was to leave and asked if I had a date or something. I think he was a little surprised when I told him I wanted to meet my girl for lunch!" His quick wink made Vonda smile. Leanza loved being witness to the relationship those two shared.

"He laughed and told me to go ahead promising he'll get it going. He's one of the best electricians I've ever known. Otherwise I'd still be over there. I told him to come find us when he gets done."

Marshall and Vonda stood facing Leanza as they waited for their lunch orders. Looking past Leanza Marshall suddenly said, "Oh, good, there's Chrystian now. He must've gotten things up and running."

"Chrystian!" he called out while waving his hands in the air, "over here."

Leanza turned to follow Marshall's gaze and saw the young man approaching. Her eyes met and held his gaze as he walked up to join them.

"You! It's you?" she said aloud seemingly unaware that she had even spoken.

Being about five inches taller than her he was gazing downward into her face. His lips slowly curved into a smile. "That it is," he said with a chuckle. "Actually, I don't know who else to be."

Marshall looked at Vonda questioningly and turned back to see the two still intently looking into each other's eyes.

"Do you two know each other?" Marshall asked and immediately felt as if he'd broken some kind of spell when they turned to look at him.

"No, actually we don't," Chrystian said turning back to meet Leanza's eyes again, "but I sure have wished we did."

Leanza's cheeks flushed a beautiful shade of pink as she asked "You have?"

"Why, yes, ma'am, several times, I have, in fact. Haven't you?" he asked her pointedly.

Vonda had never seen her friend look the way she did at that moment. The confident, professional, independent young woman she'd known for the past six months had never appeared the least bit shy or vulnerable. At this moment, however, she looked as if she were in junior high school and had just been noticed by a boy for the very first time.

It was actually quite adorable.

CHAPTER 63

A few seconds passed before Leanza seemed to get her bearings. She then reminded Vonda of the pup and owner they had come across on the hiking path a while back. Looking at the man more intently Vonda realized Chrystian was indeed the same man. He was the pup's owner.

Chrystian went on to share that the two of them had caught a glimpse of each other at the Christmas Festival but were then lost in the crowd. After these explanations Chrystian ordered lunch and the group found a place to enjoy them.

Marshall managed to spend most of the afternoon relaxing with his friends. They took part in the dart throwing and corn-hole competitions and enjoyed the raffle ticket gift presentations throughout the rest of the day.

When dusk was about to fall Marshall took center stage as was customary at the company picnic. Addressing the crowd, he thanked everyone for coming out for the day and for their faithful commitment to Davidson Construction. He talked about the growth of the company over the past year and shared its goals for the coming year. He expressed his thanks to all those who had temporarily joined the construction crew to get the new hospital addition completed. He then shared that they had come from various locations and asked them to stand when he named their home state. To Leanza's surprise Chrystian stood for the state of Virginia.

Marshall ended his speech with an announcement. Tomorrow's Logan Tribune newspaper would have a front page feature article on the completion of the new addition to the Myrtle Beach General Hospital. Pictures from the ribbon cutting ceremony, which had taken place on Friday, would be featured.

It was an exciting time for the company, the healthcare system and the community. Marshall said he felt blessed, being a part of it. On that note, he turned to Vonda and asked that she join him. Taken by surprise she smiled and walked over and stood at his side. Addressing the crowd again Marshall said, "Since I was just talking about feeling blessed I can't let today end without introducing all of you, my work family, to this important lady in my life. We've been friends for quite some time. I'm always talking about the company and our latest projects with her. She prays for me and for each of you so I just wanted all of you to meet her. I have a feeling that once you get a chance to chat with her and get to know her better you'll grow to love her just the way I have." He looked lovingly into her eyes and said "Everyone, this is the special lady in my life, Vonda Graham."

Not knowing what else to do Vonda looked out at the crowd and said simply, "Hello everyone. I'm so very happy to meet you all."

Everyone began to applaud and Marshall put his hand up to shush them. "Okay then, thank you all for being here today and being part of the Davidson Construction family. Please enjoy the fireworks show and be careful heading home this evening."

Putting his arm around Vonda's shoulder he pulled her toward him in a gentle hug as they walked away.

"You sure took me by surprise," she told him. "I didn't know you were going to do that."

"I didn't know either," he chuckled. "It just didn't seem right not telling everyone about you since you've become so important to me."

They shared a brief hug and sat down to enjoy the fireworks show.

Not far away Leanza and Chrystian sat chatting and enjoying the show together.

"I was surprised to learn you're from Virginia," Leanza said. She then asked, "What part?"

"Norfolk," he answered. "I'll be on a flight home tomorrow morning."

"Are you kidding me?" she said, not quite able to believe her ears.

"No, not at all," he answered, looking at her strangely. "Why would you ask me that?"

"Because I'm from Norfolk, Virginia," she answered not taking her eyes off of him, "and I'll also be on a flight home tomorrow morning."

CHAPTER 64

The next day found Leanza making her way back home. After six months of living in Logan, South Carolina and working with the A413TF team her life was changing yet again.

She was returning to Norfolk and she was ready. She felt proud of the work she'd done and its results. It was good to know the organ trafficking operation was out of commission. Realistically, she knew that a half a dozen other illegal and terrible practices would rise up to take its place. But at least she'd had a part in taking this one down. It gave her a great sense of accomplishment just as Vonda had once predicted it would.

Living in Logan had been an adventure and her life was richer for the relationships she'd formed there.

Leanza had said goodbye to Marshall after the fireworks show. She and Vonda said their goodbyes on the drive home and shared a long last hug in the driveway. Vonda stood watching as Leanza walked across the street. Then the two friends waved to one another from their front doors for the last time as they stepped inside their homes.

Leanza was glad in the morning that she had the goodbyes out of the way. It was one less distraction as she prepared to go. She was anticipating the flight home even more now that she knew she'd be sharing it with her new friend, Chrystian. What a pleasant coincidence to learn they both lived in Norfolk. When she asked about his pup, Chrystian admitted he'd had no plans for a pet while on temporary assignment. The pup had basically found him. He'd never flown with a pet before but he had it all worked out.

Meeting up at the airport, they enjoyed getting to know each other better on their flight home. While making definite plans to stay in touch they had exchanged contact information before parting ways.

Leanza was settled back in at home by six o'clock that evening. After a relaxing hot bath she rested perfectly in her own bed. She was pleased not to remember any dreams when she awoke the next morning.

She drove to Megan's for a sweet reunion with her mother and the two of them spent the day together. As Leanza filled Megan in on the details of solving the case her mother was, yet again, very proud of her daughter and the work she did.

After hearing all about the happenings in Megan's life Leanza updated her mom on her continuing dreams, especially the most recent in which she'd actually seen her father's face. A short time later, Leanza said she wanted to go downstairs and sit for a while. She couldn't help wondering if being in the actual place of her dreams and hidden memories might somehow be helpful.

Of course, Megan agreed.

Watching her daughter walk toward the basement doorway Megan asked God to go down those stairs with her, to help Leanza open her mind to the things that were trapped inside. If there's something she needs to remember, Lord, she prayed, please help her grasp it; if there's not, please help her find peace and closure.

Megan loved her daughter so very deeply. She wanted nothing more than for Leanza to be able to move past all of this and get on with her life.

As her mother prayed for her, Leanza stood at the foot of the stairs thinking. She then walked over to the washer and dryer near where her parents had kept the easy chair. Pulling a piece of paper from her pocket she read what she'd written after her most recent dream.

Looking at the furnace in the center of the room she could see the brick wall underneath the stairway in the background. Her mom's storage tubs of Christmas decorations were still stacked there. That will never do she thought and went to move them out of the way. Returning to where she'd been standing she realized it was exactly where her dad had been sitting in her dreams.

She willed herself to relax and focused her mind on what she'd written. She was riding her tricycle around the furnace. With each circle around she looked at her daddy to be sure he was watching.

A Brick to Remember

Picturing it in her mind's eye she began to feel happy. For the first time in her life she could almost see him. He was leaning forward watching her, smiling and clapping.

Her dream had changed at that point. She was under the stairway putting her dolls into the toy baby bed. This was when he'd called out to her, "Hey, Little Dove, do you remember what we found when we played down here before?"

Next she was standing in front of the brick wall lifting her hands and placing them flat against the bricks. She then looked down toward her feet and saw her pink tennis shoes.

Leanza felt almost as if she were there, in her dream, or in her memory, whichever one it really was. She was about to close her eyes and go with it when she decided she needed to be closer to the brick wall. She walked across the room. Thinking of the child she had been back then, she sat down on the floor and scooted in as closely as she could to the bricks. Deciding this was about the right height for a four-year-old she closed her eyes and tried to return to the memory.

She'd been standing in front of the brick wall and had just looked down at her tennis shoes. She remembered seeing four very small toys lined up on a ledge and feeling something strange in her hand.

Having no idea what she was doing she reached up to place her hands flat against the bricks in front of her. Eyes still closed, Leanza sat there thinking through the dream again. Feeling as if her memory was picking up where the dream had left off she went with it. She remembered turning her body away from the wall and looking toward him. She kept her eyes closed while making the movement.

"I feel it daddy!" the happy Leanza child had said. Feel what? She now asked herself. Turning her upper body back toward the brick wall she looked at her hands as they rested on the bricks in front of her. Slowly she began to slide them across the brick wall. Whatever it was perhaps she could feel it now....

CHAPTER 65

Concentrating intently while trying to stay in the semi-dream state of memory, Leanza gently pressed the palms of her hands against the bricks. Moving her hands ever so slightly she slid them slowly across the bricks to her right. Feeling nothing more than sharp edges from the bricks and mortar she began to feel foolish. What are you doing? She asked herself condescendingly. But almost immediately she said aloud "no, don't do that. Yes, this seems crazy but just stay with it. Stop thinking and just feel."

Closing her eyes again she continued very slowly sliding her hands across the bricks. Her palm butted up against something. She lifted her hands just a fraction before continuing to move them along the wall. Something was still protruding into her palm. Opening her eyes she looked straight ahead to where her hands rested on the wall. Lifting her hands away, it became obvious, although it was almost unnoticeable, that one brick was protruding further out than the others.

In her mind's eye, she immediately saw a little girl's fingers reaching toward the left bottom corner of the brick. Mimicking the memory she placed her finger there and immediately noticed the missing mortar. Gently she placed the pointer finger of her left hand into that opening and pressed. The brick jutted outward at a sharp angle to her right. The right side of the brick was now very obviously sticking out from the wall. Using her right hand she grasped that end of the brick and gently pulled. The brick slid outward. She continued pulling and the brick continued to slide outward until suddenly she was holding it in her hands. She could then see into the opening in the wall where the brick had just been. There was something inside. Leaning her head downward she leveled her eyes to the opening. It was dark inside but she could make out what looked like a ledge with several very small items on it. Reaching into her back pocket she retrieved her cell phone and pressed the flashlight icon. Shining the light into the

226

opening she was stunned to see a huge opening behind the wall. It held a level shelf and on the shelf standing neatly in a row she saw four cobweb covered tiny child's toys. There was something else lying flat at the end.

What is that? She asked herself.

Reaching into the opening with her right hand she began to pull the toys out one-by-one. She gently laid them on the floor beside her. Looking at each toy as she brought it out of the opening she felt the stirrings of remembrance. These were her toys. She had played with them. What's more she had specifically chosen each toy to put into the hideaway.

She immediately recognized that word from her sleep-typing and realized her memory was returning. Touching the item at the end she suddenly remembered having held it long ago. She could actually see herself looking down into her little hand at it when her daddy first gave it to her. Pulling it out of the opening she looked at it and her memory returned completely! This was exactly what she had been dreaming when she'd awakened just a couple of nights ago.

She was looking at her daddy's toy!

She stared at it in wonder. It was wrapped tightly in plastic bubble wrap which was taped securely in place. Looking back into the opening she saw nothing else. Quickly but gently she picked up the other four toys. She stood up and hurried up the stairs calling out for her mother as she went.

"Mom!"

"Mom!!" she called out again as she came through the basement door.

Megan was rushing through the kitchen to meet her.

"Leanza?? What is it? Are you alright? I'm here. What is it?"

"I don't know, mom. But *it's something!!* I've found something. Look mom. Look!!" Leanza said, holding her open hands out toward her mother.

"What in the world?" Megan asked, leading Leanza to the kitchen table where Leanza gently laid the toys and the plastic wrapped item.

"Those are your toys." Megan said incredulously. "Where did you find those? You used to have several tiny sets of toys like these." Megan was looking from her daughter's face to the toys in complete bewilderment.

"I found a loose brick in the wall, mom. These were lined up on a shelf behind it. *I remember!*" she said excitedly. "I remember it all now! Daddy and I found that loose brick. We called it our hideaway and we were hiding toys in it for me to find the next time we played downstairs." She was smiling and at the same time tears were streaming down her face.

Even in the confusion of the moment Megan loved the joy on her daughter's face. The women hugged each other and laughed. They then turned and stood looking at the items Leanza had laid on the table.

"Mom," Leanza suddenly said, moving in the opposite direction of the table. She was purposely trying to get her mother to look in her direction.

"I remember now! Look at me, Mom." She said and waited for Megan to face her before continuing. "I remember! Daddy asked if he could put a toy in the hideaway with mine."

She gently reached out and took both of her mother's hands into her own. She felt very protective of Megan at that moment. She knew her mother needed her protection now. This was huge and she wasn't sure how Megan was going to take it.

"What?" Megan said clearly confused. "What kind of toy would your father have had?"

"I know what it is, mom." Leanza answered. "I don't know what's on it yet. But I've just realized what it is. Daddy gave me a computer flash drive. It's there on the table, mom. It's tightly wrapped in bubble wrap so *I've just this moment* realized what it is."

Megan's head jerked toward the table and her hands pulled against her daughter's. She was trying to get away but Leanza was holding on tightly, gently, but tightly. Megan looked at her daughter in confusion but almost immediately her head returned to the table as her eyes sought for the item.

"I see it!" she all but shouted. "Let me go, Leanza. Let me have it. I have to know what's on it! I *have to know*!"

"Mom!" Leanza was pulling against her mother.

"Mom!! Look at me mom. PLEASE, look at me. I need you to hear me before I can let you go."

Megan tore her eyes from the table and looked into her daughter's eyes.

"I know you want to know what's on there. *So do I*. Believe me, mom. I do! But I've done this too long to just be reckless. We've got to think clearly. We've got to be careful and wise right now. Are you with me mom? Do you hear what I'm saying?"

Megan felt as if she were shrouded in a heavy fog but her daughter's words were sinking in.

A Brick to Remember

'Yes, yes, Leanza." She said in a calmer voice and her hands went slack. "I'm okay. I'm calm. You can let me go now. I understand."

Leanza released her mother's hands and immediately Megan collapsed into her daughter's arms.

CHAPTER 66

The realization that years of not knowing might now come to an end was too much for Megan to handle. Leanza helped her mother to the sofa and comforted her until she got her bearings. Then they called Wade who came to the house immediately.

The three of them went downstairs and marveled at what Leanza had found in the wall. Of course, they were all desperate to know what was on the flash drive Denvel had hidden. Still, they knew this had to be handled correctly.

They couldn't call the police for fear the drive would immediately be taken as evidence before they even got to see what it contained. There must be some extremely important information there for Denvel to have hidden it the way he did. It may hold some kind of legal evidence, in which case, this had to be handled very carefully. They were in agreement that every precaution had to be taken. After all, protecting whatever was on that flash drive was the last act Denvel had taken in his life. For all they knew it *had* *cost* him his life.

That was why Leanza had stopped her mother and herself from tearing the bubble wrap off and plugging the flash drive into a computer immediately.

Being educated and employed by legal and government organizations both Wade and Leanza knew the integrity of the flash drive had to be preserved. After much discussion they agreed to contact two people whom they could trust with documenting the opening and viewing of the flash drive for the first time.

They chose Chrystian Park and Tiffany Lee.

Leanza and Chrystian hadn't known each other long but Marshall had spoken of his exemplary work ethic and outstanding personal character. Chrystian was basically an impartial person. He had no history with the family. This played into the fact that he didn't know them well enough to have a motive for covering anything up or lying for them.

When Leanza placed the call she briefly explained the situation before asking if he would be willing to come to her mother's house to film the action. She emphasized that by agreeing to participate he could be subjecting himself to being called to testify in a court of law in the future.

Wade called Tiffany Lee. While Tiffany's natural beauty was the talk of many of his colleagues, Wade saw so much more. Tiffany had served as a court reporter during his early years of practice. Later, as a paralegal, Tiffany often assisted Wade in preparing for trial. She had never failed to impress him with her excellent work ethic and professionalism. Bottom line – Tiffani was a person of great integrity. Wade trusted her.

Placing the call Wade asked if she were willing to participate in a professional capacity, bringing her stenograph machine to record the entire exchange. He emphasized this meant she could, and would, most likely be called to testify in court if needed. Tiffany agreed without hesitation.

Both were available and came that evening to Megan's home.

Chrystian filmed while Tiffany typed as Leanza shared how and where she came to find the flash drive. Chrystian filmed the toys and flash drive as they lay side-by-side on the kitchen table. He continued filming as Wade carefully cut away the bubble wrap and inserted the flash drive into the computer.

As had been previously discussed, he continued filming and Tiffany continued recording as they opened the flash drive contents. Wade spoke clearly as he read the titles of a variety of files and documents which instantly appeared on the monitor. The largest icon was a video labeled "Open only in the event of the death of Denvel Wade Williams".

Wade, Megan and Leanza were seated near the computer monitor, in that order. Tiffany sat at the stenograph typing and Chrystian stood slightly to the side where he could film the screen as well as the three family members watching it.

Wade opened the video file.

Immediately an empty chair was seen in the center of a room. Denvel appeared and walked over to the chair. He sat down and looked directly into the camera.

231

Megan's breath caught in her throat. Leanza reached out and placed a hand over her mother's. Simultaneously, Wade placed his arm around his mother's shoulder.

CHAPTER 67

Denvel cleared his throat, ran his hand through his wavy dark hair and began to speak.

"Hey Megan," he smiled and winked.

Leanza watched as her mother's lips curved upward. Her eyes were glued to the monitor and a single tear spilled out and slid down her cheek.

Looking a little stressed, Denvel took a deep breath and said "I hope you never see this video, Megs. If you're watching it – well, it means only one thing; I'm gone. Megan, I am so sorry!"

He lowered his head for a second before raising it again. Looking into the camera he continued.

"There's been a lot going on. I'm sorry I couldn't tell you about it. I wanted to. So many times I wanted to. I sure could have used your input. But I've been afraid. I couldn't risk putting you and the children in danger. What's happening is no joke and I have to protect all of you until I figure out what to do. I'm making this video just in case I don't live to tell the story. I *really hope* you never see this but just in case….

We got a new guy down at the docks about a month ago. Dominic Bianchi. I don't like him. You know me, Megan. I like most everyone but not this guy. He's cocky. He has a smart mouth and no work ethic but mostly he's just mean. Actually, knowing what I now know, I'll go so far as to say he's evil.

I was working late about three weeks ago and I went out on the dock for a break. I was in the shadows by some crates, alone, just trying to relax for a few minutes. I heard a commotion and was about to say something when I recognized Bianchi's voice. Thank God I didn't say anything because in the next few seconds I saw Bianchi pull a knife. Before I could even move he'd run it into this guy's chest, right where his heart was. He killed the guy. Just that fast. I was sick, in shock really, but more than anything else I was

233

scared! It was a deadly thrust. It took mere seconds for that man to bleed out. There was no saving him. Even if I hadn't frozen, even if I'd snapped out of it quick, there was just no saving him."

Denvel's head dropped and he put his face into his hands, very distraught. In a few seconds he'd pulled himself together and looked into the camera again.

"Dominic called out and a couple of guys joined him. They put the guy's body in a boat along with some rope and a cement block. One of them grabbed a bucket and poured water on the dock, getting rid of the blood. Feeling like a coward but knowing it was my only way to survive I stayed hidden. The whole thing was over pretty quick and they headed out to sea. Once I was sure they couldn't see me I came out.

I almost went to the police right then. But I knew they'd never find that guy. There'd be no evidence and my life would be ruined. I went back to work like nothing happened. It took everything I had to finish my shift trying to act normal that night. I didn't know what to do so I just started watching everybody after that. It didn't take long to realize something is terribly wrong down there.

It's been risky but I've been careful and I've been sneaky. I've learned a lot and none of it good. Bianchi's running a smuggling operation out of the dock where I work. He's got an intimidation racket going, too. Bianchi's crew has threatened the owner along with a lot of other business owners in the area. They trashed their places and now the owners are so scared they're paying. It's called protection but basically they're paying just to keep running their own businesses without having them completely destroyed.

Bianchi does anything he wants. It's a mess down there, Megan. And it's gonna get a lot worse unless Dominic Bianchi is stopped. Anyone going against him will end up like the guy I saw him kill.

I've been putting everything I'm learning on this drive: files, documents, as much proof as I can gather and now, this video. It'll all stand up in court. I'm just trying to figure out how to get it to Andrew Wood. You remember him, right, Megs? My best childhood buddy - he became a cop."

Denvel sighed heavily, ran his hand through his hair and said again, "I'm sorry, Megan. Since you're watching this I guess you'll be the one taking it to Andrew now."

A Brick to Remember

Looking as if he might cry, Denvel took a deep breath. He let it out and kept going.

"Andrew is *the only one* you can trust. Some of the cops have gone bad. They're working with Dominic now. There's more and when I say this you'll know why I've been so scared. Dominic was sent to this area as an underling for Jack Chevanty."

Megan's hands flew up to cover the gasp escaping her mouth.

Everyone understood her reaction. They *all* knew that name. Jack Chevanty was the notorious mafia boss who'd taken over the docks. He had a real issue with people pronouncing his name wrong. The name looked like it would be pronounced Che-van-ty. But the proper pronunciation was Che-vaun-ty. Jack was best known for having killed a man just for calling him Jack Che-van-ty.

Denvel continued "I don't have proof on that last bit of information, but *if* it is true Andrew will find proof. You just get this drive to Detective Andrew Wood. He's solid. He's not just a good cop - he's the best! He'll see to it they all go down.

I have every intention of doing this myself.

I pray to God I still can and you never even have to see this. But I don't know. Things are getting bad now. They've followed me a couple of times acting like they're gonna run me off the road, running me right up to the edge, but never actually doing it. It's been random for the past couple of weeks. I never come home until I'm sure they're not tailing me. I'm trying so hard to keep you and the kids out of this. I really don't think they know what I'm doing. Dominic just knows I don't like him and with someone like him that's enough.

Okay, that's pretty much it. Everything I've got is on this flash drive. I just need to hand it to Andrew and this will all be over.

I hope to destroy this video without you ever seeing it. If that didn't happen and I'm not there now, you'll have to take care of it. You can do it, Megs. You're the *strongest person* I've ever known. You can do this. I know you can."

He took a deep breath and his voice softened.

"Take care of our babies, Megan. Love them enough for both of us and give them the life we planned. *I know you will.*

I love you, Megs. I love our children, Wade and my Little Dove. Hug them for me every day. You give them my love but don't you forget to keep a heap of it for yourself."

He purposely smiled into the camera then.

For just a second he almost looked carefree. Leanza had the thought that she was catching a glimpse of the man her father really was. Glancing at her mother's face again she could see she was right.

He went on, "You three are the greatest gifts God has ever given me. Thank you for always loving me. You've made me so happy in this life. You've made me proud *every day* and *you always will.*"

He smiled into the camera, winked and said "I'll make you a deal."

Beside her Leanza heard her mother laugh a soft little laugh.

"Of course you will," she said softly and Denvel continued.

"You take care of everything just like I've asked you to and I'll forever be watching over the three of you. If at all possible I'll find a way to show you I'm ok and I'm there, watching over you. *You know I will!*" He laughed then or came as close to it as a man under the kind of stress he was under could.

Smiling again he said, *"I love you. Megan,* I love you *so very much."*

Denvel sat looking sadly into the camera for just a few seconds.

Then he smiled, gave another quick wink, stood up, walked toward the camera, reached forward and the screen went blank.

CHAPTER 68

"It's so good hearing your voice," Vonda said into the phone to Leanza. Vonda had already updating Leanza on the happenings in her life. The main one being the return of her good friend Doreen whose condo Leanza had lived in during her assignment in Stokesbury.

"Yours too," Leanza answered as the two friends continued their conversation. In the process of updating Vonda she had already told her about the return flight home, getting to know Chrystian a bit better, settling back in and resting well in her own bed that first night back. She was now sharing about the visit to her mom's the following day.

Of course, Vonda was astonished to hear about the return of Leanza's memories, the discovery of the loose brick, and the items hidden behind it.

Leanza had just finished telling her Denvel had left a video she and Wade had watched with their mother.

"What an emotional day you all had," Vonda said sympathetically. "This is an unbelievable story Leanza! How amazing that your father had you put that flash drive with your toys. I'm sure he thought he was just putting it away for safekeeping until he could contact that policeman he was friends with. Have you been able to get hold of him yet?"

"No, I haven't. When I contacted the police station I was told he'd transferred out. He hasn't worked here in Norfolk for years. I don't know if it's a policy or not but they weren't forthcoming on where he's moved on to. So I'm currently faced with the challenge of finding him. I'm just not at all comfortable taking the information we have to the local police. I don't know if the man he named is still involved in what's happening at the docks. From the sounds of it, what happened with my dad back then was just the beginning of the mess that's still going on there. And he was right - it's gotten a lot worse. For all I know that man is still the one in charge down there. Dad was very clear that some of the cops had gone bad even back

237

then. I'm not sure how to go about it, but I've got to follow dad's instructions. He was very clear that Andrew Wood was the only police officer he trusted."

"Wait a minute, Leanza. Did you just say Andrew Wood?" Vonda asked incredulously.

"I did. That's the name dad said in the video. He went to school with Andrew. They were apparently good friends. In fact, I was just thinking his family might still live here in Norfolk so maybe I could find him that way. Why do you ask?"

"You're not going to believe this Leanza. In fact, I'm having trouble believing it myself. This is such a wild coincidence if it's the same man. There's a Detective on the Stokesbury police force by the name of Andrew Wood. I only know this because the accountant in Marshall's construction firm went missing several years ago. Andrew Wood was the Detective who headed up that investigation."

"Are you serious?" Leanza asked.

"Completely," Vonda answered. "Do you want me to call the station and see if he's still there?"

"No. But thank you for the offer. I'm actually thinking I need to hang up now and call there myself. If it's dad's friend I want him to know about this immediately. I'm sorry to be so rude but...."

"No!" Vonda interrupted her friend. "No apology needed, Leanza. I totally agree with you. Hang up *right now* and make that call! I hope it's him and I'll be praying you make a connection."

Leanza hung up and stood looking at her phone. She was almost in shock. What were the chances her dad's friend had ended up at the police force of the town she had just spent six months working in?

"Life is unbelievable sometimes," She said aloud as she dialed the number for the Stokesbury police department.

Leanza had been asked who the person on the line may tell the detective was calling.

"This is Leanza Williams," She said simply. "Would you please tell him my father was Denvel Williams."

After being on hold for a few moments a male voice said "Hello, this is Detective Andrew Wood. Denvel was your dad?"

238

"Yes, he was." Leanza answered proudly. "If I'm not mistaken you were a childhood friend of his."

"I sure was. We were *very close friends*. I'm so sorry about his disappearance. That's one cold case that's been a continual frustration to me through the years. Is there something you, your mom or your family need that I can help with? I'm happy to help Denvel's family, of course."

"Yes, we do need your help actually. If you're not already, you may want to sit down. I've got quite a story to tell you."

Leanza filled him in on finding the flash drive containing her father's specific instructions that no one but Andrew be trusted with its contents.

Not ten minutes after that call ended Andrew was in the process of booking the first available flight home to Norfolk. He would be at Megan William's home in an official police capacity as soon as it could possibly be managed. Since he no longer worked in that jurisdiction there were certain legal hoops to be jumped through, but he was on it. He had been impressed and pleased to learn that the integrity of the flash drive had been correctly protected. Without having seen it, he could only hope the evidence it contained would go a long way.

Andrew was, of course, grieved to know, after all these years that his friend was dead. At the same time he was anxious to see what the drive contained since he had cautioned Leanza not to speak in detail over the phone.

For the first time in years Andrew felt hopeful that some real changes could be made to the dock area of his hometown.

Wow! He thought as he rushed home to pack for the trip, this is incredible.

CHAPTER 69

Marshall was excited about tonight's ball game. It was the first game of the season for the Old Timer team. He couldn't believe it had been three years since he'd gotten that started.

Knowing Vonda would walk to the field and cheer for the players tonight, as she always did, left him feeling happy. He loved looking over to see her smiling at him from the bleachers. Marshall wasn't sure he had ever felt happier than he did in his life right now. It seemed to him that the older he got the better life became. He sure had a lot to thank God for.

He smiled as he thought of the day he first met Vonda at the ball field. He had just finished talking with a few friends when he turned to walk away and startled her. She was carrying food back to the bleachers, lost her balance and ended up spilling her soda all down the side of him. Marshall couldn't help but laugh at the memory of his arm covered in soda and her hot dog and fries spread on the ground at their feet. She was profusely apologizing when Marshall looked up from his wet, sticky arm into her lovely face. He liked her immediately. Of all the changes in his life these past several years that was the one thing that hadn't changed.

We've been through a lot together since then he thought as he headed out the door.

Vonda was, at that exact moment, clearing her table after her evening meal. Noticing the dishwasher was full she put a detergent tab in, shut the door and pressed the start button.

Glancing at the clock she went to get ready for tonight's ball game. She chose a light lavender shirt that was a little dressier than she generally wore which prompted her to do something different with her hair. She combed it and pulled a bunch up into a messy bun leaving about two thirds hanging loosely around her face and over her shoulders. She clipped a decorative silver butterfly clip to the front of the bun. She found her silver butterfly dangly earrings and put those on. The effect was lovely and left her feeling pretty.

She put a light dusting of natural powder make-up on just to cover the imperfections of aging and ran a light pink lipstick over her lips. With one last look into the mirror she pronounced herself ready and headed out the door.

Walking through her neighborhood she found herself feeling a little reminiscent. It had been a long while since she'd given any thought to when she and Stanley first moved to Logan. A smile played at her lips as she remembered the excitement of house hunting. They'd been so anxious the day they made the offer on the house and excited when they came to terms with the seller. She remembered sitting in the car with Stanley in front of the house deciding to get windmill palm trees for the front yard. Stanley would sure be pleased to see how well those had grown.

She had learned long ago not to let herself dwell on the memories of Stanley's sudden passing. Thankfully, the pain had subsided with time and life's changes since then. Still, she didn't think she would ever be able to remember those days without twinges of sadness. Stanley was such a good man and they had shared such a happy life together. His loss would never stop being tragic. It was still hard, sometimes, to believe how long she'd been living in Logan without him now.

As the ball field came into view she had to laugh at the memory of spilling soda on Marshall the first day they met. Their friendship was such an unexpected blessing. Marshall had made her feel safe and protected when she'd been afraid. Those were memories not worth revisiting except for the reminder of God's promise to use all things for good in the lives of His children. How clear it was that God had used that uncertain situation to draw her and Marshall to one another. He was such a good man. She felt warm and happy thinking of how naturally her love for Marshall had taken root in her heart and grown. Recognizing that she loved him God has shown her that this was all new for Marshall. She chuckled now at how patient she had been as she waited for him to realize what they shared was more than just a deep friendship.

If anyone had been watching her face at that moment they would've noticed the glow of happiness. She was thinking of Christmas morning when he'd surprised her with the wind spinner in her yard. Her smile widened at the memory of the moment he told her he loved her and she was finally able to say it in return.

Arriving at the ball field Vonda waved to Marshall who'd been watching for her to arrive. Since he wasn't on the field yet she rushed over to him and they shared a brief hug. Laughing he then hurried out to the pitcher's mound. Turning back to the stands, Vonda was surprised but pleased to see Marshall's family there. It had been a little while since she'd seen Mitch or Mason, Stacy and the boys so it would be fun to sit and watch the game with them tonight.

The night passed quickly and the game was enjoyable for everyone.

At the end of the first Old Timer's game of the season the spectators usually got up from the bleachers and headed to their vehicles while Marshall addressed the team. Vonda noticed no one seemed to be in a hurry tonight and stayed seated herself. The players gathered around as Marshall thanked them all for coming out again this year. He was commenting on the fun they were going to have this season when he suddenly looked confused.

Looking toward Vonda he called out, "Vonda, would you mind helping me out? Could you go to the dugout and get that clip board for me. I wanted to go over something on the schedule with the players."

She jumped up and hurried to the dugout and grabbed the clipboard. Rushing out to the pitcher's mound she handed it to him and started to turn away.

"Oh Vonda, could you just wait here a moment in case I need anything else?" he asked her.

"Of course," she said, smiling and taking a few steps back to get out of the way.

Marshall clumsily dropped the clipboard and leaned down to pick it up. Vonda noticed the players smiling when instead of rising back up Marshall went down on one knee.

Thinking he'd stumbled she started toward him. When he looked up at her he had a huge smile. She felt confused as she sensed the players moving back a few steps.

"Vonda, I have something very important to ask you," Marshall said, reaching his hand toward her. "Here at this ball field, the place where we first met, I want to ask if you'll spend the rest of your life with me."

Realizing what was happening Vonda's mind stopped.

242

She stopped noticing what was going on around her.

She stopped thinking of the players.

She stopped doing everything except meeting Marshall's eyes with her own.

He was the only thing she was focused on as a smile graced her lips. He was all she was thinking of as she listened to what he was saying.

"Vonda Graham, I love you. Will you marry me?" As he spoke Marshall lifted his hand further toward her. Between his thumb and forefinger he was holding up a diamond ring.

Unaware of the smiles on the faces watching and the hush that had fallen as the world waited for her answer Vonda took a step toward him. She looked deeply into the eyes of the man she loved as a soft whisper escaped her smiling lips "yes".

And the crowd roared!

CHAPTER 70

Leanza was sitting at her mother's kitchen table looking down into the creamy delicious coffee in her mug. It was warm against the palms of her hands cupped around it. The warmth added to her sense of wellbeing. No matter what else had ever happened in her life or the world around her it had always remained true that she felt comfortable and safe here with her mom.

Her mother's kitchen, more specifically her kitchen table, may just be Leanza's favorite place in the entire world.

Denvel and Megan had gotten the blue Formica topped table with yellow chairs when they'd first married. It was extremely outdated now but still perfectly functional. Leanza's happiest memories had been made right here with her mom and brother. Here they ate their meals, played board games, did homework, worked on school projects, wrote Christmas cards and as they were doing today, just sat together having coffee and talking. In this family the kitchen table was the center of the home.

Feeling warm and happy, Leanza raised her head to watch her mother moving about the kitchen. Megan lifted the coffee pot and poured herself another cup then turned and began walking toward Leanza.

Seeing her daughter watching her, Megan said simply, "I'm so glad you stopped by Leanza. I love hearing the happy news of Vonda and Marshall's engagement. What a blessing for both of them. I still can't believe he proposed to her on the pitcher's mound of the baseball field, but considering how they met, what could be more perfect?"

"I know, right?" Leanza answered with a smile. "I almost hope they get married there, too. What a fun wedding that would be!"

Megan laughed out loud. "Oh, I hadn't even thought of that. That *would* be fun!"

Sitting down across from her daughter she smoothed out the placemat and set the mug in its center. "I can't get over that Detective Wood now works at the Stokesbury Police Department, the very place you were living and working on your last case. I mean, really, what are the chances?"

"I've been asking myself that question ever since I located him. I'm just thankful I said his name when I called Vonda. I hadn't intended to. I was pretty intent on saying as little as I could over the phone. I thought it best if he learned the details when he had the flash drive in hand. Just imagine, mom, if I had never said his name. Who knows how long it could've taken me to find him. Instead he was on the next flight and got here to see the video and take the flash drive the next day. Well, he's got the evidence dad gathered and I'm sure he's building a case with it now. He's expecting to make some major arrests based on everything dad documented. It's amazing what dad did, really."

"Yes it is," Her mother said "I'm so very glad you realized what your sleep-typing has been trying to tell you all these years. I'm so thankful you remember it all too, especially your dad and the way he talked to you and played with you and *loved you*. I'm truly happy about everything that's come to light. God has been so good to us.

Still, there's the void of not knowing what actually happened to Denvel. That's been one of the hardest parts of all of this. But, maybe that's for the best, too. I don't know. I mean if he were tortured and killed in some horrible way by that evil Dominic Bianchi or another of Jack Chevanty's people. Well, I'm sure I'm better off not knowing those details."

"That's true, mom." Leanza answered in a caring voice. "As hard as it is not to know, it might be better if we never learn what happened. We'll just have to keep trusting God with that."

Leanza's phone rang and she looked at the screen.

"It's Andrew," she said, sounding a bit surprised. She hadn't expected to hear from him this soon. "I'm going to answer this, mom."

Her mother smiled and nodded affirmatively.

"Hello Andrew." Leanza said into the phone. "Yes, I'm actually at mom's house right now. We're here together. No, Wade's not with us. What's going on?"

Megan watched her daughter closely wondering what this was all about. Leanza was listening intently, occasionally nodding her head slightly. She made a few vague comments.

Leanza's expression was becoming more intense. While slowly coming to her feet she reached one hand out and placed it on the table top as if she needed the extra support. Her eyes were staring straight ahead, not focusing on anything in particular as she listened. They now moved slowly in Megan's direction. She was purposefully seeking her mother's eyes. Her face looked grave and yet somehow relieved which didn't make any sense. Megan couldn't read her daughter's expression at all, she didn't know what was happening but something told her it was very important.

CHAPTER 71

"Yes, I'll call him as soon as we hang up and we'll do exactly as you've suggested. Thank you, Andrew. Thank you so very much," Leanza said before adding, "Yes, I'm fairly certain we'll be seeing you very soon. Goodbye Andrew."

As Leanza hung up the phone she slowly sank back down into her chair. "What is it?" Megan asked, looking very concerned.

The stunned look on Leanza's face told her mother her mind was still processing whatever she'd just been told. Turning toward Megan but again not appearing to really see her, Leanza shook her head from side-to-side ever so slightly, as if to say no. With empty eyes she lifted her phone to her lips, pressed the SIRI button and said, "Call Wade Williams."

"Calling Wade Williams" her phone repeated back to her in its cheerful voice as a musical dial tone began to play.

Looking in Megan's direction unseeingly, Leanza said into the phone, "Wade, Andrew Wood just called me. There's been a development in dad's case." Her eyes began to gain focus as they again sought Megan's.

Looking directly at her mother now Leanza continued, "You've heard of those dive teams devoted to cleaning lakes up, right? You have? Yes. That's right. They dredge the bottom of the lakes. Sometimes they find some pretty interesting things."

She wasn't taking her eyes from Megan's face as she spoke. "Apparently a dive team has been systematically cleaning up the lakes here in Virginia. They're currently working the one between here and the docks where dad worked."

Leanza now looked directly into Megan's eyes.

She reached out and took her mother's hand in her own as she continued, "While dredging the lake the team found a car. In cases like this the standard practice is to clear the license plate and run it. If it comes back in connection to a missing person or criminal case they contact the police before bringing the car up....."

The implication there was clear.

Leanza squeezed her mother's hand and appeared to be studying her face as she continued speaking into the phone. "Wade," her eyes focused on her mother's. "Mom," she took deep a breath, "they've found dad's car. Andrew just called to let us know. They'll be bringing it up within the next hour if we want to be there."

Understanding exactly what her daughter was saying Megan began nodding her head up and down to confirm that she wanted to be there. Understanding and agreeing Leanza's head began to nod up and down in unison with her mother's.

"Yes, I agree," she said to Wade, "We both agree. We want to be there. Yes, you're right Wade. It's out of your way to come here. That would just take more time. Ok then, we'll meet you at the lake. We'll see you as soon as we can all get there. We love you, too, Wade."

Leanza ended the call, laid the phone on the table, turned and embraced her mother.

"It looks like they may have run him off the road after all, mom, right into the lake. If he's in that car we're finally going to know what happened to dad."

Denvel had driven past that lake going and coming from work every day. There was a deep curve in the road and the lake lay directly beyond it. Leanza was driving but as they approached it both women were looking at the curve in the road in a way they never had before. It wasn't hard to imagine Denvel being forced off the road, losing control and careening into the lake.

Megan softly said, "I never thought about him being this close all these years. Of course, I had no idea how he died or where. It's just really hard to imagine he's been this close to us this whole time."

As they got out of the car they saw Wade pulling in behind them. He parked, got out and hurried forward to hug them.

"Mom, are you okay? Sis?" Wade asked the women, looking from one to the other with a worried expression.

"We're fine," both women answered. "Are you?"

"I am. Actually, in a strange way, I feel more relieved than anything else. I'm almost excited. Is that weird? I guess I'd come to believe we'd never know what really happened with dad."

Leanza said, "I feel the same way, once we saw dad's video we knew *why* something happened but we still didn't know what or how."

Looking toward the lake they spotted Andrew. He was talking with one of the clean-up crew not far from the big equipment that would hoist the car up and out of the water. A couple of cables were protruding from the water up to the hoist. Apparently, swimmers were securing the cables to the car at the bottom of the lake.

Megan said, "If Denvel's in his car we're finally going to have all the answers. That makes this a good thing and today a good day."

She smiled as she looked from one of her children's faces to the other. "I'm so proud of both of you," She said. "Your father would be so very proud of the people you've become.

I want to remind you that I've known he's been gone for a very long time. Ever since that day so many years ago, when God and your dad sent me the sign I had begged for. Remember? Denvel's visit, when he came to me in the form of a yellow butterfly. That was the day I was able to start moving forward again.

Today, right now, if they find him in that car, it's going to be the last step in this part of our journey. We'll *finally* know what happened all those many years ago and that his earthly remains have been here all this time while his spirit has been in heaven."

Standing between the two of them she reached up and placed the palm of her right hand along the side of Wade's face. Lifting her left hand she placed that palm along the side of Leanza's face. She looked from one to the other of her children, smiled, took a deep breath and asked, "Are we ready then?"

Wade and Leanza looked at each other. They nodded 'yes' to one another and looked back at their mother.

"Yes," they said in unison.

"Alright then," Megan said. "Let's go."

She slid a hand into each of theirs and the three of them took the first step forward. They'd gone no more than ten steps when Leanza noticed a cluster of butterflies floating toward them. There may have been fifteen or twenty altogether. They were flying as a tight group toward the trio.

"Will you look at that?" Wade asked in a whisper. The cluster was nestled very close together in a way none of them had ever seen done before.

As they got closer the butterflies began to separate, flying outward from the center of the cluster.

A sound escaped from Megan's lips causing Wade and Leanza to turn simultaneously to look at their mother. It was a gasp but then not really.

Following her movements they watched as Megan lifted her arm and turned her hand palm upward. All three of them looked on in awe as the butterflies fluttered away leaving just the one that had been in the center of the cluster. It floated in place for a few seconds gently lifting and lowering its large beautiful yellow wings. Turning slightly it seemed to be looking straight at them as it softly alighted into the palm of Megan's hand. As it gently closed its wings Andrew Wood's voice called out, "There's a person in the car. We're pretty sure it's Denvel."

Readers are invited to contact VS Gardner through Messenger (Facebook Author page VS Gardner) or via email to **vsgbooks2020@gmail.com**. Reader referrals to other readers and/or Amazon / Goodreads book reviews are greatly appreciated.

The setting of this book echoes VS Gardner's home in beautiful South Carolina where she lives with her best friend/husband. She loves spending time with her family and is thankful for life's many blessings.

In 2020 VS Gardner was excited to achieve her lifelong dream with the publication of her first book _A KILLING ON HARDEE STREET_. Although each is a stand-alone book which can be read without the other Vonda Graham's story continues in _A BRICK TO REMEMBER_.

If you enjoyed this book be sure to follow the Author on Amazon and/or her Facebook Author page VS Gardner for notification of future publications.

Made in USA - Crawfordsville, IN
37728_9798763454956
03.19.2022 1219